THE GHOSTLIGHTS

Gráinne Murphy

Legend Press Ltd, 51 Gower Street, London, WC1E 6HJ
info@legendpress.co.uk | www.legendpress.co.uk

Print ISBN 978-1-80031-9-417
Ebook ISBN 978-1-80031-9-424
Set in Times. Printing managed by Jellyfish Solutions Ltd
Cover design by Kari Brownlie | www.karibrownlie.co.uk

Gráinne Murphy grew up in rural West Cork, Ireland. At university she studied Applied Psychology and Forensic Research. In 2011 she moved with her family to Brussels for 5 years. She has now returned to West Cork, working as a self-employed language editor specialising in human rights and environmental issues.

Gráinne's debut novel *Where the Edge Is* was published by Legend Press in 2020.

Visit Gráinne
www.grainnemurphy.ie

Follow her on Twitter
@GraMurphy

and Instagram
@gramurphywriter

*For Dee
and all the sisters
everywhere*

AUTHOR'S NOTE

In June 2009, a man's body was found on the beach in Co. Sligo. Despite checking into a local hotel under the name Peter Bergmann, that did not appear to be his real name and his identity remains unknown. *The Ghostlights* was inspired by the story of Peter Bergmann, but the characters, location and circumstances in the story are entirely fictional.

CONTENTS

THREE WEEKS LATER

GOOD FRIDAY

It was too early for breakfast. Perhaps he didn't mind. After four days, who would miss another portion of poached eggs on soggy toast? Or perhaps something about the four triangles of toast held apart from one another in their silver rack saddened him. Reminded him of other places. Other times.

He didn't go directly to the lake. It was enough, at first, to know that it was waiting. Water had all the time in the world.

He might have hoped to meet someone but instead found himself outside alone, his face held up to the feeble morning sun as if for inspection. The wind held spring inside itself. A person could nearly hear nature stretch and wake.

The bag would have been the first thing to go, dropped into the black maw of the bin on the edge of the village, the plastic strings uncuffed from his red-ringed wrists. A feeling of freedom then, or something close to it.

He would have walked the length of the village to the hill where the statue stood. Her eyes the same blue as her cloak, cast resolutely upwards, seeing nothing but sky. No flicker of recognition in his direction. How long does a miracle take?

Another turn took him along the lake path, his pockets empty but for his hands. Clutched inside his fingers, the tags he cut earlier from his shirt and jumper, rubbing their edges together, feeling them slide and crack. As a child he likely had a comfort blanket. Long gone from him now but still somewhere. Little that is man-made can ever truly disappear. Except maybe man himself.

At the marshy corner, where the tadpoles were about their mysterious transformation, he would have released the tags, watching them flutter in the lift of the breeze and scatter like starlings from the eaves.

He could have continued on his way. Followed the path all the way around the lake, watching the swan in its solitary majesty. Then back to the house with the primroses around the door. Instead, he left the path and stepped towards the water.

His glasses he might have put in the bin, or, more likely, placed with careful habit on one of the rocks that hid among the reeds on the edge of the lake. Without them, everything was less distinct, but he could see well enough for today.

At first the water would have been a cold reproach. Welcome, in its way. An initial tightening, then loosening the sadness. Allowing a roll-call of his life, maybe. Of people and places and moments. With his eyes on the horizon, he saw low lights dancing. Sunrise, his brain told him, but his heart said they were the ghostlights. Like the girl said, lighting his way home.

The breakdown of the body is the most private thing. He persisted, and who knew but there was one final miraculous pleasure to be found in his own resolve. Deeper and deeper he went until he lost his footing and descended, clothed in the very lake itself.

THREE DAYS EARLIER

HOLY TUESDAY

MARIANNE

You never knew what you might find cleaning the rooms. That was why Marianne liked it, although that wasn't something she could ever admit without risking ridicule. Over the years she had found the oddest items – she would go to her grave remembering the baby octopus in a jar, its little purplish face pressed against the glass. Try as she might, she couldn't shake the idea it was pleading for help. What would drive a person to buy such a thing? And, having bought it, to pack it in a suitcase and bring it on holiday? You couldn't make it up, her dad used to say.

There was a certain satisfaction in observing the guests at the breakfast table, all the while knowing what she had seen of them in private. The woman putting the tiniest little spoon of low-fat yogurt onto her grapefruit as if she hadn't a suitcase full of Toblerones upstairs, the giant airport ones that people bought themselves as consolation for returning to their real lives. Or the couple barely speaking to one another, despite several condoms in their bathroom bin. There was simply no knowing until you looked below the surface. If the job had any kind of beauty, that was it.

What would her own room say about her? Since leaving Ed's apartment – whether technically or temporarily wasn't something she could even think about right now, not with his *You can't take it out on me if you are unhappy* ringing in her ears – that only left her childhood bedroom here for examination. A grim thought. No matter how well loved, a few dusty books and stones brought home in pockets from beaches up and down the west coast did not a successful picture paint.

'What's seldom is wonderful,' was all Liv had said last night by way of welcome. Marianne's feet and suitcase were barely inside the door and the smell of fresh laundry and furniture polish was threatening to take the legs from under her and throw her on the comfort of her sister's shoulder.

She was poised to retort that it had only been a few weeks and she had a busy life but bit her tongue. The last thing she needed was Liv to take offence at the idea that she herself wasn't busy.

'I had a week's annual leave to use, so I thought I could come and help with the start of the season.'

'It's quiet,' Liv warned. 'There won't be much to do.'

'Then there will be less for you to redo after me,' Marianne joked and even if her sister didn't join her laughter, oh! the relief of coming back to the very place where all the jokes began.

She dragged her cloth along the windowsill, poking into the corners to dislodge any tendrils of web that might be invisible to the naked eye. Sorry, spiders, no home for you here.

Home is where the heart is.

Home is where they have to take you in.

Home is where the Wi-Fi connects automatically.

'There's no place like home,' Marianne told her reflection in the window. She clicked her heels together three times and waited. Nothing changed.

She gathered up her bucket of cleaning supplies and moved into the tiny en suite bathroom that Ethel had insisted on fitting back when they were fashionable rather than obligatory. That was her mother all over. Forever wanting to be that bit better than everyone else.

Marianne sprayed the bathroom surfaces and wiped until she was breathless. That was one of her father's tips when she railed at her mother's exacting standards. 'Keep going until you're good and warm,' he advised. 'Let her see the work on you.'

Today's most interesting find was a package of corn caps on the little glass shelf above the sink in the bathroom. Hardly worth noticing, although she did find herself taking a second glance at the neat size five shoes and wondering if the woman was really a reluctant six. She would have to get a look at her gait later.

There was nothing else left to do, but Marianne lingered in the room. If she went downstairs, Liv would be sure to work ostentatiously around her, her tight topknot quivering above her smock (and when, exactly, would her sister stop dressing like a college student?). At best, she would find somewhere else for Marianne to hoover, when all she really wanted was to curl up with a comforting book and nap the morning away. She had announced her intention to take her mother and Liv out for lunch – Coolaroone had a new restaurant, if you could believe it – so at least there was that to look forward to. Irritating though her mother's lack of enthusiasm had been – if she had time, she said vaguely, and Marianne had wanted to shout that she was inviting her out for a meal, for fuck's sake, not to witness a root canal. Still, Ethel was always good about sharing desserts and never raised her eyebrows at Marianne ordering wine at lunchtime.

Cheered, she dragged the hoover down the stairs into reception. With her back turned, she didn't see the man approaching and his voice made her jump.

'Good morning.'

'Jesus Christ tonight!' Marianne dropped the head of the hoover onto the flat of her foot. 'Where did you jump out of?'

'I'm so sorry. I didn't mean to startle you.' The man moved to pick up the hoover.

Marianne remembered herself. 'You took me by surprise is all. My apologies for swearing.'

'Not at all. Is your foot okay?' He pointed, as if she mightn't know which part of her body was which.

If the accent hadn't given him away as a non-native speaker, the gesture would have. She found herself doing the same thing whenever she was abroad and trying to make herself understood. Her attempts at communication equal parts words and mime. Marianne smiled. It was hard not to feel protective of his efforts.

'Nothing a little soak in hot water won't fix – and who doesn't love an excuse for that?' She surprised herself by winking at him. Not forty-eight hours without Ed and here she was eyeing up elderly gentlemen. Mid-sixties, she thought. Or a well-preserved seventy. Tall but with a slight stoop that gave him a charmingly apologetic air. Brushed overcoat, with a scarf tucked carefully into the V-neck. And a hat, a trilby no less! Like something out of a film.

'I'm Marianne.'

He tilted his head towards her in a tiny bow. 'Fred Stiller. I wonder if you might have a room available? I don't have a booking, I'm afraid.'

'Let me just check the system.' He swallowed his Rs, she noticed. A little bit like Ed. Did it make her racist if her brain automatically divided people into accent/no accent categories? That was the problem with living as a sensitive person, a *thinking* person. Every thought was likely to mortify you eventually.

'Is it possible to stay for five nights? For cash.' He leaned forward, as if confiding some great secret.

'Of course,' Marianne said and waited while he counted a pile of notes onto the desk. 'You're most welcome here to

Gaofar! That means "windy" in Irish, but we're having a good run of weather so you shouldn't see much more than a stiff breeze.' She could recite the spiel in her sleep – where the lake path started and finished, no bank but there's an ATM in the garage or any local business will give cash back with your purchases, fishing trips arranged by the hotel. Her mother had trained them long ago not to ask whether business or pleasure brought visitors to Coolaroone. The only business anyone had here was someone over at the drying-out centre in Willowbrook, and, as for pleasure – where better, as long as moving statues were your thing.

'You'll walk the lake path,' she said. 'Everyone does. The trees are particularly beautiful. Lots of legends and stories about them – you'll find an information leaflet in your room. And, of course, the statue of the Virgin Mary in our grotto is something of a local...' *Don't say legend*, she reminded herself, *the faithful might be offended.* 'Something of a local *cause célèbre*, you might say. Over the years a lot of people have seen it move and believe that it is a message from the heavens.'

'My goodness. What sort of message?'

'That's between people and their conscience.' Marianne gave a merry little laugh. Her Bord Fáilte laugh, she thought of it. Her Coolaroone laugh. 'You'll have to go and see for yourself. Be sure to come and share any wisdom she imparts.'

She waited until he had gone upstairs before gathering the notes with a rubber band and putting them into the desk drawer.

With the addition of Mr Stiller, that made four rooms occupied out of nine. Ten, if you counted her own. Not bad for the first real week of the season. A soft opening, you'd call it. The way Liv went on about the recession, you'd think they were on the poverty line. Last year, her sister even went so far as to wonder if they should sell the remaining land.

'Land?' Marianne said, frowning at the phone as if Liv could see her. 'You mean the acre out the back? It would be a better idea to expand, build a couple of small cottages out there. A rural retreat kind of thing. We were talking about it at work only recently, the upsurge in corporate rural retreats. It's the new mindfulness, apparently, to deal with all of the pressure and burnout.'

Liv gave a short bark of laughter. 'We're a long way from executive rural retreats, if you haven't noticed.'

The cheek of her! Marianne bloody well grew up here too. She was every bit as familiar with it as Liv. She counted to five before speaking. 'That's the whole point,' she said. 'To offer something new. Maybe do a pop-up restaurant one night a week—'

'And have the hotel Dillons accuse me of stealing their business?'

'A high tide lifts all boats,' Marianne said. But Liv was already ending the call and the call-to-arms of their father's words went unheeded.

Marianne looked at the hoover and pushed it in under the desk. She could put it away later, after a coffee. If Ethel was around, maybe she could raise the idea of rebranding again. She might be here for a while – and miracles could happen. Just ask the statue.

HOLY TUESDAY

ETHEL

'Grand and early for a walk, Ethel.'

Everyone that passed her said the same thing. If a person hadn't a spark of creativity in themselves, they'd go mad. It amused Ethel to say the same thing back every time. Let them think she was one of them.

'Up with the lark, that's me.'

The duplicity pleased her. It took her mind off the fizzing in her blood. Drink did that to her, or, she supposed, the absence of drink did that to her. It was important to be precise. You were nothing in this world if you hadn't the ability to express yourself accurately. No matter how ugly the world got, there was elegance to be found in a clear sentence.

In that selfsame spirit of honesty, she had to admit to herself that there were few enough larks around, up or otherwise. The mice must be finding their nests and destroying the eggs before they had a chance to hatch into baby birds. If she was still doing the bit of work with Birdwatch Ireland, she could alert them to it, but time had been called on that particular bit of community spirit. It was agreed that it might be better for all concerned if herself and Jennifer Keefe kept their distance from one another. It mightn't be the mice at all anyway.

Coolaroone was close enough to the water that the blame might equally be laid at the feet of the voles. Which raised the question of whether or not voles had feet, a diversion that brought her to the end of the road and onto the lake path proper. There, the wind met her with the exuberance of a pup, nosing between the buttons of her coat and making her glad that she had pulled her socks over the lip of her boots before setting off. Still, cold or warm, wet or dry, the beauty of the light on the water was a balm to the soul. *Aren't we two-thirds liquid?* her mother used to say, and wasn't she right?

It was cold for April and the trees were bare enough yet, but there was nevertheless a sense of unfurling, of the greenery poised in the wings, waiting for its entrance. It put Ethel in mind of going to friends' houses to get dressed for dances when she was a girl, the little group standing before the mirror in their underthings but with the finery all laid out on the bed, ready to step into at the appointed hour.

She continued on, the gravel underfoot crunching in time with her step and the growing thrum of her blood. It was the brandy, of course. Irresistible when someone else was paying, but brown spirits made for brown spirits.

'What are you having to drink, Ethel?' Dr Nolan had asked her the previous evening, placing a fifty euro note on the bar where Alan the barman could see it. 'Although you're clearly drinking from the fountain of youth.' He laughed, as if that would hide his eyes flicking down her blouse. It was a trick that used to drive Martin mad, God rest him. Even the time he had pneumonia and was nearly drowning in his own phlegm, he waited for the doctor to come from the next town over rather than let Dr Nolan inside their bedroom door. 'We might never get him out,' he said, and she thought the fit of laughing between them might carry him then and there.

'You're very good,' she told him. 'A chivalrous man is God's own creation. I'll have a brandy and port, please.' There might be another one in it for her yet, if she could put up with his insinuations. His knowing everyone's business.

While he turned to order, she checked her blouse, placing her fingers on the bottom button and tracing them all the way up to be sure she had them done right. She couldn't be peering down at her own cleavage. It was uncouth. Not to mention the double chin it bestowed. Doing it by feel was discreet and, if she was caught, faintly alluring. Fifty was the new forty they said and sure she was in her fifties for another few months yet, which meant forty was practically in the rear-view mirror still.

Halfway along the lake path, she stopped for her customary look over the water. The morning light was pale and grey, her favourite, she would swear, until the next time she saw it in moonlight, when the bright silver would take the breath from her. She leaned on the paling, and it shifted under her. The council had the money to put it up a few years ago but none to maintain it and the rot was setting in. Ethel looked about her at the seagulls wheeling overhead, the pike jumping. It did a body good to see it. The first time Martin, God rest him, brought her for a walk there, it as good as sealed the deal. To the young Ethel, having such peace within a stone's throw of home let her draw in a full breath for the first time in a long while.

A jogger thundered past, decked out like a highlighter marker, with headphones and sunglasses blocking everything good about the place. Ethel was tempted to trip the little fool just to bring her closer to it. Small good it would do. There was no telling some people. Instead, she stood in the classic irritated pose, arms akimbo and her fists resting on her hip bones. Martin, God rest him, used to tell her they were like two little shelves. 'You could balance a stack of coins there,' he said admiringly when she undressed in front of him on their wedding night.

'Penny for them, Ethel,' called a voice behind her.

She turned to see the Dempseys ambling along the path towards her.

'Gentlemen. Fine day for it.' *Grand now, thanks be to God,*

John Paul the father would say, and John Paul the son would add that the forecast was poor.

''Tis grand now, thank God,' John Paul the father said.

'Forecast is poor,' John Paul the son added.

'But sure they get it wrong as often as they get it right,' she said.

With the required conversational loop closed, she was free to go on her way. This would be the ideal place for a stroke victim. There would be no need to learn to speak fully, a few key weather-related phrases and nobody would be able to tell anything had ever happened. 'Stroke?' they would say, wonderingly. 'Old Dempsey? Hardly. Wouldn't we have noticed?'

Hey presto, no more rehabilitation speech therapists. Wouldn't the health service save a small fortune? She should write to the minister.

This last part of the path always annoyed her. Rowan trees on one side to ward off spirits, aspens on the other to communicate with the next world. That was Coolaroone all over, wanting to be all things to all people and succeeding in none. Her mood spoiled, there seemed little point in finishing her walk. She'd be as well ducking under the fence and across Powers' two fields until she hit the main road into the village.

Mother of God but she could hardly hear her thoughts above the hum in her blood. She needed no clock to tell her that the shutters of the pub would shortly lift, waiting with open arms to succour the weary. Her whole body felt like it was flickering. That was brandy for you, caramel on the tongue but sherbet in the veins. Was that the kind of kick they said Skittles gave small children? Lord but Olive killed her when she found out she used to let Shay have them whenever she was minding him.

She climbed the gate that separated Powers' field from the road and paused at the verge of the road. A left turn would take her home, where Olive would be running around with the harried air of someone overseeing a multinational.

Having Marianne home made her snappish. Marianne would be looking for someone to drink coffee and listen to whatever she was running from this time. A right turn would take her to Naughtons, where she could have a quick Irish coffee and be in better humour to face home.

Her body moved without her, it felt like. The scientists would say it was adrenalin. As if such a prosaic thing – the gift of Everyman, of common animals, for heaven's sake – held within it such magnificent insistence. *Two-thirds liquid.* Her mother was closer to the mark.

Just the one, she promised herself, knocking lightly on the side window so that Alan would come and unlatch the door for her.

One, then home for lunch with her girls.

HOLY TUESDAY

LIV

Liv lifted her hair high onto her head, letting the warm water gush down between her shoulder blades. Waiting until after breakfast to shower was worth it to purge the smell of cooked breakfast from her skin. Maybe Marianne was right and they should upgrade the place. Bircher muesli and a fresh honeycomb wouldn't take the same toll on her pores. Liv turned up the temperature as high as she could bear until the steam engulfed her entirely.

Shay could fail his exams again and become a shut-in. She would have to leave his meals on a tray outside his door until such time as drones could deliver them through the window and he didn't need her any more. In the steam of the shower door, Liv wrote: '1. Shay = recluse.' She hadn't heard Ethel come in last night, which meant she could be in a heap at the bottom of the front steps with her neck broken. She was still at the stumbling-home stage of this particular descent. Liv sighed and added: '2. Ethel = awkward death.' Marianne was home, which meant there was heartbreak or divilment or wounds of some sort to be licked. It also meant high-flung suggestions for unnecessary improvements, all delivered with a world-weary air, with the rest of them expected to bow down in gratitude for her wisdom. Liv traced: '3. Mar = drama.' She read the words aloud, shivering as the too-hot water ran red rivers down either side of her neck. Only when she turned off the water did she swipe her hand through the steam, obliterating the words and her worries along with them.

That was the theory anyway. Affirmations for the self-conscious. For the not-quite middle-aged mortified.

Liv closed the door to the final room. Marianne had done a surprisingly thorough job and she herself needed only to add a few small tweaks so that the beds were perfectly made, the towels neatly arranged, the bathrooms neat as ninepence. Why was it, she wondered, that ninepence got to be neat while sixpence was crooked? Who decided that? Did the coins themselves get any say at all? Maybe the sixpence was bored by neatness, the ninepence terrified of disorder. Ethel would say that such questions were the sign of an idle mind.

'We're going out for lunch,' she announced to Shay, arriving into his room with the barest hint of a knock. It might not have been exactly audible, she conceded to herself, as he snapped the computer shut and sprang backwards, narrowly avoiding Lucky's tail. But that was the way with teenagers, wasn't it? You had to surprise them into engaging with you. Softly, softly or they saw you coming a mile away, like flies with rolled-up newspapers.

'Wh...at?'

Jesus but she hated when he stammered. Man up, she wanted to order. Except you weren't allowed to say that any more. It was too emasculating. Or was it too masculine? Anyway, it was too something and was therefore Not Done if you didn't want to end up like the mother in that book about the child who killed his classmates. The story whose suggestion got her kicked out of her book club. It was worth it for the looks on their faces when they arrived to discuss it, each of them more puffed up than the last. 'And you having a son!' they hissed. It was their liveliest meeting by a long shot, building to a denouement that saw them rise as one, each placing her copy of the book by Liv's seat, ceremonially almost. After they left, she finished both bottles of wine before going into each of the empty bedrooms and adding the offending item to the obligatory Bible in the bedside lockers.

Looking at Shay now, in the bedroom that hadn't changed so much as a poster since the previous year – if she wasn't mistaken, his final year exam timetable was still tacked to the wall under the windowsill – she wondered if it was too late to contact any of those women and ask what it was that had freaked them out so badly.

'We're going out to lunch,' she repeated. 'Perk of the B&B trade. Afternoons off.'

Like his room, Shay seemed to be frozen. The same routine as the previous year, the same friends. And yes, she knew she should be grateful that he had a real-life social network, but, honestly, with most of his group gone off to university, it was hard not to see the remainder as exactly that. The leftovers. The dregs. Granted, they weren't junkies or drug dealers – as far as she could tell – but they had an air of hopelessness about them that might be catching. Every time Shay opened his mouth, she was afraid he was going to tell her he had decided not to bother resitting the exams. She would be expected to say that it wasn't the end of the world, when what she really wanted to do was sit beside him in the exams and nudge his arm every time he stopped writing.

'You are a terrible mother,' she told herself sternly in the mirror on the landing.

'In fairness, you learned from the best,' Marianne said, from behind her.

Liv jumped. 'You're worse than a bloody cat!'

'I'm less needy though.'

Liv couldn't help but laugh. 'Fish Bar for lunch, so?'

'Only B&B perk there is. I didn't see Ethel – is she around?'

'I'm sure she'll meet us there if she has time,' Liv said carefully.

As they passed through reception, Marianne stopped. 'I forgot to mention – someone checked in earlier. An older gent. I put him into the system, but he paid cash, if you want to take it to the bank.'

'I'll deal with it later,' Liv said. 'Dealing with it' meant noting the cash in her expenses column and then putting a bit back into the drawer under the desk where Ethel would be sure to find it. Marianne would be outraged if she knew. She would tell her if there was any point to it, Liv reassured herself. But she was the one that had to call down to Moran's shop and settle a tab, or return a phone call to the bank about a bounced cheque. Filing Ethel under 'expenses' was the most practical solution.

Liv had a little rush of giddy joy walking down the street with her sister. Whenever she told someone she had a twin sister, they looked around Liv as if she might be attached at her back. No, really, I do, she always wanted to insist.

No lunchtime rush was evident in the Fish Bar and Liv had a moment's worry for Joely. She had invested so much, wanted so desperately to make a go of it and stay in Coolaroone. She hugged her extra warmly and introduced her to Marianne, before following her to a window table with an eagerness that suggested they were on display as much as the lobsters in the tank by the counter.

Marianne nodded at the tank. 'Has anyone ever ordered one?'

'No chance,' Liv said. 'One of the young Cotters named them the day the place opened, so the odds are good that Bert and Ernie will be enjoying a long retirement here.'

'What do you think they think about?'

'Lobsters? Or the young Cotters?'

They shared a giggle at that one. 'I never gave it much

thought,' Liv said. 'Do they have a brain to think with or is it something more primitive? Wouldn't that have been a more useful thing to have on our biology exams than the earthworm? At least we'd know whether or not to feel bad about what we're eating.'

'You just said nobody would eat them,' Marianne pointed out.

'True. But if they got new ones in, who knows? Or some tourist might take a notion.'

'What's her story?' Marianne nodded at Joely, who was writing specials on the chalkboard.

'Joely? Why does there have to be a story?'

Marianne shrugged. 'People don't usually move here.'

'Ethel did,' Liv pointed out.

'Anyone would have moved here for Dad,' Marianne said fondly. 'Is Joely after hooking up with a local, is that it?'

'Nope. Damien is South African as well.'

'Jesus. Really?'

Did she have to sound so surprised? Liv bit back her irritation. This was the way it always was with Marianne – if you wanted a nice time, you swallowed a certain amount.

They were silent while Joely recited specials and poured wine.

'I'll have Bert,' Marianne said, pointing to the tank. 'Plenty of butter, please.'

'Plenty of butter,' Joely repeated faintly.

'Maybe some lemon mayonnaise as well. But on the side,' Marianne added. 'Lobster can be terribly sweet.'

'Lemon,' Joely agreed, her pencil barely touching the order pad.

'I'm only messing with you. I'll have the mussels, please.'

'Thank goodness!' Joely clapped her hand to her heart. 'I don't know how I'd explain it to Ernie. Or the young Cotters.'

'She's making herself at home,' Marianne observed as Joely bounced away. 'Knowing the young Cotters, imagine.'

'It is her home,' Liv said, taking a grateful slug of wine.

They were silent for a few minutes.

'Shay said we'll be eating insects next,' Marianne said.

'What?'

Which part had thrown her, Marianne wondered, the idea of eating insects or her son volunteering information?

'When did he say that?'

Marianne shrugged. 'We had a bit of a chat earlier on.'

'What else did you chat about?'

'Why the Spanish Inquisition? Does he have an allotted number of words per day and you're afraid he wasted them on me?'

That was closer to the mark than Marianne might realise. Although any imagined limit was imposed by Shay himself. 'No. It's just that... Shay's not very chatty at the moment.'

'He seemed perfectly sociable to me.'

Liv willed herself not to lean across and throttle her sister's casual confidence out of her. Or drop to her knees and beg to know what they had talked about. 'Was that all he had to say for himself, that we would all end up eating insects?'

Marianne shrugged. 'I don't know. Don't get all mother-monster over it. It was just random chat. I didn't exactly make a mental note of the topics covered.'

Topics? Liv thought. Plural? She forced herself to laugh. 'I worry too much, I know. It's just that it's a bit of a funny year for him, repeating his exams and that. I often wonder if he feels he's missing out—'

'Here we go.' Marianne rolled her eyes.

'Here we go what?'

'Just because you regret not going to university doesn't mean it's the be-all and end-all.'

'And just because you went doesn't mean you can be casual about what it might mean to other people.'

The food arrived before things could disintegrate any further. Joely was at pains to explain the ins and outs of their meal to them, where the fish were caught, how they were killed, how long they spent in the bucket of ice.

'Thanks, Joely. It looks great. We can't wait to tuck in,' Liv said eventually, cutting her off mid-sentence.

'Oh, right. Enjoy!' she said over her shoulder as she went to hover by the bar, casting looks between them and the door as if they might suddenly double in number while she glanced away.

'A bit of The Waterboys,' Marianne said, leaning in close.

'What?'

'"Fisherman's Blues". That's what the mussels chose to listen to as they went into the pot.'

And just like that they were six years old, laughing until Liv thought she would pee her pants.

'Shay is a great kid,' Marianne said when they calmed down. 'You've done a good job there.' She nudged Liv companionably.

'I just wish he would give me a bit more to go on. I look at him and I haven't the first idea what he's thinking. If he's thinking. A stray word here and there and that's it.'

'They have to be more concise these days. All the texting and Twitter shortens their thoughts down to staccato. I'm sure half of them couldn't expand a thought if their lives depended on it. You should see some of the emails I have to deal with at work. Half-illiterate, some of them.'

'How is work?' Liv usually enjoyed her sister's stories – Mar could be bitingly funny about the nonsense she claimed accompanied corporate life. She had a seemingly inexhaustible fund of meetings going horribly wrong, marketing disasters averted, emails sent to the wrong people. Today, however, she didn't seem to want to play.

Marianne made a face. 'It's work. I keep showing up and they keep paying me.'

'Except you're not showing up. You're here. Everything all right?'

'I told you. I had a bunch of annual leave days to take before they went into the big void in the sky.'

Her voice was far too casual. Whatever had sent her

running home wasn't up for discussion yet. Unless – the thought was uncomfortable – she was here to talk about the business. About the future. 'What about Ed?'

'What about him?'

No wonder Marianne and Shay had got on so famously over breakfast. They were probably just batting the same sentence back and forth.

'He didn't want to come with you?'

'He wasn't asked.' Marianne pointed over to the counter. 'Look!'

Joely was sticking a sign to the lobster tank. 'Hi! We're the Fish Bar mascots, Ernie and Bert,' it said. 'Together since 2016.' Underneath it, she had drawn a little rainbow flag.

'She's made it sound like they're a couple,' Marianne said. 'If she's not careful, she'll have protesters with placards outside the door.'

Liv shook her head. 'The marriage referendum crowd were on fire around here. You couldn't move for "Love is Love" badges. Everyone was spoiling for a fight, only there was nobody voting against it. Even the priest, allegedly.'

'Go on Father T,' Marianne said admiringly. 'Who would have thought?'

'Father T retired. We have Father Mike now.'

'How did Coolaroone swing that? I thought priests were as rare as hen's teeth.'

'He rotates between four parishes,' Liv said.

'A timeshare priest.' Marianne raised her glass. 'Modernity in rural Ireland.'

Marianne insisted on paying, so Liv let her, even though she felt like pulling up her bank balance on the phone to prove that she could well afford it herself.

'Do you fancy walking the lake?' she asked Marianne. Experience suggested her sister was more likely to share confidences when they weren't face to face. At one of her antenatal scans with Shay, she had looked at the curl of him on the screen and wondered whether all the time herself and Marianne had grown facing one another had worn out their closeness.

Marianne shook her head. 'I'll head home. Shay is downloading a series for us to watch.' She caught her sister's eye and burst out laughing. 'You should see your face. Actually, I have to make a work phone call.'

'I thought you were on holiday.'

'Nice lunches in fancy fish bars don't pay for themselves you know!' Marianne wagged her finger and left Liv standing in her own annoyance.

The breeze off the lake pulled the top of the water into little peaks. Toy waves, they looked like, incongruous with the depth and chill of the lake. *Bottomless*, they used to whisper to each other as schoolchildren, shivering with dread or anticipation or some delicious mix of the two. Liv found herself worrying that the season's tadpoles tempted to the surface by the warmth of the sun might be blown further than their ability to return.

The air held the promise of rain. She should go home before it started. In the distance she could see the gable wall of Naughtons and she wondered if Ethel was in there or if she was at home behaving herself while Marianne was around. It was a tough trade that put Ethel and Marianne both at home. Tough enough to send a person pleading intercession from the statue.

'Statue, statue, move for me. Or grant me wishes one-two-three.' Liv sang their childhood rhyme, skipping alternate feet, then jumping the final step with both feet together, getting a pebble in her shoe for her trouble. It hadn't worked then and it wouldn't now.

As if proving her point, the rain arrived with the suddenness of a toddler's tantrum. Liv pulled her hood tight around her face and ran for home.

HOLY TUESDAY

ETHEL

In the daytime, the snug was hers. It wasn't much, but it had its own little hatch that gave onto the back end of the bar, allowing a modicum of discretion for days when the thirst came early. The crossword and a coffee, what could be more respectable? The merest raise of an eyebrow and Alan knew to add the brandy to the mug. They didn't call it making it Irish for nothing. Weren't they born to it?

Who would begrudge it to her? Wasn't she a lady, a businesswoman in this community? Hadn't she worked hard enough and long enough, rearing two fine girls after Martin died, God rest him?

She took a swallow. A good drink – a drink you'd earned – hit you in the legs first, like you were only the vessel. Like you were hollow before it.

'Are you all right awhile, Ethel?' Alan stuck his head into the tiny hatch.

Was she all right awhile? She needed to be getting home if she was to go for lunch with the girls. Although they hadn't said they would all leave together. Maybe their intention was to meet there. 'I'll take another coffee when you get a moment, Alan. There's a few clues in today's crossword have me foxed. No rush.'

'Right you are.'

With a glass in her hand, time took its time. That was what people didn't understand. The way time moved. As if the alcohol split it into a hundred tiny different moments. Refracted, Shay would say. He was a smart boy, Shay, if he could only make up his mind to it. His father's brains but his mother's confidence, God love him. She would share that wisdom with him, she decided. Tomorrow morning. He only ever talked to her in the mornings now.

The glass slowed everything down, reminded a person to live moment to moment. Take the dust motes dancing in the sunlight coming through the window there: if she wasn't prepared to find the beauty in whatever was on offer, she would have been in the ground long ago.

'The next one will have to be the last, Ethel, I'm afraid.'

She had dropped the coffees a few hours ago when she realised it was well past lunchtime, but surely the peel of notes in her purse should have stretched further?

'I don't suppose…?'

He shook his head with every sign of regret. 'House policy, Ethel. Nothing personal.'

She closed her eyes rather than look at him. He was a bad bastard, Alan, when he let the power get ahold of him.

She got to her feet and tucked her handbag carefully under her arm. She couldn't go staggering into the bar like one of the poor Twomeys. She patted her hair and caught a glimpse of herself in the side of the glass. Nothing to be ashamed of there, wasn't she a fine-looking woman, all told? There would be plenty out in the bar that would appreciate her, even if Alan couldn't see further than his next euro.

'Dr Nolan,' she said, making sure to stand close enough that their elbows grazed. Men like him liked to hear their title. 'Is your good lady wife with you this evening?' A necessary question even though it nearly killed her to attach the term 'lady' to that common trollop he married.

'Good evening, Ethel. She may join me later, but I'm on my lonesome until then.'

'A handsome man never has to drink alone. You'll have the whole town lining up for your company.'

'To tell the truth, Ethel, they can be a little dull for my taste.'

And so the evening went, or some hours of it, at least. There might have been real talk mixed in among the rest. If there was, she didn't hold onto it.

'You're a fine-looking woman, Ethel,' he told her at some point. Or maybe she told him, it had a ring of the familiar. 'You haven't changed a jot as long as I've known you.'

She leaned in as if imparting the third secret of Fatima. 'I can still fit into my wedding dress.'

'I remember your wedding day,' he told her. 'We all thought Martin was the luckiest bastard alive.' This time it was his turn to lean in. 'There was more than one of us in town stayed awake that night wishing we were in his place.'

'Little good I was to him that night.' She looked him right in the eye. 'I knew next to nothing then.'

He half-groaned and shook his head.

'I suppose you keep a key to the surgery on you all the time?' she asked.

'For out of hours emergencies,' he said.

Ethel nodded. 'Give me five minutes and follow me over.'

'I'll put your name on a bottle behind the bar.'

He pushed his keys towards her and signalled to Alan to take an order. She kept her back ramrod straight as she walked to the door. She had the posture of a ballet dancer, Dr Nolan panted into her ear, later. A ballerina, she wanted to correct him. The word is ballerina.

The door to the B&B had something done to it since she left that morning. They had put some kind of fancy lock on it that moved every time she tried to put in the key. Some kind of newfangled anti-theft device, it must be. She bested it in the end, finding herself on her knees in the hallway when it gave way suddenly before her. The reception desk was only a few metres in front of her; it was hardly worth the bother of standing to walk to it. Out of habit, she opened the little drawer underneath the desk and was rewarded with a neat little roll of tens, paper-clipped together, the way Olive did. That girl was born old. Ethel pushed the money into the toe of her left shoe – she must have already taken off the right one – and wedged it back onto her foot. She could buy her own bottle tomorrow. It would have been handy to her today, it would have saved her… well, never mind. You couldn't unring a bell, as the man said. Lord knew, the good doctor's bell had rung fine and loud. It was as well there weren't many passers-by on the street outside. She giggled and it turned into a yawn. She would need to be up and out with the larks shortly for her walk. Couldn't miss her walk. Nothing like fresh air for keeping a woman at her best.

She pulled down the cushion from the office chair and curled up on the carpet under the desk, the way the day might find her all the sooner.

SPY WEDNESDAY

MARIANNE

Marianne woke early. Whatever her sister might say about afternoons being the perk of the B&B trade, the mornings more than took their pound of flesh. Her options, as she saw them, were either to lie there dreading getting up or to just bloody do it. *Better to find the day than have it find you*, her father used to advise her when she was a teenager and prone to sleeping in. That and *an hour in the morning is worth two in the afternoon.*

Her phone buzzed once, twice, making the whole bed vibrate. It would be Ed, she told herself. There was really no need to be scrabbling around looking for it like some kind of crazed gameshow contestant.

She found it eventually, half-tucked under the pillow. That was the beauty of sleeping without Ed: she didn't have to listen to anyone telling her she would burn the house down. 'Burn us in the bed' were his actual words. Was it any wonder she worried what exactly it was that remained between them, other than some scenic photographs and a shared weekly food shop?

She should be grateful that he was limiting his concerns to fire, having seemingly let go of the crackpot theories about ionising radiation and fertility that had so absorbed him a few months back. In vain, she had pointed out that the whole thing was a grand conspiracy theory, simply an insidious encroachment of the Internet of Things into bodily matters.

It wasn't as if the question of her ageing ovaries was solely Ed's concern. She had a passing interest in the topic as well. *Not now* wasn't necessarily a synonym for *never.*

Coming home to take a break from it all had made such sense forty-eight hours ago. Here, however, she was confronted with Shay – literally endless evidence of her sister's fertility! – and the queer sensation that Liv was crossing the finish line while she herself wasn't even out of the starting blocks. She had never thought much about this particular race, beyond a casual assumption that the decision would be hers whenever she was ready. The idea that her body might make the choice for her, that her level of control over all aspects of her life might fall somewhere short of her customary absolute, was unimaginable. What advice would her father have for her? Without him here to ask, she would have to settle for the comfort of his memory all around her.

She pulled a jumper and socks on over her pyjamas and went to find some breakfast. In the mornings, hot water was for the guests. Another B&B rule. If they wouldn't let her shower, then they would just have to take her as they found her, to hell with any early bird that might see her wandering the corridors.

The hallway and reception were less dark than the stairwell, the brightening sky outside faintly visible through the bevelled glass over the front door. It was light enough for her to see where she was going, bright enough to see the shape of her mother on the floor behind the desk.

'Fuck,' she swore under her breath. Her phone was still upstairs. Was it heart attacks or strokes where literally every second counted?

'Ethel.' She shook her mother. No reaction. She leaned close and shook a little harder. 'Ethel!' This time, her mother groaned, sending a powerful waft of brandy Marianne's way.

One too many, that was all, Marianne thought, already inclined to laugh at her own apocalyptic thinking. The host of whatever bingo night or book club her mother was at last night must have poured with a heavy hand.

The clock on the wall told her it was 1 a.m. in New York, 7 a.m. in Italy, and, more pertinently, 6 a.m. here in Ireland. Almost breakfast time for a certain kind of B&B patron. The frugal kind. Was there really any other among the people who chose to holiday in what were essentially other people's spare rooms? They were the type to rise early to make the most of their day, which meant putting away enough breakfast to fell a competitive eater in training.

'Come on, Ethel.' She caught her mother's two arms and tugged, but there was no way she was getting her down the corridor to her room by herself. That left her with two options, each less palatable than the other: leave her mother where she was and trust that the smell of frying would wake her, Lazarus-like, before the guests saw her, or wake Liv for help. It was not to her credit, she knew, that she considered the former for a shade longer than she should have.

'I say we ground her or take away her phone. What do you think for a first offence?' Their mother was safely deposited in her bed – thank God she had moved to a ground-floor room after Dad died, claiming she was unable to stomach their room without him – and Marianne was prepared to find the humour in the situation.

'Fourth,' Liv said.

'Fourth what?' Marianne looked at Liv. 'You don't mean that this happened three times already?'

'Of course not,' Liv said calmly.

'Good because—'

'It has happened *many many* times before. Four is simply the count in the last twelve months.'

'You're joking. Right?'

But Liv was already moving along the corridor, leaving Marianne no choice but to follow.

'Liv. Stop. Tell me what's going on.'

'I just told you what's going on.'

Her sister's face was composed and entirely serious. Marianne felt her anger rise. 'Do you mean that this is a regular occurrence? This… this is why Ethel missed our lunch yesterday? To get so rat-arsed she slept where she fell?'

'You know what, Marianne, it would be really helpful right now if you could try not to make this about you.'

Marianne recognised her sister's attempt to deflect from the real issue. Of course she would, when the fault – no, the blame – was indisputable. 'Why the hell would you not tell me something like this?'

'When?' Liv rounded on her. 'When you were to visit last summer but cancelled at the last minute? Or at Christmas? No, wait, you cancelled at the last minute.'

'You. Could. Have. Phoned,' Marianne enunciated carefully.

'Leave a message on your voicemail, you mean? Or send a text, so you could reply telling me you were too busy to get away so I should do what I thought was best? That's what I did, I simply skipped the middleman.'

'Don't you dare try to lay this on me. How have you let things get this out of hand?'

Liv closed her eyes and took a breath, making no effort to hide the fact that she was counting to ten.

'I'll phone Willowbrook,' Marianne said. Let Liv see how hurtful an overreaction could be. How stupid it could make a person feel.

'Willowbrook.' Liv had a strange little smile. She walked behind the desk and was flicking through a large diary, muttering dates under her breath.

'Here,' she said, stabbing her fingernail onto the page. 'She went in on the Monday and was out again on the Wednesday.' Back went the pages, and back, and back. 'And here. See? She made it about a fortnight once. I actually thought she might stick with it. Go ahead. Look. See for yourself how I let it get out of hand.'

There it was, in black and white. Willowbrook. The great unspoken community resource, hidden away on a demesne about twenty miles outside the town, housing those otherwise unable to manage themselves.

Babies, Marianne knew from having to listen to her married friends, were sometimes given the label 'failure to thrive'. Willowbrook was the adult version, a failure to live appropriately in the world.

'Who else knows?'

'That's what's bothering you? Who knows?'

Marianne took a breath. 'Who. Else. Knows.'

'Shay lives here, of course he knows. Other than that, I haven't told a soul,' Liv said. 'Which means the whole village knows.'

'When—'

Liv held up a finger and shook her head. 'Not now. I need to do breakfast,' she said.

Marianne dressed so fast she must, she thought, look like a children's cartoon, with her feet and arms whizzing in circles, pulling and dragging and smoothing. Even so, Liv was in the kitchen before her, cracking eggs into a pan. Wordlessly, Marianne scalded teapots and cafetières and placed toast racks into the top oven to warm. Their movements were still perfectly synchronised. It was like getting up to dance at a wedding and discovering you could remember every shake of 'The Birdie Song'. They even smiled at each other once, when Liv swung a rasher-laden spatula onto the counter-top to find Marianne standing there with a paper-towel-covered plate ready for her.

'Mr Stiller, how are you this fine morning?' If she were a stranger, Marianne thought, she would find her own bluff heartiness suspicious.

'Very well, thank you.'

'I hope you'll get a chance to enjoy the town today.' She

was suddenly painfully aware how much of their morning patter was carefully designed to avoid asking guests what their plans were for the day. To avoid the awkwardness of their visits to a relative or friend in Willowbrook. A kindness learned at her mother's knee, ironically. *Discretion is the better part of valour* was one of Ethel's by-laws. Was she an inmate? What was even the right word – a client? A patron? Too late, she realised she was standing staring into mid-air. Mr Stiller was looking at her with his eyebrow raised.

'Excuse me,' she said brightly. 'I seem to be away with the fairies this morning. Which reminds me, did you have a chance to read about the trees down by the lake? There's quite a wealth of local fairy legends, if you have any interest in that sort of thing—' And she was back on track again, explaining that they planted primroses around the door because the fairies could not pass through them on May Eve.

By the time the four tables had their refills of tea and coffee and their second rounds of toast (to set them up for the day, like good economical holidaymakers), Marianne felt she had run a marathon. In the kitchen, her sister was angry-cleaning. Marianne knew if she opened the bin, she would find at least one glass with a cracked rim.

'Has she really tried four times?'

'She says it "doesn't take",' Liv said, flatly.

'If we both talked to her, explained that she has to give it a chance, stay the twenty-eight days—'

'The twenty-eight-day thing is a myth. It works if you believe in it, it doesn't if you don't. Simple as that.'

'What about AA?' Marianne felt stupid even suggesting it, as if it was something her sister wouldn't have heard of.

'That calls for believing in something bigger. "A higher power".' She made air quotes. 'And Ethel doesn't—'

'I know.' Marianne had to work hard not to snap at Liv that of course she knew her mother was a cultural Catholic, at best. She didn't exactly have the high moral ground when it came to who knew what about Ethel. She had a flash of the old resentment. That was how it was with twins, always competing, always compensating.

'Is this... she didn't used to be like this.' She hated the questioning tone in her voice, but there was no way around it.

'No. She can be fine for a long time then go off the rails. This phase will last a few weeks then she'll go cold turkey, straighten herself out... If you come back in six months, she'll swear blind that this morning never happened, that you dreamt the whole thing.'

'What can we do?'

'Keep her away from the guests. Give her enough money that she doesn't make a show of herself in the pub begging people to buy her drink. But not so much that she's a real danger to herself. Wait it out until she's ready to hear it.' Liv sighed. 'In the meantime, hope she comes home in one piece.'

Marianne left Liv to do the rooms and headed out for a walk. She needed the air, she said. It was more polite than saying she couldn't stand to do the morning's work knowing that her sister would only check it and find it wanting. Liv's controlling tendencies could be dismissed as quirky if not quite endearing. Today, however, they were just another symptom of how far apart they were. 'Give her something to come home to.' Marianne mimicked Liv's voice. As if she hadn't wanted to come home a bit more often. But Ed had his family to see too and there was only so much a person could do, for fuck's sake.

On the street ahead of her, a gaggle of women were blocking the footpath. Five abreast, for fuck's sake, and walking slowly enough that they were all within hearing or arm-grabbing distance. Marianne sighed. Judging by the mid-height heels and layered highlights, these were her generation. What was it about staring down the barrel of forty that drove women back to the teenage need to look like everyone else? Odds were these were women she had gone to school with and would be expected to know. Just as she tried to sidle past on the inside, they stopped entirely, and Marianne ducked left and in the church gate rather than face them.

Once she gained the little porch, she risked a glance back over her shoulder, only to see them coming along the path after her. Dammit. She took a breath and stepped past the unsettling sign proclaiming 'Holy Wednesday service 12 p.m.' – whatever happened to Spy Wednesday? – and into the church proper. Inside, it was gloomy but warm and Marianne slipped into a side pew, loosening her scarf with a pleasurable shiver. She would give it a few minutes and then head back out before the service started. The group of women that had come in behind her busied themselves arranging hymn books and choir sheets. Their glances passed over her from time to time, but they showed no recognition, although Marianne recognised at least two, which meant they must know her as well. There was an undeniable flicker of annoyance. Take it as a compliment, she told herself. Wasn't that all she wanted as a teenager? To swan back in to Coolaroone so glamorous as to be unrecognisable? It was worth the high maintenance sharp-edged haircut, the three-weekly fringe trims. She was no longer Mar, one half of the *Gaofar* twins, but Marianne O'Callaghan, kicker of ass and taker of names, with her pick of jobs and salaries.

She straightened her back and lifted her head to look around. The altar was flanked by two statues. The obligatory crucifixion scene, Jesus on the cross, his ribs showing, blood trickling down his face, arms and chest. How did it not give children nightmares? Herself and Ed had visited Brussels together once. When they passed the famous statue of the little peeing boy, he was all decked out in an Irish costume for St Patrick's Day. There he was in his little tam-o'-shanter and Aran sweater, weeing away gaily. Would they consider something similar here? Jesus in a bathrobe? Or would that only interfere with the realism of their Caucasian Jesus?

There was no statue of Mary on her own, she noticed. No need, not when she had the grotto to herself. If they were out for a drive on a Sunday, Dad would always stop the car at the grotto on the way so they could say a quick decade of the rosary for a safe journey. While they recited the words, Marianne would look at Mary's peaceful face and envy her. She didn't look like she would be one bit bothered by the fact that Mags and Lorraine had spent Friday whispering in corners, glancing over at her and shushing one another when she came up to ask could she play too. Mary would just toss her head and find something else to do. Although, Marianne thought gloomily, she would probably go and sit beside that awful Ellen Ghoul, who ate her sandwiches facing the wall so nobody would see they were just bread smeared with brown sauce and who had nothing interesting to say because she wasn't allowed to watch television in the evenings. Beside her, Liv would have her eyes closed, thumbing rosary beads dutifully through her fingers. Marianne would have to guess where they were and hope that she wouldn't be caught out by starting an accidental eleventh Hail Mary instead of the Glory Be.

The grotto was transformed utterly that one summer, of course. The summer of the moving statue. The older girls saw it first, their excitement spreading through the village like German measles. There was no doubt that it conferred an aura of specialness on children generally – the idea that it was their purity that attracted the attention of the Virgin herself held a kind of scientific power for the first few days – but how Marianne longed for the more specific specialness that could only come from being an actual witness. For days, Ethel refused to let them anywhere near the place, despite Marianne – and even Liv – telling her over and over that there were tour buses, *actual tour buses from the actual city*, coming to see something that was rightfully theirs. Marianne could hardly sleep at the idea that some other eight-year-old would have the vision that should rightly be Marianne's if only she had been there. As if the Virgin would co-opt Santa's bold child policy of passing over the house and leaving the gift with the next child instead.

In the end, even Ethel couldn't hold out against the fever that gripped Coolaroone, and when Dad suggested that they go along one evening to join in with the nightly rosary, Marianne knew that would be enough. Her father didn't often overrule Ethel.

Like all the evenings of childhood, it was sunny and warm, the sunburn and midges bleached out of the memory by the kindly hand of time. During the rosary, Marianne stared at the statue so hard that her eyes watered. Should she pretend she saw something? she wondered, but the risk was too great that she would be found out. What if the other girls had some sort of secret proof, some signal or code word that Mary gestured or whispered to them? Disappointment was better than shame. When the rosary was over, Dad suggested they get a burger from the van and Ethel nodded her agreement. They would be over on the bank, she told the girls, and there had better be no messing. Liv started crying to go home, and for one awful minute, Marianne was sure they would all have to go and wanted to cry too. But, again – and if there were ever proof that the grotto was a place of miracles, this was surely it – Ethel agreed that Liv could get a lift home with Tadhg Hayes, their neighbour. Marianne had a flicker of doubt – Tadhg was a bit creepy – but Liv still seemed to want to go home and this way they both got what they wanted, which was almost as rare a miracle as the statue herself. Marianne found herself among the other children, playing a sort of muted numbers game that gradually emboldened into tag and, once Father T's underpants-blue Ford Escort disappeared into the distance, graduated into daring each other to jump off the side of the bank furthest from the grown-ups. When it was her turn, Marianne glanced over to where her parents sat, drinking tea from her mother's flask and talking mostly to one another. Ethel didn't like the way other women gossiped. They weren't looking at her, so Marianne held her breath and jumped. She landed badly, knocking the breath from her body and fighting back tears.

It was worth it. She was the only girl brave enough to try, a small fame that she could see in the eyes of the local boys for long months afterwards. She was glad, though, when Ethel called her to go home before she had time for a second go.

Marianne was still smiling to herself when someone poked her in the shoulder to move her knees so they could pass by her into the inside of the seat. Around her, the church was beginning to fill. The women that had followed her into the church had emerged from the sacristy with a portable stereo – an amusing throwback – that was filling the church with the sounds of Taizé music.

Jesus, remember me, the monks chanted. *When you come into your kingdom.*

This was the Easter of her childhood. A week of daily church visits, each with the promise of meeting her school friends and, at the end of it, the Easter Sunday crowning glory of spring lamb with mint sauce and roast potatoes and as many chocolate Easter eggs as her childish belly could accommodate. Uncomfortable, now, to remember her parents' tradition of opening a bottle of wine with that dinner. Herself and Liv with their glasses of Lilt ('made of snots and water', her sister told her, and Marianne was half-thrilled, half-traumatised, and drank it anyway, because Liv did), hoping against hope their parents would refill their glasses and keep the party going.

'Ethel is a drunk,' she mouthed to herself. If anyone saw, they would think she was praying.

Jesus, remember me, the monks replied. *When you come into your kingdom.*

'My relationship might be over,' she added, but even that didn't shift the single-minded monks. *Jesus, remember me*, they pleaded.

The women didn't remember Marianne. Their schooldays had no social media posts ensuring she would never be fully forgotten. Liv wouldn't have to beg to be remembered. She had it all sewn up. Everything about her sister was immutable.

Was it any wonder that next to her, Marianne felt like air? Like she could be hit by a bus and all she would leave behind was a healthy bank account and the perfect capsule wardrobe.

She got to her feet and made her way to the door. When she got there, one of the Twomeys held it open, but when she smiled her thanks, he nodded and looked into the distance.

She stumbled out, feeling like a ghost. Whoever rebranded Spy Wednesday as Holy Wednesday missed one crucial point: the past shouldn't – couldn't – be sanitised.

SPY WEDNESDAY

LIV

'I only asked where you were going.' Liv looked up at her son, who was trying to shrink his six-foot-two frame into something unnoticeable. Jesus Christ, it was an innocent passing question and here he was, practically cowering, as though she were the Gestapo and not his mother. How was he to ever survive in the world?

'Um... out?'

If there was one habit she would wipe out among the youth of today – if she were omnipotent for a day, say, or if she was granted three wishes, unlikely though that was, it was toilets she was scrubbing, not heirloom silver – it would be upspeak. Hands down. What it must do to their collective psyche to put themselves into the world with that degree of uncertainty of their own most basic opinions. No wonder teen suicide was through the roof; they were barely sure of their own names.

She didn't share those thoughts with Shay. Instead, she opted for the more acceptable shorthand. 'Tone!'

He hung his head. On someone so tall, the gesture looked ridiculous, as if he were being an animal in a school play. 'Out,' he said, finally.

Was that so hard? she wanted to ask but didn't. Sometimes you had to take your win where you got it.

'Are you taking Lucky for a walk?'

'Um… no?' He cleared his throat. 'I mean, no. She had a walk earlier and, you know, her hips, the vet said…'

Jesus wept. Eighteen years old. At his age she was… Well. There was no point in comparing.

'I'll be back later.' And he was gone.

Looking at his diminishing figure, she couldn't see how he might ever move out and find a life for himself. He would still be here at forty, holed up in his room doing incomprehensible things on his computer and coming out only to be fed, like some kind of zoo creature. What did it say about her that she could picture it so readily? Maybe that was why 'Shay = here forever' ended up on her shower door with alarming frequency.

It was, she told the banisters sternly, different for her. Obviously. Eighteen and pregnant didn't give a person many options. Correction: didn't give a *girl* many options. Seamus carried on as if nothing had changed.

Instead, she watched as he and Marianne sat their exams and went off to university without a backward glance. Marianne came home at weekends for a while, purely to moan about the hardships of studying (of which she seemed to do very little; complaining seemed to be the biggest part of it, as far as Liv could tell). Liv, worn out from night feeds, hadn't the energy to tell her to fuck off for herself. Marianne must have done enough, though, because she came out of it with a glowing degree. That was just like her, to look as if she was doing nothing and then come out on top. Everything came easily to her sister, it always had.

Liv mentally shook herself. Didn't she have a grand dollop of self-pity on her porridge this morning! A job she enjoyed, a fine healthy son, a roof over her head. These were not small things. So there were days when knowing the name of the newest Donegan baby, or what happened to the Sacred Heart statue outside the national school the night before Halloween didn't seem like much. So what? Life had space to hold all sorts of moments.

Her mother's room was empty. The bed was carefully made, suggesting Ethel was passably functional when she woke and left. If her mother had snuck back out, it meant they were still at the keeping-up-appearances stage.

Her mobile rang. Seamus. Her body did that complicated thing that came with seeing his name, two competing reactions leaving her vibrating in place, as if she herself were the device.

'Seamus!' Her voice was worthy of hospitality awards. If she entered the Rose of Tralee pageant, she would win it on her voice alone. 'Couldn't be better, thanks. Heading into the busy season. We were hoping for a little lull over Easter but no such luck. Ha! First world problems, am I right?'

This, to the first man ever to see her naked. Her sixteen-year-old self would never have believed that life could be this weird. 'Shay isn't here at the moment. He's taken Lucky out for a walk.' It annoyed her that she was pretending to know where her son was. She had got him this far, she didn't need to justify her parenting to anyone. 'You might get him on the mobile. Or did you try already?'

'Actually, I wanted to talk to you first.'

Liv's heart vibrated again. He was going to be late, which meant another excuse to Shay. Or he was going to be early, which meant something else entirely. 'What's up?'

'What? Nothing. I mean, nothing much. Ruth – I – we were just thinking that since it's Easter, maybe Shay could come to us instead? The girls have a few things on, and I know they'd love to have their brother there.'

Liv tapped her nail on the thigh of her jeans. She didn't need to know the ins and outs of his family life. Circumstances kept him in her family, she had no business in his. 'He's about to resit his exams, Seamus. He can't waste six hours of his weekend on the bus, it's not practical. You need to come here, as arranged. He's looking forward to spending Easter with you.'

'Surely he can decide for himself?'

'He'll say the same thing. The boy has hardly left his room these holidays.' It was both a lie and not a lie. The Schrödinger's cat of dodges.

God forgive her but she couldn't go through another week of post-results depression. The previous summer, on finding out how badly he had done, Shay had locked his bedroom door and refused to eat or talk. So it wasn't a lie. Not really. Not like *I love you*. Not like *I'll be back for you*. Not like *it'll be your turn soon*.

'Another weekend will hardly make any difference, so. Will you let him know that it's not my fault? Explain about Easter, the girls and all that,' Seamus said.

Liv closed her eyes. She could still picture him at eighteen, peering sideways at her, his eyes pleading. *What are you going to do?* Waiting for her to decide what they were asking his parents for, their blessing or money for the boat to Liverpool. He hadn't lost the habit of that sidelong glance, although the fringe and glasses had been outfoxed by laser surgery and a head that he pretended was shaved by choice.

'He's looking forward to seeing you, Seamus. To tell you the truth, he's been a bit quiet in himself and I think it would do him good to blow off a bit of steam.' She didn't know which was worse, having to talk Seamus into coming at all or pitching it as some sort of lads' weekend.

'I suppose I could come down early Saturday. The egg hunt isn't until Sunday evening…'

Liv let him talk himself into it. She would have jumped in with reassurances if it were only her own feelings at stake, but Shay was a different matter.

'I'll square it with Ruth and the girls, so. You can tell him not to worry, I'll be there.'

As if she would tell Shay anything about this conversation.

Seamus' own father had been the same, the kind to complain that someone else's funeral arrangements were designed deliberately to put him out. But when you put yourself at the centre of everything, what is everyone else, only peripheral?

They gathered around the lunch table, drawn there by fresh bread and years of conditioning. Ethel and Shay had arrived home within minutes of each other, neither keen to talk about their morning. Marianne toyed with her soup spoon, looking sidelong at Ethel as though she were an alarm about to go off.

'What are you working on today, Shay?' Liv asked, when it became clear that it wasn't enough to make lunch, she must also power them through an hour in each other's company.

'Physics, mostly,' he told his bowl.

Marianne managed to look away from Ethel for long enough to shudder. 'I hated physics. At least in maths you weren't expected to understand the why behind it all. You just plugged the numbers into the formulas and away you went.'

'I sort of like it,' Shay said. 'The why part, I mean. Maths always seems a bit... clinical.'

'I hadn't pegged you for a romantic,' Marianne said, poking his shoulder.

Liv watched poor awkward Shay blush up to his two ears. People who nudged other people should, in her humble opinion, have their elbows ceremonially snapped and the pieces handed back to them. *We are who we are*, she told herself. That stupid mantra was all that was left of her yoga phase (strikes one and two were the coldness of the village hall and the indignity of contorting beside the postman while he executed a better sun salutation, respectively).

'The radiator in number three is making that noise again,' she said, to move things along.

'Did you ever think about plumbing, Shay?' Ethel said, buttering bread with the focus of a woman thinking in terms of soakage later in the day.

'Ethel.' Liv's voice was a warning.

'I'm only saying.'

'Well don't. Shay's decisions are his own.'

'Who're you telling?' Ethel said.

'Maybe we should overhaul the whole thing,' Marianne said, pushing her soup away half-eaten.

Liv let her talk. What she wouldn't give to tell Marianne that it had nothing to do with her one way or the other.

Shay was the first to finish, dropping his bowl in the dishwasher and mumbling something that might have been 'study'.

'I'm going to head out for an hour,' Ethel said. She made a production of taking Shay's bowl back out and rinsing it before replacing it together with her own.

'Weren't you already out this morning?' Marianne asked. 'I thought maybe we could have a bit of a chat—'

Ethel sniffed, 'It's Holy Week, whether you like it or not. We're taking it in turns to do an hour in the perpetual chapel.' She shook her head gently at Marianne. 'City life has you ruined. Here you are, neither fish nor fowl.' There was a blast of cold air as the back door opened and closed behind her.

'That was uncalled for.' Marianne looked as if she might cry.

'She needs a cure,' Liv said, enunciating every word as clearly as if her sister was a middling foreign exchange student.

'She's never gone this early. It's barely two.'

'She was wearing her good shoes,' Liv said wearily.

'Should I go after her?'

'Unless you're planning to buy your round, I wouldn't. There'll be a scene.'

'For fuck's sake. How long has it been like this? Since Dad died?'

It would be easy enough to say yes, that's exactly when it started. It was grief or loneliness or a solace-seeking of some kind. It would be easy, certainly, but would it be true? If she were to look further back, if there existed some kind of *Black-Mirror*-type playback device for real life, would she find her mother reaching for the glass and then the bottle around the time that she told them she was expecting a baby? That she wouldn't be finishing school but would continue to live at home like an overgrown teenager, only it was her baby roaring at night that kept them awake and not the stairs creaking when she crept in after a night out.

No matter what angle she came at it from, she couldn't decide to her satisfaction if it was shame that first drove her mother to drink. As she crept up from the kitchen after warming Shay's bottle, was her mother waiting to creep down to her own bottle? She was too busy with her own portion of shame back then. Now, she read the stories of the Magdalenes and gratitude for her parents' acceptance of the situation nearly bent her double. It made her irritable, that fullness of heart. It was worse than indigestion.

'I didn't notice it for a long time after Dad died. Years, even,' she told Marianne. There was truth enough in that. If her sister noted the subtle shift in focus from Ethel's behaviour to Liv's, she said nothing.

But later that evening when Marianne poured them both a glass of wine, then paused, Liv knew what she was thinking before she said it.

'It's one drink,' she said. 'Don't make it into something it's not.' She took a defiant gulp from her own glass and began to dice the peppers.

SPY WEDNESDAY

ETHEL

The air had a spring feel to it, either fresh or chilly depending on your bent. Decidedly the kind you would have to be walking briskly to appreciate. Ethel would have stopped in for the paper, only she was anxious to get to the bar and claim the snug. Early afternoon on a Wednesday meant dole cheques and child benefit were burning holes in pockets all through the village. There was a song in that, Ethel thought, if a person had a mind to sing it.

'Alan.' She banged the door shut behind her and glanced around. As predicted, most of the tables were taken. She made to walk around the bar to the corner that housed the snug, but Alan shook his head apologetically. Typical. Only for Olive and her bloody soup, she could have been here an hour ago.

'What'll it be, Ethel? Coffee and the paper?'

She made a show of looking at her watch. 'It's nearly three. I'll chance a vodka and Slimline please, Alan,' she said.

'Right you are.' He nodded as if he wouldn't have known what to pour for her otherwise.

That was the sign of a good barman in a small town; he didn't confuse service with discretion. Ethel surveyed the room for a good spot. The Donoghues were in the window seat, billing and cooing like a pair of fifty-year-old lovebirds. In three hours' time, they'd be elbow-deep in each other's faults and failings and inviting comment from all and sundry. It was a foolish man that weighed in, but Coolaroone wasn't noted for its prizewinners.

The smaller central tables were peopled with young men, taking a day off from the job search to drink several days' worth of social welfare before going home to hand the rest over to their mothers. The Kavanaghs and Keatings were all represented, the Twomeys, of course, one of the PJ Mullinses – who was rumoured to be heading for Canada but based on the look of him today would be hard pressed to find his own backside – Teddy Dwyer and one of the Neilus Macs. She sighed and took a second look around. The non-nationals had no time for her or anyone else; they were only there to make money and take it home. Spilling out of the backs of lorries in port towns, willing to make their own start, whatever it took. It would do Shay no harm to see a bit of their work ethic, she thought, but Liv would go mad if she started bringing him here with her.

The fellow nearest the door was sitting alone. One of the Timjoe Sweeneys, she thought, the lad that was a couple of years behind the girls in school. He was clean enough looking that he couldn't have been there long, but she couldn't share a table and small talk with cleanliness alone. Dr Nolan avoided the place on a Wednesday. 'The day after dole day is a free-for-all,' he told her once. 'Everyone with a hangover thinks they can have my medical expertise for the price of a pint.'

The man in the chair by the fire looked vaguely familiar, and harmless. He must be from out the country, she decided. She crossed the floor and gestured to the empty seat on the opposite side of the fire.

'Could I trouble you to sit?' she asked.

'Please.' He made a little bow and gestured to the chair.

She arranged her coat on the back of the chair and placed her glass on the cardboard coaster. 'Another item whose days are numbered,' she said, tapping it with a fingernail.

'Excuse me?'

'The environmentalists will have them banned shortly, mark my words.' She tapped it again. 'They'll be gone the way of the dinosaur, the dodo and the plastic straw.'

He nodded, solemn as if they were in church. 'Am I to understand you believe that the environmentalists are wrong?'

The full flow of his sentence gave him away as a foreigner. That explained the small glass of beer in front of him. No self-respecting Irishman would order less than a pint. Even poor Martin, God rest him, when he had a headache or a bug and had no mind for it. Yet look at this little fellow sitting here with his woman's glass and not a bother on him. That was Europeans for you, content in their own skin.

'Wrong, no. Misguided in their belief that it will change anything, yes.'

He raised his glass. 'On that point we are agreed.'

'What brings you to town this fine spring day?' she asked.

'The new restaurant was recommended to me,' he said, shrugging. 'I thought, "why not?"'

'How was it? I haven't made it there yet. Work and so on,' she added, lest he think she was a common housewife, boozing in the middle of the afternoon.

He took a moment to reply. That was another thing to like about European men; they believed that conversation was real in itself, not merely a means to an end. Sex, usually, in Ethel's experience, or in Martin's case – God rest him – the peace waiting on the far side of an acceptable amount of small talk. Ask any other man in town, the Dempseys for example, about their meal in the Fish Bar and they would choose their answer from the twin pillars of local taste: *plenty of it* or *a bit pricey*.

'The food was very good,' he said at last. 'But the server hovered more than necessary.'

What a wonderful concept, Ethel thought. That everything, even eating out, could have a necessity quotient that might be surpassed. Poor Joely, with her notions of fine dining.

'Did you have the lobster?'

'Sadly not. They did not appear to be on the menu. Rather the opposite, in fact. There was a series of postcards on the wall, attesting to their travels together.'

'We have our own way of doing things,' she said, lifting her glass.

'There is no story unless somebody defies expectation,' he said, in apparent agreement, clinking his glass against hers.

Ethel would have been hard pressed afterwards to say exactly what it was they talked about or how they got from one thing to the next. At some point she became aware that the little fold of notes Olive had given her was beginning to look rather pitiful, suggesting that rather more of the day lay behind than before her. The knowledge gave the conversation a certain edge, nudging it from the general to the more specific, as it were.

'I was just admiring your hat,' she told him when he returned from the gents. She couldn't see why he needed to go at all. He was only on his second small glass of beer, for heaven's sake. She was on to her however-many-th vodka and tonic and hadn't yet had to leave the table once. She wondered if he had prostate issues. Common enough, in men of a certain age.

'A hat makes a man look more... finished, somehow,' she said, nodding again to where it was hooked jauntily over the side of his chair. 'I bought my Martin – God rest him – a hat like that once, years ago when we were first married. I thought it would give him a certain gravitas. *A man is never fully dressed without his hat*, I told him. He had his flat cap of course, but you know exactly the look *that* is – but he had the farm then, so the cap was in keeping you might say, and I let it go. Then he gave up the farm but lo and behold the cap stayed. More fool me, I suppose.' She laughed her lightest laugh for fear he would see how much it had mattered. She drained her glass. 'He wore his good hat to funerals,' she conceded. 'That was something.'

'In a marriage you learn to read between the lines,' the man said. 'The apology in the cup of tea made without asking.'

Ethel nodded at that. It was a page right out of Martin's playbook, God rest him. He had a powerful belief in the little things. No matter the bitter words spoken, time passed and they moved on.

That seemed to wear the man out. He stood to leave, thanking her for her company. He didn't offer her one for the road. Maybe he was afraid she was going to continue to talk about her dead husband. She nodded to Alan, and he brought her over another drink.

'A relative, was it?' Alan said, clearing the empties. 'He had a look of Martin about him.'

'A lady can drink with a gentleman without blood involved,' Ethel said frostily.

'It's just you don't normally socialise with the B&B guests.' Alan shrugged and moved away.

In her consternation, Ethel handed over her last tenner without a murmur. She cast her mind back over the conversation, looking for anything out of the way. She was charming, she decided. From a certain angle, she might have been simply a hostess who went out of her way to entertain her guests.

Around her, the early evening crowd had begun to gather. No Dr Nolan tonight, she reminded herself. But there was still a seat going begging with the youngest of the Timjoe Sweeneys. She rose and picked up her glass – there was a respectable amount left, so she couldn't be said to be going with her hands hanging – and made her way to the table.

'Is this seat taken, Mr Sweeney?' she asked, leaning in a little.

His face fell when he saw her. Not that it had far to go – he looked like a man whose Lotto numbers came up on the one day he had forgotten to play.

'It's yours if you want it, Mrs O'Callaghan,' he said.

The Timjoes were all well reared, Ethel thought approvingly. It was a start.

SPY WEDNESDAY/HOLY THURSDAY

MARIANNE

The night sky was bright and clear and cold as fuck. What was she thinking when she packed a couple of power cardigans instead of an extra fleece? Marianne looked at the moon, an impossible distance away, and wondered if the whole thing was just an elaborate prank on the part of some mischievous god. Earth – humanity, she guessed she meant – all seemed so *unlikely* when you stopped and thought about it. So unsettlingly random. If she were creating the world, she would start with a nice clear rule book so that everyone knew what was what.

She stubbed out her cigarette on the gatepost and turned to go back inside. It had made her a bit light-headed and sick-feeling, if she was honest. She didn't smoke often enough to have any kind of nicotine tolerance. The emergency packet she had dug from the bottom of her little suitcase was the remnant of a work jolly the previous year. She liked the feel of it more than the feeling, the little layer of drama it added to things. Having believed her mother's lies about going to the Easter devotions, Marianne had spent the evening in a swelter of anticipation that worsened the longer Ethel stayed out.

'I'll go down and bring her home,' she told Liv, shivering pleasantly in the heat of the living room.

'You'll do no such thing,' her sister said.

'Are we to just let her below in the pub, to make an old eejit out of herself?'

'That's better than going in to haul her out of the place,' Liv said. 'It would kill her to be seen as no better than the Twomeys.'

Marianne had a sudden memory of the Twomeys. The mother parking across the road and dispatching one of the endless children to drag their father out of the pub. Sometimes the first child would fail, and a second would have to be sent in. They mustn't have ever heard the definition of madness. Or seen a horror movie. The TV was probably hocked for drink money, along with anything else of value, including – if the rumours were to be believed – Mrs Twomey's virtue, dubious a prize as that might have been. Eventually they would emerge, supporting the father between them, only for the mother to rev the engine and drive off, leaving them to walk him the cold mile home.

'Ethel is hardly in that league,' Marianne said. She bit back the rest of her sentence, that, like the rest of the village, her sister was infected by the need to appear normal. *Aren't you just as bad?* a little voice inside her head asked. *Why else haven't you told Liv that you might have finally fucked things up with Ed?*

'Just sit down, would you? You're making me nervous.' Liv snapped her newspaper for emphasis.

Marianne scrolled through her phone to find something to read, succeeding only in annoying herself. Everything was either too heavy or too light. The world either in shite or deserving to be. She hesitated for a moment over Ed's unopened texts – all eight of them – then swiftly deleted them all. She had enough to deal with.

She was wrong to kiss someone else, no question about it. To go back to his house, take off his shirt, let him take off hers. Even though it ended there, it was wrong and she knew it. But Ed drove her to it. Unquestionably. With his chinos and his Sunday papers and his drawerful of plain white socks. She was a young woman trapped in a middle-aged life; that was the long and the short of it. Actually – and here she felt her temper begin to rise – it wasn't even a life that a proper middle-aged person would appreciate. For God's sake, her own mother was still out gallivanting, and it was nearly midnight. If she phoned Ed right this minute, it would go straight to voicemail because he was already in bed, a solid ninety minutes into his mandated seven-and-a-half hours. So, yes, okay, she sort of strayed – just once! – but if she was honest with herself, it was really only to push things to a head. Constructive dismissal, as it were.

She confessed it all to him over dinner three nights ago. He broke a glass, in fairness to him, even if she strongly suspected that it slipped out of his hands in sheer fright at the prospect of change rather than being hurled at their inoffensive beige tiles. That was perhaps the most pleasurable part of the whole enterprise. Everything else was surprisingly prosaic, from his refusal to ask for sordid details to her packing her suitcases while gulping white wine. He offered to help her pack. It had always been his department in their polite division of labour: she researched the best deals for a week away, he prepared their luggage. *Luggages*, he still said. One of a handful of words that still caught him out. The small wheelie had come here with her, the others were stored in their – his? – spare room, where he would no doubt move them next Saturday morning so he could hoover underneath. When he was finished cleaning, he would make a pot of coffee and drink it while listening to the review of the week on the radio.

But she hadn't time for sadness; there was Ethel to think about. What they needed was a plan of action. Liv's idea of dealing with it was clearly ineffective. It needed a fresh pair of eyes, a slightly more objective perspective. Maybe Willowbrook itself was the problem. People were in and out of the place at a rate of knots, it seemed, which was hardly a ringing endorsement. Marianne opened the notes app on her phone and began to make a list. Once she started, there was no stopping her. *1. Research Willowbrook success rates. 2. Research alternative facilities. 2a. Waiting lists?? 3. Find out cost of private facility. 4. Find out if sober coaches are a real thing or only on TV shows. 5. Set out a recovery timeline, including likely times of the year for relapses (Christmas? Dad's anniversary?) and book annual leave accordingly. 6. Make list of successfully recovered alcoholics and buy their autobiographies (personal stories best). 6a. Consider leaving books in prominent place for Ethel to find? 7. Isn't there some kind of medication you can take that makes you vomit at the taste of alcohol? Search reputable website or phone the health insurance helpline. 8. Find out if Ethel has health insurance and, if so, what supports or services are covered.*

By the time she went up to bed, she had almost succeeded in banishing thoughts of Ed. As she lay there trying not to listen for Ethel's key in the door, she had the unsettling thought that perhaps gentle boredom was, in fact, a sign that they fitted together too well for sharp edges.

The following morning, when Marianne opened her mother's bedroom door, she found Ethel snoring gently on the bed, fully dressed except for her shoes. She must have fallen asleep before Ethel came home; she hadn't heard a thing. If she were a guard dog, she'd be on her way to the pound by now.

'I'm going out,' Liv said when the worst of the breakfast rush was over. 'Can you finish up here?'

'If you're heading into town, I could come with you?' Marianne offered.

Liv shook her head. 'I'm meeting the accountant, that's all. Nothing exciting.'

She was gone before Marianne had a chance to suggest she go along and ask the accountant some questions about the level of private care Ethel might be able to afford. It was typical of Liv to assume that Marianne wouldn't be interested; she only ever saw what she expected. Marianne poured boiling water into the two frying pans and left them steeping in the sink. If Liv wanted to have everything to herself, she could have the breakfast dishes too. Marianne had better things to do than stay behind in the kitchen like some kind of home help. She would go and get a proper coffee, for a start.

The petrol station was sluggish at this time of the morning. After rush hour, it was only housewives surreptitiously buying biscuits and the sales reps pacing the forecourt, phones glued to their ears. A couple of hours earlier, cars would have lined the pumps while their owners trudged bleary-eyed to the till with takeaway cups in their hands, ahead of their ninety-minute commute to work. She couldn't imagine what possessed them to want to live here that badly. No amount of light on water or birdsong was worth three hours a day in the car. Unless they were waiting for another miracle.

Outside, the sun was still struggling to heave itself above the horizon. It had its heavy boots on, as her father would have said, and she would have replied that a person only needed three shades of green and brown to paint Coolaroone.

She stood on the footpath for a minute. The trouble with takeaway coffee was that she had nowhere to go with it. She would take it to one of the benches on the lake path, she decided. Since the path was finished a few years' back, people never stopped talking about the wonderful resource it was, right on their doorstep.

Whoever designed the bench wasn't quite such a wonderful resource. Who in their right mind would place the seat so that it had a view of the trees and the ditch rather than the water? Someone from Coolaroone, evidently. Marianne sat side-saddle on the back of the bench and sipped her coffee, trying – as she always did – and failing – as she always did – to find the sweet spot between scalding and warm. She recognised Fred Stiller walking towards her while he was still a hundred yards away. He crunched along rhythmically, as neat in his movements as in his dress. Dapper, that was the word for him. For a lot of foreign men, really. Although, she thought, as he drew closer, maybe it was simply that they had the knack for hats. On more sophisticated heads they looked like accessories instead of simply something to block the weather. Ed, to give him his due, could carry off a hat with aplomb. It was his only stipulation about couples' Halloween costumes: they had to feature a hat.

'Hello, Mr Stiller,' she called when the gentleman was within earshot. 'Fine morning for it.'

He tipped his hat in response and she thought for a moment that he might continue on his way.

'May I sit?' he asked her.

'Be my guest.' They both laughed a little awkwardly.

'It is very beautiful here,' he said. 'But might I ask the reason not to face the water? Is it…' He smiled self-consciously. 'Local fairy lore, like you mentioned?'

'Not at all, I'm afraid. I suspect that logic might not have had a lot to do with it.'

Marianne climbed down onto the seat proper, and they sat together in silence for a few minutes. It was odd, she thought, to sit in relatively comfortable silence with someone she didn't know from a hole in the ground.

'I read the leaflet in my room,' he told her. 'It struck me that there were rather a lot of foolish young men.'

Marianne laughed. 'There certainly were. They were always chasing magical women and following the ghostlights.'

'The ghostlights?'

'An ethereal light that rises to guide people home. Or to a life of music and dancing in an eternal fairy kingdom, depending on who you listen to.'

'These foolish young men, they believe in the eternal dancing, I imagine?'

'They do,' Marianne agreed.

'And your young man, is he foolish?'

Marianne thought of Ed, carefully applying factor 50 from April through to October. 'He is a great many things but not foolish,' she said. 'Although he may not be my young man any more, so perhaps I'm the foolish one.'

He was kind enough to look out over the water while she composed herself.

'If you're interested in fairy stories,' she said, 'have you come across the idea of changelings?'

'Changelings?' He rolled the word, pronouncing the 'e' and adding an extra syllable.

Not American at all, Marianne realised. Not quite Ed's Netherlands but not a million miles away either, she would bet. 'If the fairies liked the look of a human baby, they would steal it and leave a weaker version in its place.'

'Goodness me. How does a person know the child is a changeling?'

'They are cranky the whole time. Bad-tempered,' she explained, seeing his uncomprehending face. 'They feel they don't fit in.'

'That is more psychology than fairies,' he pointed out.

'True. Around here it used to be the teenage version of wishing you were adopted.'

She and Liv used to hurl it at one another during arguments: which of them was the changeling, who should just *piss off and find your real family.* It never failed to make Liv cry. Ethel's explanations that fairies were not real only served to increase her sister's hysteria. *That's what they want you to think*, she would howl. Only Dad could calm her, taking her outside and showing her the rowan tree, soothing her with explanations of how it protected the house. On Good Friday, Liv's room was the first to get its protective rowan branch.

'Adults know better, naturally,' she added, in case he thought she was nuts.

'Of course. It is not the adult who changes, but the world around him.' He gazed off into the distance, the bright sun making his old eyes water.

'A swan,' he said, after a moment, pointing. He sounded pleased, as if it was his discovery. 'They mate for life, you know.'

'Yes. The second one must be around here somewhere,' she said. A kind tourist myth when the truth was the second swan was dead. The first spent its days sailing majestically up and down, whether lonesome or relieved it was hard to tell. Its emotions, like its feet, did their work in private.

Marianne glanced at her watch. Ed should be on his coffee break around now. Unless he had an anxious patient and worked through, unwilling to rush them. She stood and stretched. 'I'll leave you to enjoy the sun,' she said.

Mr Stiller nodded and tipped his hat again before returning his gaze to the swan.

A hundred yards down the road, she glanced back over her shoulder and saw that he had remained stock still, looking over the water. Pour concrete over him, she thought, and he could be an arts grant come to life. Ed would appreciate that joke. She took out her phone, pulling up his unread message from that morning and hitting reply. 'Come for Easter', she tapped out quickly.

Too foolish or not foolish enough?

She would know tomorrow.

HOLY THURSDAY

LIV

Thursday was Liv's favourite day of the week. Even at Easter, with the privations of Good Friday – notional though they might be these days – looming. There was something special about the feeling of having the weekend to look forward to that was nearly better than the reality of it.

Which went some – albeit roundabout – way to explaining how she ended up visiting Seamus' mother in the nursing home every Thursday. She used to take Shay in the beginning, but when he got older and less biddable, he often refused to go. Liv kept it up, careful to ask each time if he wanted to accompany her. Sometimes he agreed and she was grateful that her small sacrifice of an hour's peace every week set a good example. It made her laugh to hear married friends complaining about taking on the burden of caring for their husbands' families. She never even married bloody Seamus yet here she was dancing attendance on his mother.

'You're very kind to always come,' Jasmine, the staff nurse, told her when she came to buzz her in the front door of the nursing home. 'Mrs Lucey looks forward to your visits, you know.'

Oh but she was good, Liv thought. That little nudge was

worth a hundred public service broadcasts about respecting the elderly. Half the reason she kept coming was so Jasmine wouldn't think badly of her. 'How has she been?'

'Your mother-in-law is doing very well this week. She had a touch of a cold over the weekend, but she shook it off no bother. She puts the rest of us to shame.'

Liv used to correct them at the start. 'I'm just bringing her grandson to visit,' she would say, but the staff turnover was such that she had started to wonder who her insistence was for. Without Shay, it was easier to leave her title in the hands of their collective memory.

'How are you, Mrs Lucey?' Liv said. She leaned in and kissed the papery cheek, trying not to think of a younger Shay saying that his grandmother's skin gave him the creeps.

'Olive. How good of you to call. Jasmine! We'll take some tea when you're ready.'

Liv let Mrs Lucey have her gracious-hostess moment.

'Is Shay not with you today?'

Her speech had never corrected itself after the first stroke, the words running together slightly, making it 'Ishshaynot witooday'. It must drive the woman mad, she who was always such a stickler for things in their proper places. 'He's studying hard for his exams. He sends his love and he'll be in someday soon.'

'Such a hardworking lad.' The old lady nodded approvingly. 'He gets that ambition from his dad.'

Liv smiled thinly. Be kind, she told herself. That's what you're here for. She's an old lady and this might be the last conversation she has with anyone. From her mouth to God's ears. The thought was gone before she could catch it back and pretend she never had it. Dammit. If she still went to confession, it would be one for the list. She sighed and assigned herself a decade of the rosary. It would give her something to do at the Holy Thursday ceremony later on. Anything was better than looking at the wet bare feet of Coolaroone's finest as they recreated Jesus' humble foot-washing ceremony.

'Seamus has done very well for himself. It helps that his wife is a career woman. She understands that drive to succeed.'

'He's a lucky man,' Liv said, looking around for the tea trolley and wondering if she could convince Pauline it had already been and gone.

'There's many young men go out into the world to seek their fortune, but it isn't many can say they've found it.'

'It's just a shame that he can't get back more often to see yourself and Shay.' The teenage spite burst out of her. She was no better than the wild streel Mrs Lucey labelled her the day they told Seamus' parents about the baby.

'That strap will never be welcome in our home, Seamus.' The words were as clear in Liv's mind as if they had been uttered only that morning. Well, Pauline's home was now among drooling strangers and she was damn glad to see Liv's face when her son and his career-woman wife couldn't bother their fancy arses to come and visit. She breathed in-one-two-three. Out-one-two-three.

'He'll be here tomorrow for Easter. Jasmine said he might take me up to the church for the Stations of the Cross at three o'clock.' Mrs Lucey sat back with a smug expression.

The thought of her sitting and waiting in vain shouldn't have made Liv happy, she knew, but she was only human.

'Tell me how Shay is getting on,' Mrs Lucey ordered.

'He's after flying up another inch—'

'Tall like his father.' Again, the self-satisfied nod.

From the minute Shay was born, they were all over him, demanding she bring him to visit, suggesting that he stay for a night or a weekend, trying to edge out her own poor parents. It was a relief to be breastfeeding and thus to have a ready excuse. If Shay was to stay, she would have to stay with him, Liv explained politely and watched the invite turn to dust in Mrs Lucey's mouth. When Mr Lucey was killed in a car crash on a golfing holiday in Portugal, the question of Shay spending nights and weekends there was mercifully settled for good. *I couldn't possibly*, Pauline told her, her hand to her heart, as if Liv had been begging. *Not now. Not on my own.*

'Although your own father, God rest him, had height enough too,' Mrs Lucey said grudgingly.

Liv glanced discreetly at her watch. Ten more minutes of Shay, then a bit of gentle village gossip – who had emigrated, who was back, whose garden was gone to rack and ruin, who had stopped going to Mass – then a final ten minutes on Shay and she would be out the door. Was it boredom that killed old people in the end? she wondered. Repetition of the same things over and over. Life's way of saying *nothing new under the sun, you're safe enough to move along now.*

Liv never went straight home after leaving the nursing home, instead driving to the nearest shop and letting her inner teenager eat her feelings. Often, she caught an early evening film, working her way through a bag of pick 'n' mix with no one to judge. Today, there was nothing she wanted to see and she took her bag of sweets to go, driving home with one hand digging in the bag every couple of kilometres. To passing cars, she thought, she must look like she had a fierce itch. She laughed out loud: such was the power of the Thursday feeling and her duty done.

Even while she was parking in the village, she was telling herself that she was just going to have a quick look in the playground to see if Shay was there. He used to hang out there with his friends and she worried that she might find him there. The red flag it would present. At half past six on a darkening April Thursday, there would be nobody there but the degenerates of the village. Handsy Tadhg Hayes, old enough now that Shay might seem young enough for him. Groups of ne'er-do-wells from the ghost estate on the outskirts of the village, the Dwyers or the Timjoe Sweeneys, their lives already shattered and nothing more to lose. She pictured Shay in the middle of them and began to jog. What would take him there, only things that would break a mother's heart?

At the kissing gate, she slowed and stopped. The playground

was mercifully empty. She stood there for a few minutes to be sure, but not so much as a fluttering crisp wrapper disturbed the peace.

Liv closed the door with a little more force than she had intended.

'Where were you?' Marianne asked.

'Up at the church for the Easter week ceremonies.' Liv didn't add that she had spent the entire time conjuring images of her son come to harm. By the time Father Mike blessed and released them, Jesus' impending crucifixion was nothing to what she had imagined for Shay.

'I didn't think you still believed all that.'

'It's comforting.'

'Leave-a-light-on-for-Jesus kind of thing, is it? Next thing you'll be calling over to the grotto for a chat with the statue.'

Liv closed her eyes while she had her back turned to take off her coat. Was it too much to ask that her sister leave one single solitary thing unmocked?

'Sorry, sorry.' Marianne held her hands out in surrender. 'I'm used to being on my own in the evenings. Having someone to ask about their day is a bit of a novelty. Yikes.' She stopped. 'Do you think this is what it's like to be old? Even after you retire, just days of talking endless crap for the sake of it?'

'Work going well then?' They shared a little laugh at that.

'They're talking about rationalising but sure that only means they'll get rid of a few and pay the rest of us a bit more to keep the show on the road.' She shrugged.

'Do you remember when you wanted to be an explorer?' Liv remembered.

Marianne snorted. 'Weren't we awful little eejits? You wanted to be a doctor.'

It wasn't the same thing, Liv wanted to say. Marianne might have been a century late, but Liv's own ambitions had been well within her grasp. At her Christmas exams in Leaving Cert, she made medicine with points to spare, despite Seamus pawing at her night and day. 'We made our choices,' she said, slowly.

'Children only ever pick the things they read in books anyway.' Marianne was dismissive. 'Nobody ever grows up to be a fireman or a rocket scientist.'

'Some people do,' Liv pointed out.

Marianne laughed again.

That little laugh. If her sister were ever to take up poker, Liv thought, she would have to be gagged. Or only allowed to play with deaf people. It was the worst tell of all time. If Liv heard that little laugh once more, she would take Marianne out and drown her in the rainwater butt by the back door, like Ethel did the time Pusscat had kittens.

She should ask, she knew. Turn to Marianne and say, gently, 'You seem tired. Is everything okay?' But where was anyone to ask Liv if she was okay?

And the distance between them was of Marianne's making.

HOLY THURSDAY

ETHEL

Ethel woke at half past five to the B&B quiet around her and the taste of the young lad's misery in the back of her throat. Brian, that was his name. It had come to her when he was telling her how his mam was doing. She was a nice woman, his mother. Low-sized but nimble. They used to do the church flowers together.

If she was the kind of person to think about their life in terms of low points, well, she might be in for a miserable day. But it wasn't in her nature or she would be dead and buried long ago.

Not that she had anything to be ashamed of, she reminded herself. Here she was, at home in her own bed, in the business she built off her own back. Brian Timjoe would be waking up in a house made of the next best thing to cardboard and not even a footpath outside the window. If she were French, nobody would take a tack of notice at someone her age passing the evening with a fancy man. Not that poor Brian was fancy. Or anyone in Coolaroone, indeed. Despite poor Joely's best efforts, it was no fancier now than when Ethel first arrived. *Gaofar* was still Callaghan's farm in those days, out at what was then the edge of the village, before the housing estates sprang up beyond them and shifted them closer to the centre.

There was shit everywhere, she remembered. Shit and the unmistakeable smell of chickens. It was no wonder Martin, God rest him, thought their honeymoon – two nights on Achill Island, hardly worth the drive – the last word in exotic. Everything is relative, wasn't that what the smart people believed? Marianne would know, but Ethel wouldn't give her the soot of asking. She was already looking sideways at Ethel. Clearly Liv had been talking out of school.

She stretched in the bed. The older she got, the earlier she woke. Some carpe diem Mother Nature programmed to kick in once a person got past fifty-five. Martin, God rest him, had started to remark on it before he died, and now here she was, catching up and shortly outstripping him. Well, she would give herself the same advice she gave him: if you can't sleep, get up out of it. If she was quick – and quiet – she could be out the door before having to face Shay. The scrubbed morning innocence of him.

Walking on her tippy-toes was becoming more of an ask, but she got to the front door without going over on an ankle. She quenched the light at the door, blessing herself and thinking of Martin. It was he who had first told her that if they left a lamp lighting all night, the fairies couldn't cross the threshold and leave a changeling behind. Laugh he might, but he still wouldn't have dreamt of going to bed without switching on the little low lamp there for the purpose. The guests loved it, even the ones here for the statue. If nothing else, the Irish were well practised at holding two contradictory belief systems at once.

Out in the pale grey morning, she began to feel better in herself. The crunch of gravel on the lake path was pleasant underfoot and the blue-white glare of the halogen lights had the sting taken out of them by the approaching dawn. If she could stop time, this would be the moment she would choose, with the world caught in a state of possibility and grace, its failings not yet revealed in the harsh light of day. Dawn was like the second drink of the day: the dark edge gone, everything full of soft potential and all still ahead of you.

She set out at a smart trot, breaking stride only to nudge a plastic bag with the toe of her shoe in case there was anything in it that shouldn't be. She would have done it even without Brian's grim lecture the night before. He used to drive a forklift, he told her, at the bring centre in the big town. He liked it. He could spend the day lost in his own thoughts.

'I'd say you'd learn a lot about people from what they throw out,' Ethel said.

'At the interview they asked if I liked working with people. It would have been more in their line to ask if I was good at keeping my mouth shut.' He laughed bitterly.

Ethel knew what he meant. The rubbish bins were far more instructive about her B&B guests than anything they themselves might tell her. 'Anything you're allowed to share?' she asked, leaning forward as if rapt.

'Since they let me go, I can share whatever the fuck I like,' he said. He was a bit further on than Ethel initially thought but so much the better; he might be that bit more likely to stand his round. She sat through a rambling litany of *poor me*s, interspersed with horrible vignettes of human nature. The bag of puppies dumped inside the barrel of a tumble dryer. The man who hurled all of the family photo albums over the lip of the embankment while a brace of children cried in the car. The child's wheelchair that a woman nearly threw herself in after, requiring him to drag her back by the scarf, and what thanks did he get, only fired for handling a customer. An endless stream of everyday misery. Even when she led him out the back, he kept talking, talking, talking. His jeans smelled of lavender. His mother was always a divil for the floral fabric softener. When they did the church flowers, Ethel used to joke she was competition for the blooms.

Ethel glanced at her watch. It was barely seven and already the day felt long. She would do two laps of the lake, she decided. After Martin's funeral – God rest him – when the hours were hanging heavy, she found the lake had a way of moving time along.

As soon as she turned onto the path itself, the trees quietened the traffic and the space filled with lake life. Everywhere was growth, fierce and green, consumed by its own survival. The rain in the night had left behind the mulchy green-brown smell that perfumed Coolaroone ten months of the year. If that wasn't the smell of Ireland itself: dark and wet and hankering.

In the distance ahead of her, she saw a shape. Nearer-to, it turned out to be that solitary gentleman guest. Lord but that man was everywhere. Martin, God rest him, would have him pegged as a spy.

'Hello again, Mr Stiller!' she called out as she approached, not wishing to startle him. She had made sure to look at the register last night and his was the only name there on its own. A Danish guest told her once that 'stille' meant 'quiet' and she considered joking that she didn't want to creep up on him with a name like his, but if he wasn't Scandinavian, it would take too much explaining. For some odd reason he was sitting side-saddle on the back of the bench, his knees tucked sideways like a little old lady in the seat at Mass. If the fox cubs peeked out of their den inside the grove of trees facing the bench, he would miss it all. The Wildlife Trust would be horrified to see their sponsorship wasted.

'Good morning.' He raised his hat.

No mention of either the earliness of the hour or the weather forecast for the day. No mention either of their conversation in the pub. That was foreigners for you, forever bucking the odds.

'The birds are very beautiful this time of morning,' he offered.

'The swallows are back, so there's divilment afoot,' she said. Seeing his puzzled look, she explained. 'Swallows are said to have three drops of devil's blood in them. That's what livens up the summers.'

He nodded.

'You picked a good spot to read.' She gestured at the book he held in his lap.

He nodded once, slowly. 'Sometimes I find that reading beautiful words does not just add beauty to my day but also to my thinking.'

His gravitas was sadness, Ethel saw now. 'I'll leave you in peace,' she said, and was gone before his hand found the hat brim.

When was the last time she'd had a beautiful thought, she wondered. The morning she woke and found Martin, God rest him, dead in the bed beside her, maybe. Her relief that he didn't suffer in the end – not a day sick in his life – but was gone, swift and unfussy, the way he admired in others. Was that a beautiful thought or simply the prosaic wish of the ordinary person? Ethel found herself walking faster, her heart loud in her ears. Mr Fred Stiller, with his sorrow and his eye for the world's beauty, wouldn't dream of engaging in... lewd acts, let's say, in the junk-strewn yard behind a licensed premises well before last orders. He was too... the word came to her finally – *prim*. That was exactly it, he was too bloody prim.

Towards the end of the lake path, Ethel ducked under the fence to shortcut back to the main road. The church would be open and warming up, Father Mike already seated in the confessional, ready to absolve all comers. It was Easter week after all, what better time for redemption? There was nothing simpler, nothing *cleaner* than the human capacity for starting over.

The church smelled of damp and lavender – Mrs Timjoe Sweeney's work, no doubt – and the plasticky odour of three-bar electric heaters. Not for the first time, Ethel wondered at the engineer who thought it appropriate to mount the heaters so high on the walls that only the birds roosting in the eaves felt the benefit. Maybe it was God's toes he was trying to heat. She snorted laughter and had to turn it quickly into a half-cough. That was one benefit of getting old; all sorts of noise were accepted, the elderly understood to be at the mercy of everyone and everything, their own bodies included. Their own bodies *especially*. She sighed and made her way along the central aisle to the altar, quick genuflect, and into the side chapel where the confession boxes loomed. There was no rhyme or reason to the seating, so it was a matter of guesswork to figure out who was ahead of who. The ones on their knees with their heads bowed were likely to be the penitents doing their homework. Ten Hail Marys here, five Glory Bes there. The odd rosary thrown in for the worst offenders. Did the priest ever get a mad notion to mix it up, she wondered. Three times around the lake barefoot, say. Or walk the length of the town ringing a bell. It would be no less public. Anyone who had a mind to could sit here and time their neighbours' penance and get a read on the breadth and depth of their wrongdoing. That was where the Church was going wrong, Ethel thought. They pretended that penance was an individual matter, which missed the global potential of the thing entirely.

After fifteen or twenty minutes, during which time two of her neighbours emerged in their turn from the confessional – judging by the length of their confession and penance, they were getting in a good spring clean of the soul before the Lord died for them tomorrow – she was no closer to deciding how exactly to get what she needed. As an opener, *Bless me Father for I have sinned* didn't lend itself to truth. Not when the truth needed lower, coarser speech. *I sullied the temple of my body* was only hiding in words and would free her of nothing. *I caught my breasts in my two hands, Father, and offered them to a young lad like two old oranges in the bottom of a crate in exchange for a night's drink, Father.* Jesus wept. The man would fall down dead and so well he might. No amount of Hail Holy Queens would ever reunite her with Martin then, God rest him.

Father T, before his fall from grace, might have heard her out. He was a priest of the old school, outraged by even small transgressions, so that it was much of a muchness whether a woman was confessing to adultery or passing off shop-bought scones as homemade. He was shocked at everything and was, by extension, unshockable by anything specific. Father Mike, on the other hand, didn't even take a drink. A couple of years ago, in Moran's shop, she heard Sharon Moran pointing to the single serve bottle of wine in Father Mike's basket and telling him that the full bottles were on special offer. It's better value, she said. Father Mike held up his hand as if warding off the devil himself. 'If I bought it, I'd only drink it,' he said, shaking his head as if that were the worst sin imaginable. God placed a fierce burden of loneliness on his servants, it was true, but weren't they worse fools to take it on? She got to her feet and edged her way along the seat to where Mrs Neilus Mac had her eyes thrown to heaven and was pretending not to see her. Running the launderette in the village, there was a lot that woman pretended not to see. You could say it was an occupational hazard.

Outside, the breeze caught her certainty and flung it skyward until she felt she might lift off the ground. She held out her two arms and spun with it. 'Festina lente,' she told the sky. *Make haste slowly.* If she had something to say to God, she had no need of a middleman.

Going home was out of the question, it being Thursday and nursing home visiting day. Olive would be waiting to fall on her knees before Pauline Lucey, thundering around in anticipation, with a face like a slapped arse and the urge to take it out on someone. Ethel would be damned if she was going home to that.

She looked at her watch. Nine o'clock. Fourteen hours until a respectable, non-geriatric bedtime. Perhaps she should walk up to the café. Easter meant hot cross buns. Thickly smeared with butter and with a pot of strong tea, it would settle her stomach.

'Morning, Ethel. Sit anywhere.' Gen was the ideal server, cheerful enough to say hello but too busy to expect her customers to pass the day for her.

Ethel took the corner table. She could still see out the window, but the chances of someone spotting her and coming in to chat were slim.

'Season's nearly on us,' Gen said when she brought Ethel's tea and bun. 'We'll soon be run off our feet with tourist buses.' She took a newspaper from the basket on the counter and put it on the table. 'I'll leave you alone to enjoy the quiet while we have it.'

If someone had told her forty years ago that the day would come when a none-too-bright school-dropout who had turned the front room of her mother's house into a tea shop was what she would consider ideal company, Ethel would have laughed in disbelief. But even that long ago would have been too late to get out. She was tied to the place by then, with two small girls and a farm that was killing her husband. Martin, God rest him, saw nothing. She had to sit him down and explain it, step by step, year by year, the things their girls would have to do without, the uncertainty they would face as the years advanced. Then she took him on a tour of the smallest B&Bs she could find in the four corners of rural Ireland. By the end of the week he was pointing out things they could do better and would have sworn blind it was his own idea. The day after they got back, he contacted the auctioneer to sell the farm. That was Martin, God rest him. Decisive when he needed to be. He would have been the perfect husband, she reflected, if he had held on a couple of decades more. Or if he had the grace to die younger, when she still had a chance at something else.

'I see Marianne is around for Easter,' Gen said, replacing the pot of tea with a fresh one. 'Nice to have them both home.'

'Her boyfriend is coming for the weekend,' Ethel offered. She had found a note to that effect under her door while she crept out. Olive, marking her card for her. Best behaviour and all that.

'You'll have a houseful, so,' Gen said.

Ethel would have sworn when Marianne arrived to stay for

a few days that her romance was all off. She only ever came home as a last resort. 'She'll settle into herself eventually,' Martin used to say, God rest him, when she left in high temper.

If the boyfriend was coming to join her, she must have been mistaken. As long as he wasn't coming to do anything foolish, like ask her permission to marry Marianne. Ethel would be hard pushed to know what to say if he did. When Marianne herself had never known what she wanted from life, how would Ethel be any the wiser?

Ethel checked her watch again. Half past ten. Christ on the cross. Was this to be her day, moving from one miserable minute to the next? She flicked through the newspaper. Page after page of doleful updates, dire warnings and lamenting, it seemed like. She closed it again, wincing at the crackle, and began instead to line up the condiments according to size.

Of course, today didn't have to be the drink-free day, necessarily. She could always do it tomorrow. The thought was so welcome she could almost ignore the fact that she had barely enough money on her to pay for the tea and bun. She could nip home and have a discreet root around the desk drawers. Olive would still be clearing up after breakfast, so the coast would be clear. If all else failed, she could ask Shay to drive her to the ATM in the next town. It was a sad day for the village when they got rid of the one in the petrol station. But, then, three burglaries in a season was no joke. She could curse them, but she couldn't blame them.

'Keep the change,' she told Gen, rattling her twenty cent into the bowl by the till to make it sound more robust.

She made her way home, saluting every person and magpie with gusto. Wasn't it as well to put it off? It would be far more polite to be at home tomorrow when Ed came. No one could ever accuse her of being less than welcoming.

'I'll take a vodka and tonic please, Alan,' Ethel said, taking off her coat and settling herself on a stool at the bar. To look at her, she thought, nobody would guess that she had been ensconced in the snug this past few hours, thanks to Olive's little rubber-banded pile of twenties in the desk drawer. Only one crossword clue eluded her, didn't she deserve to celebrate? *Worries about stringed instruments.* No matter, it would come to her.

Everyone was in great form, what with it being Easter and the long weekend. Ethel hardly had to put her hand in her pocket all evening. By seven-thirty, however, the crowd began to thin, the great and good of the parish heading up to the church for the next of the Easter week ceremonies. When the door closed behind the last of the sheep, there was only herself and Peter Clifford left. There was another alternative penance idea for Father Mike, she thought: half an hour on the stool next to Peter. The place would be full of saints in no time.

'You're not going up to the church, Ethel?'

'I am not, Peter.' She snorted. 'Who would want to be perched above on the altar having their feet washed? For what?'

Peter shrugged. ''Tis ceremonial, I suppose.'

'It would be more in their line to have a ceremony apologising to people for all the wrong they've done. Those mother-and-baby homes, pretending to help families in their hour of need and then what do we find out? Women and little babies thrown into unmarked graves, that's what. And they have the cheek to think they can dictate who people can bury in consecrated ground.'

'True for you.'

'Did you hear – anyone who wants to be cremated has to be buried in the graveyard after? Sure the whole point in cremation is being scattered to the four winds and lifting up to meet the birds.'

'Jesus would be no poster child for cremation, mind,' Peter said. 'Didn't he rise and came back in his recognisable body?' He sat back as if he had scored some sort of point.

Ethel sighed and rooted in her wallet. There was only bruss left, hardly enough to make up the price of a mixer. She could have sworn she had another twenty, but it wasn't there now. She felt around the lining of her handbag. If there was a little rip, the note might have got caught somewhere. She tipped her handbag sideways to see better and managed to upset the entire thing, spraying all of her personal bits and bobs onto the floor of the bar. Peter was down by her ankles, pawing through receipts and tubes of mints. Ethel's face flamed. 'I can manage, thanks,' she said, scrabbling the things back into her bag and succeeding only in knocking a tube of lipstick back down onto the ground. She bent to pick it up, but the world seemed to tilt with her and the ground came to meet her faster than it should have.

'Are you all right there, Ethel?' Alan was out from behind the bar. 'Do you want me to call one of the girls?'

'I do not.' Call home, indeed. The temerity of the man! As if she was a common drunk, no better than one of the Twomeys. 'Low blood pressure is a curse.'

'It is, that.' Alan's tone was perfectly even.

'But it is probably time I was getting home. Olive will be expecting me. Marianne, too.'

'Before I forget...' Alan rummaged beneath the bar and came out with a brown paper bag. 'A friend left it in for you the other day.'

For a second she thought Alan was talking about himself, then she remembered Dr Nolan. Ethel could feel Peter's eyes on her. She should just tell Alan to hold onto it for another time. But the clock behind the bar said it was only half eight. And Ed was coming tomorrow.

'Thanks, Alan. I'll pass it on to Olive,' she said. 'She mentioned something about sponsorship for a raffle.' At least Dr Nolan hadn't witnessed that little performance, she thought. He would still be below in the packed church, perched in the front seat beside his wife, sweat pooling in their creases, waiting their turn to have their feet fondled by the priest.

The bottle was a pleasing weight in her handbag. She never understood the men sitting in the car parks and corners of the town with their cans. Nothing that flimsy could give the requisite comfort. She would walk down to the playground and tell them, Ethel decided.

But the playground was deserted. More peace to be had here than at home, Ethel thought, with Marianne glowering and muttering darkly about lunches that were promised and Olive smarting from Pauline Lucey's judgement and only spoiling for a fight about disappointments and letting people down. She could feel a confrontation coming the way an arthritic knee heralded rain before the clouds ever appeared.

She sat on the end of the toddler slide, tucking her back into the curve. It made a fine discreet wind block, she realised. No wonder the derelicts liked the place. It was shabby now, in the way that these sorts of municipal efforts so often were once the politicians lost interest. Let it all go to hell in a handcart, so long as they got the photo of the sod being turned. She twisted the cap on the bottle – that thrilling crack! – and took a contemplative swig.

'Frets!' she said out loud, in delight. That was it, of course. *Worries about stringed instruments: frets.* It was the noise in the pub that had clouded her judgement.

She looked around her at the rusting equipment. A square of the rubbery surface missing over by the roundabout. One swing listing sideways like an insurance claim waiting to happen. If it ever did, it would shut the place. Still, she would have appreciated something like this when the girls were small. They were lonely times; she could admit it now. Martin, God rest him, had the farm and she had the girls. That was the way it was. Although, she thought, opening the bottle again – no thrill this time – and taking another drink, he stood firm behind her decisions. They're Olive and Marianne, she told him, her voice wobbling. Earth and sea. One for each.

'Marianne and – did you say Eve?' the priest asked hopefully.

'Olive,' Martin repeated.

'Would you not go with Eve?' The priest spoke to Martin as if Ethel wasn't there. No need to guess *his* views on the recent abolition of the practice of churching women to absolve them of the sin of childbirth.

'No, Father. Saddle a child with that kind of torment?' Martin looked as shocked as she had ever seen him. 'There's a Saint Olive of Palermo,' he added. 'I looked it up in the library.'

Bless him, those weeks of tears and tiredness were a lot for him to deal with. Stalwart, that was him. He was the same when it came to the B&B.

'It's not that different to the farm,' he told her. 'You move with the seasons. Get the livestock up and fed and watered in the morning, make sure there's no broken fences and that they're safely in at night. Although there's no slaughterhouse, I suppose.'

Ethel laughed aloud at the memory, tilting sideways off the slide. 'Whoops-a-daisy,' she whispered, and righted herself.

What really sold him on the B&B was the idea of having something to leave to the girls. 'Can you see either of them taking on the farm?' she asked him, and he had to agree that, no, he couldn't. Later, after Shay came along, he said it every time he had a drink taken. 'Something for the little lad to be proud of,' he would say, tapping the wall beside his chair. Well, in the decade since his death, she had managed to keep the place going. It was still there for Shay, no matter where he went or what he did. Safe in Olive's hands. Martin, God rest him, couldn't fault her there.

Little lights curled in her peripheral vision. She stiffened and drew in on herself in case it was some late-night walker with a torch and dubious intentions. But no, she blinked and the lights vanished. When Ethel was a child, her mother would lean in close and explain that when someone went missing, if their families saw pinpricks of lights dancing in the darkness outside the window, they knew they were lost. 'Ghostlights,' she would whisper, her breath sweet with gin.

Years later, watching *Peter Pan* with the girls, the flickering light of Tinkerbell took the breath from her and set her heart racing. Marianne loved that film. She dreamt of escape, even then, while, beside her, Olive worried about the trouble the children would get into for sneaking out at night. Look at them now, each the other's road less travelled. You were who you were, neither doubt nor choice about it.

She woke with a start, her hands clutching the empty bottle. It was still dark, and the cold and damp had crept well inside her coat. Ethel stumbled to her feet and out the playground gate. It was officially Good Friday, which meant going the long way home by the rowan tree. Martin, God rest him, would haunt her if she forgot to leave a branch in the girls' rooms. Against the fairies, they used to say, but these days people talked about warding off 'negative energy'. Jesus wept. Decisions were the thing. Make one, then another. Today, for instance, she wouldn't have a drink. She simply wouldn't bother. Wouldn't even think about it. It was never too late to find another way. She would tell Shay over breakfast. It would do him good to hear it.

She was almost home when she saw Mr Stiller – *Mr Quiet*, she thought to herself. His trilby was unmistakeable even in the pre-dawn gloom. A man of his years would have his pick of reasons for not sleeping. Besides, she was cold to the bone and wet through to her knickers. A hot shower and two coffees and she would be ready for breakfast with Shay and her two girls.

Better to find the day than have it find you, as Martin used to say, God rest him.

GOOD FRIDAY

MARIANNE

'You're like a hen on an egg.'

Marianne counted to ten. Then again in Irish. And Dutch. Irritating as Liv's particular brand of snarky knowingness was, if they had a falling out now it would set entirely the wrong tone for Ed's arrival. She couldn't deal with tension coming at her from all sides. She needed Liv in her corner until she got a read on Ed's frame of mind. He was coming, which, if he were Irish, could be taken as a giant clue that things would be okay. With Ed, though, it could simply be that he was coming to talk it all out. She groaned and quickly turned it into a throat-clearing so that Liv wouldn't pry.

'I'll go and get the lunch on,' she said. She pantomimed pointing to her throat. 'I need a glass of water anyway.'

If Ed did want some deep and meaningful conversation, what could she say? Was it even possible, Marianne wondered as she cracked eggs into a bowl, for two people to ever see a single event in the same way? She remembered reading the Sapir-Whorf hypothesis at university and seeing only the romance in it: two people with different mother tongues trying to understand one another. How much more noble, nineteen-year-old Marianne had thought, to have to try harder, to focus more closely on the person you loved. To create your own world of meaning and understanding. Now, in the wake of what was rapidly coming to feel like a giant relationship tantrum, the idea of a heart-to-heart was unimaginable. All she wanted was for Ed and herself to tacitly agree to leave it as a somewhat blurred piece of the past. Like getting his mother's name wrong in her birthday card or the first time she walked in on him having a wank. (She was mortified. Ed, of course, was amused. God, the memory of it still made her blush.)

'Shay!' she called, seeing her nephew skulk past the kitchen door. 'Come and give me a hand with lunch, will you?'

With him standing close beside her chopping onions and tomatoes, she noticed the shadows under his eyes.

'You've been working hard. How's the study going?'

He shrugged. 'All right I suppose.'

'Are you getting any break at all?'

'It's my weekend with Dad so...' He trailed off, leaving Marianne to wonder whether time with Seamus was a restful or a taxing enterprise. Taxing, she decided. Even when they were all in school together, the gospel according to Seamus needed a lot of active listening.

She thought of Ed, methodically packing his case at home. Filling a reusable water bottle for the journey. Rinsing an apple under the tap, cutting it into segments and putting a rubber band around it to stop it going brown.

'You'll have lunch with us before you go?' she said, aiming for casual.

'I'm not going until tomorrow,' Shay said. 'Dad had to work today after all.' He cut into a cherry tomato, the juice bursting out of it and splashing onto the bread bin.

Marianne's heart broke for him. 'I used to hate working Good Friday,' she said. 'Everyone calls it a public holiday, but it's not really.'

Shay just shrugged and began to peel the outer layers from a pile of spring onions.

'Do you ever wish things were different?' she asked.

'How do you mean?'

'That he and your mother had stayed together, maybe?'

Shay shook his head. 'That would be miserable for everyone.'

'Your generation thinks everything has to be fun,' Marianne chided him, nudging his arm to take the sting out of it. 'There's more to life than YOLO.'

He winced. 'I know that. But it's not all about doing sh… stuff you don't want to, either.'

'There's such a thing as responsibility, you know.' Marianne knew how she must sound, but Liv would kill her if she let that one slide.

To her surprise, Shay shook his head emphatically. 'If it means being stuck in a job you hate? You can keep it.'

Marianne held up her two hands in mock surrender. 'Okay, okay. Your generation can live its responsibility in any way it chooses.'

He flushed. 'I just meant it's a waste to live your life for other people, that's all.'

Marianne waited until Ed had unfolded himself from the car before opening the door. She felt self-conscious enough without racing out to greet the car like a spaniel.

'Hi, Ed.' She crossed to greet him, absurdly aware of her arms and legs.

'Hello, Marianne. I can carry my own bag,' he said mildly as she reached to take it from him.

She laughed to cover her embarrassment. 'Old habits die hard in the B&B world.' Thank Christ Liv couldn't hear her; she would break her hole laughing. She took his arm as they went indoors. 'I've put you in Room 3.' She sighed inwardly at his resigned nod. 'It was a joke, Ed. You're up in my room with me. Unless you would prefer not—?' She waited until he shook his head. This was going to be harder than she thought.

Marianne sat on the bed while he unpacked his pyjamas, unrolling them from their packing position and folding them into a neat square. He placed them under the pillow, lifting out a rowan branch and looking at it in surprise.

'Good Friday tradition,' she said. Was it possible he had never been here for Easter? Surely not. 'My dad used to do it. It keeps the bad fairies away. Here, I'll put it on my side.' She put her hand out to take it, but he shook his head.

'Perhaps I need it more than you do,' he said.

Marianne wondered if she could do something with the bad fairy idea. Throw herself back on the pillows and run a foot along his inseam. Nope. Not here among her childhood books. Not with Pippi and Anne and Jo March watching. Hazel and Fiver had survived enough without witnessing her effort to be sexy.

'It's nice having you here,' she said to Ed's back, hating the politeness in her voice. 'It's been a while.' But there was no good in trying to talk to him while he was unpacking. She watched him take out several pairs of jocks. It looked like he was planning to stay the weekend. Her heart stirred.

'We should talk,' he said, finally. 'I think—'

Marianne covered his mouth with hers. They could sort it out later – the tears, recriminations and apologies. The important thing right now was to keep moving forward.

But Ed was having none of it. 'No,' he said, pulling back. 'We have things to talk about.'

'Come and sit with me, so.' Marianne patted the bed beside her, waiting until he was settled – shoes taken off and placed neatly next to the locker – before speaking. She found she couldn't look at him and was grateful they were sitting side by side. 'I shouldn't have walked out like that. It was childish not to stay and work it out.'

'How do you know I wouldn't have asked you to leave?' Ed said.

'Would you?'

He sighed. 'No.'

She could feel his smile and risked looking up at him. 'Okay then.'

'We still have a lot to talk about,' he said.

Taking her cue, she sat up, pulling the quilt up, for warmth or armour. 'I'm sorry. Truly. I don't know what I was thinking. I love—'

He shook his head. 'Don't tell me how much you love me. How you wouldn't hurt me for the world. That does not match my experience right now and to say it is not respectful.'

Marianne threw up her hands. 'All right. I… I wasn't thinking. I was careless and—'

'It wasn't careless. You made that clear when you told me. Careless is a mistake, an accident. You were cruel. If we are to move on, then we need to be honest.'

He was right, Marianne knew. But how did you say the word *bored* without the other person hearing *boring*? Even Ed's tolerance had limits.

'I was talking to Shay earlier,' she said. 'He said that our generation acts as if life is all penance. He's right in a way, don't you think? Wouldn't it be good to have a little more fun?'

They used to have fun. Two sensible exteriors, yes, but with the occasional bout of whimsy. Holidays off the beaten track. A sick day stolen together every now and then. 'Every foot finds a shoe', as they used to say in the village growing up. It wasn't Ed's fault that she sometimes looked at him now and wished she had chosen a strappy sandal. He couldn't be blamed for taking her for exactly what she presented herself to be.

'What's so wrong with wanting to have a little more fun? We're still young… ish.' If she was trying to make him laugh, she failed.

Here was where, if Ed were Irish, there would be a handy euphemism that gave them both an out. No such luck. *If wishes were horses, beggars would ride* wouldn't hold up under the weight of careful explanation.

'There is nothing wrong with it if it is what we both want. But I have been very clear that I would like to start a family sooner rather than later. Before my arthritis gets worse and I cannot play with my child.'

My child. As if it was a flesh-and-blood thing instead of breath and wishing.

'The older we get, the higher the risk that something may go wrong. Why postpone the decision, why add risk, if this is something we want to do eventually?'

Always the fixation on risk. Was it something to do with him being a dentist? Marianne wondered. Maybe if she couched it in dental terms, he would understand the difference between now and later.

'For eighteen years, I've watched my sister put herself second,' she said, instead. 'I've seen the drudgery of it first-hand. She hadn't really lived at all before having Shay and now here she is, a grown woman with no idea who she is.' She knew it was pure horseshit, of course. Nobody was surer of themselves than Liv. It might be plausible – just – to someone who didn't know her sister all that well.

'It's not the same thing at all,' Ed said, puzzled. 'You know who you are. You have lived, as you put it.'

'I have, but there is more I want to do,' Marianne said. 'Don't you think it's better to wait just a little while longer to be sure rather than rushing and ending up resentful?' She was on surer ground here. He was Dutch; he could hear the idea of parental resentment without thinking her a monster, without making the sign of the cross and starting a rosary for her eternal soul. If he could be overly analytical, she had to admit it had its advantages.

'I am already sure.' He sighed. 'I don't just want a family, I want a family with you.'

'Still?'

'Still. I am prepared to overlook your… I am prepared to forgive you this once, but I could not do it again.'

Marianne laid her head against his shoulder. After a moment, he lifted his arm so she could cuddle in against him. 'A little more time, that's all I need.'

What harm could it do to tell him what he wanted to hear? He had time, she reasoned, men always did. It wasn't as if she was trying to do him out of his dream; if the time came and went, he could leave and find a willing woman with an equally insistent urge to replicate herself. Or plenty of women talked about the suddenness with which their biological clocks began to tick, perhaps hers would start any minute. Perhaps even now some celestial overseer was taking the batteries out of their plastic wrapping and squinting to see which pole was which. 'I love you,' she told him.

'I won't wait forever,' he said in response, tightening his arms around her.

His breath was hot on her forehead. She lay there until she could bear it no longer. 'I really should go down and see if Liv needs a hand. Afternoons can be surprisingly busy. Come down when you're ready.'

Closing the bedroom door behind her, she caught a glimpse of Ed replacing the rowan branch under the pillow with his pyjamas.

'How's work, Ed?' Liv asked.

Under normal circumstances, Marianne would have rolled her eyes, the work question being the last resort of almost-strangers. But the merits of the meal itself, slim to start with, were long exhausted and she wanted – to a depth that surprised her – Ed to feel welcome.

'Busy,' Ed replied. 'Always busy.'

'You'd swear he worked in a hospital A&E department,' Marianne said, aiming for fond and hoping he wouldn't remember that she previously had used the same line somewhat sneeringly after a few drinks.

'People will always have their teeth,' Liv said.

Marianne waited for some sort of follow-up but none seemed forthcoming. The woman had a mouthful of teeth herself, surely one of them could have excited comment.

'People only have their teeth until they don't,' Ethel said, looking up from pushing her spoon around the soup bowl.

'A kid in my class has two fake front teeth,' Shay offered.

'Football?' Ed asked.

Shay shrugged. 'I dunno.'

'I still have all my own teeth,' Ethel added.

Marianne wondered if anyone would notice if she put her head down on the table and wept.

'Have you thought about what you want to do when you finish school, Shay?' Ed asked.

Shit, Marianne thought. She had forgotten to warn him that the subject of Shay's results was taboo. That here, failure was shameful rather than bracing. Shay's head dipped lower while Liv's jerked upwards; they could have been the two sides of a cuckoo clock.

'No,' Shay mumbled.

'You could do worse than dentistry,' Ed said, oblivious. 'It's quite an exciting research area, especially now that the mouth is recognised as such an important factor in the immune system.'

'He was thinking of veterinary science,' Liv said. 'But there's plenty of time yet to make up his mind.'

Please, Marianne thought. Please, Ed, don't ask if that was what he wanted to do last year if he got enough points to get into the course. Don't even mention it.

'Do you remember the monkeys, that time in Gibraltar?' She turned to Ed, voice as high and bright as a kids' TV host. 'You had an interesting fact about monkeys' teeth – Shay might like to hear it?' *Don't ask me to tell him*, she wished silently. If she were to be hung by the toenails, she wouldn't be able to bring it to mind.

'Monkeys chatter their teeth together as a way of greeting one another,' Ed said obligingly to Shay.

'Isn't that just amazing?' Marianne said.

'I don't really like monkeys,' Shay said at the same time, in such a way that they seemed to cancel one another out.

Silence descended again.

'I like horses,' Shay offered.

'Horses' teeth need a lot of management,' Ed said thoughtfully.

Marianne screeched her chair back and started gathering half-full bowls.

Shay excused himself – to go and pack for tomorrow, he said. Somehow Marianne doubted that anything would be put into the bag until Seamus' car was outside in the drive.

On the top shelf in the pantry she found a tin of Christmas biscuits and brought them to the table with the teapot.

'No Lent around here, I see.' Ethel tapped the lid of the tin.

Marianne glared at her. 'Are we children, that giving up chocolate is the height of what we can manage?'

'Lord but you'll need a handful of them to sweeten you.' Ethel reached out and took one.

It was all Marianne could do not to slap her mother's hand. Ed was looking at her curiously, so she took the foil-covered cream-filled one – the queen biscuit, her dad used to call it – and handed it to him. 'I thought we could go for a stroll this afternoon,' she said, giving his hand a little squeeze as she passed over the biscuit. 'I don't know if I've ever shown you the—'

His watch alarm began to beep.

'Two-fifteen,' Ed said, as he always did. He reached into his pocket and shook out his little pillbox.

Marianne looked away rather than close her eyes outright at the sight of the pillbox. Like he was some kind of Victorian lady. She could be a hundred years dead, she thought, and tied to a stake in the fiery furnace of hell with Satan himself jabbing her with a red-hot poker, and she would still hear an alarm and think: *two-fifteen* and see that bastarding pillbox.

'What's that you have?' Ethel peered down the length of the table with interest.

Christ above, Marianne thought, don't tell me she has a yen for recreational drugs as well.

'Just some pills for my arthritis,' Ed told her, shaking them ostentatiously into his hand.

Aren't you very young for arthritis? her mother would ask now, because that, too, was part of this dance.

'Aren't you very young for arthritis?' Ethel asked.

'Rheumatoid arthritis,' Ed explained. 'I've had it since I was a teenager.'

'Does it affect your work?' Liv asked.

'I stiffen up sometimes—' – Marianne willed her sister not to laugh – 'but regular swimming helps to keep the joints supple.'

'Would they do anything for me?' Ethel asked.

'You don't have arthritis, Ethel,' Liv said.

'I get pains and aches like everyone else,' Ethel said, defensively. She wagged her finger at Ed. 'Never get old. Nobody has a kind word to throw or an ear to listen to an old woman's troubles.'

'You're fifty-nine. That hardly qualifies as an old woman,' Marianne snapped.

'That was all your father got, God rest him.'

Marianne drained her coffee, scalding the back of her throat. 'I promised Ed a walk,' she said. 'Grab your coat and come on.'

'Only if we can go to the pub now that they are officially open on Good Friday,' Ed said, with the air of a man who knew all about religious observance. 'Liv? Ethel? Can we persuade you to join us?'

Marianne looked at Liv in panic, waiting for her to say something. To make it clear that Ethel could, under no circumstances, be taken to the pub. But her sister just said she had some paperwork to do and would follow them down.

'Why don't you hang on here a while as well?' Marianne asked Ethel. 'We'll get in an hour or more of a walk first.'

'Not to worry,' Ethel said. 'I'll go down now and save us a seat or it'll be standing room only by the time you two get there.' She was already at the door with her coat on.

She was like Pavlov's dog, Marianne thought sourly, as Ethel nearly skipped down the path ahead of them, aches and pains forgotten. All she was short was the lead in her mouth.

GOOD FRIDAY

LIV

Liv would have liked a drink, but the prospect of letting Marianne handle Ethel was too much of a relief. Would her sister tell Ed? she wondered. Marianne was ever one for secrets. She claimed to prefer to 'keep her own counsel' when what she really meant was that she believed her own advice superior to everyone else's.

'I'll be down later to join you,' she had said. The peace and quiet was welcome.

The dishes done, she went upstairs to change the sheets in the unoccupied rooms. Once the season opened, it was simply good business to keep them fresh. It wouldn't do to have a flood of walk-ins and be caught unprepared. One damp-sheet review on Tripadvisor could ruin a season. She pulled the corners tight, smoothing her hand across it, enjoying its unspoiltness. Freud would have a field day with that. The truth was, she liked changing sheets on every bed except Shay's. When he was little, she would do it just before bedtime, then be unable to draw a full breath for fear he would die in the night and she would be left with only the smell of fabric softener where her boy should be. She couldn't relax until he had slept a few nights in the new sheets and his smell was safely recaptured.

Not that she did his laundry much any more. Once he turned thirteen, in a bid to spare both their blushes, she showed him how to change the bed and work the washing machine. In another life she would have sat him down and talked it all out, been frank and open about the whole business. Her dad might have taken it on, but he was gone by then. She had to trust in whatever Seamus told him and hope it didn't come out like wishing there were no Shay at all.

'Shay?' She knocked on his door and waited for him to reply before going in.

'Did he cancel?'

Shay was sitting on the bed, his bag unzipped on the floor beside him. He deliberately left something out each time, throwing it in and closing the bag only when Seamus was parked in the drive. It broke her heart, his childhood superstition, his fear of taking his father's love for granted. Seamus loved his son. It was just that his love was of a different, more casual order.

'No, nothing like that. I was just about to put on a wash and I wondered if you wanted to throw anything in before going tomorrow?'

'I'm okay, thanks.'

'Have you anything nice planned for the weekend with your dad?'

'Not really. The usual, I suppose.'

'Video games and pizza?' Liv hoped her voice didn't sound judgemental. Those were, after all, things they both had in common, which was more than she could say for her and Shay at the moment. 'Do you ever...' She stopped, not knowing how or what to ask.

'What?'

'Do you ever wish your dad was around more?'

'Why?'

'I just meant, you know, when you were growing up. Do you wish he had been around more?'

He shook his head and her heart lifted. 'No point in wishing that,' he said. 'Were you talking to Aunt Marianne?'

It was Liv's turn to narrow her eyes. 'Why?'

But Shay just shrugged. 'No reason.'

Liv heard them before she saw them and jumped to her feet to put her book back on the shelf.

'Ethel said she'll follow us on,' Ed announced. 'She needed to talk to someone. Should we wait to eat?'

Marianne said nothing. Much like the nothing she had said to Ed, Liv guessed.

Over dinner, Ed kept the chat going, asking questions about the people they had met in the pub and about the village itself. He was particularly fascinated by Peter, who had, it seemed, cornered him for half the afternoon to give him a lesson on the political history of Ireland.

Midway through the meal, when Seamus was mentioned, Ed pointed his fork at Shay. 'We, too, name boys for their fathers and grandfathers. That way, when the older one dies, they are a little bit reincarnated in the younger one. It is a strong tradition.'

At the time, of course, the choice of name for their son was solely a bid to placate the grown-ups. To make their teenage mistake seem more palatable, as if the unlooked-for baby was the intended scion of his father's family. Liv had wanted to call him Taylor or Ethan or Jordan. After he was born, she used to stand over his basket with the page of her diary open and whisper down the list of names until one of them cried.

'Were you named for family, too?' Ed asked Liv.

'Ethel loved the idea of opposites.' She pointed at Marianne. 'She's the star of the sea and I'm peace on earth.'

'Why opposites?'

'Individuals, not opposites,' Marianne interrupted. 'You're also the patron saint of music, don't forget.'

'Who was boiled in oil and then beheaded,' Liv said with a grin. This was familiar territory.

'At least you didn't have to work with lepers,' Marianne said.

'True, but you lived to be eighty and died of natural causes, so…'

Ed looked at Shay, who shrugged. 'They get like this sometimes.'

The truth was, they hadn't for a long time. 'Whenever anyone asked, our dad used to pretend that we were named after long-dead aunts,' Liv said.

'Neither of them had any aunts,' Marianne said. 'As far as we know. But she's a great woman for secrets is Ethel. And she's not the only one,' she added, her tone darkening.

Marianne took everything so personally, Liv thought. Nothing ever happened but that it happened to her.

'If Ethel had liked Greek stories, your father would have had to pretend to have an Aunt Persephone. Or Phoebe.' Ed was delighted with the idea.

Bless him, Liv thought. He was welcome any time, with or without her sister and her mercurial moods.

While Shay took Lucky for a last wee and Marianne loaded the dishwasher, Ed wobbled to his feet and announced that he might have an early night.

'He is a nice young man,' Ed said, breaking off four careful squares of dark chocolate before putting the bar back in the fridge. 'You did a very fine job, Liv.'

Liv smiled at the formality of his compliment. 'I didn't have to do much. He was always a good kid.'

'He'll be devastated when that dog dies,' Marianne said.

Liv rolled her eyes. 'Doesn't mean he can't be glad of her now.'

She finished her book waiting for the end of the dishwasher cycle. With any luck, a night's sleep would return Marianne to her earlier good humour. Marianne in poor form stretched the hours interminably. Even time had to bow to her, it seemed.

She held a glass up in front of her face to check for detergent streaks. 'Bitches be crazy,' she told her reflection.

'Bitches do,' Marianne said behind her.

Startled, Liv dropped the glass and it shattered on the tiles.

'Shit! Sorry! I didn't mean to scare you.' Marianne held up her hands as if to ward off her sister's anger.

'That'll teach me to talk to myself. First sign of madness, you know.' Liv bent down and began to gather the larger pieces.

'The second sign is hair on the palm of your hands,' Marianne continued, going to fetch the dustpan and brush from beside the back door.

'Third sign is looking for it,' they chorused together and for a second, Liv felt like their father was in the room with them. She shivered at the notion. 'What has you up?'

'Ed is snoring,' Marianne said. 'It's all the alcohol, he's not used to it. I got sick of lying there seething, so I came down for a hot whiskey.'

Liv caught her sister's eye and they both started to laugh. 'An Irish solution to an Irish problem,' Liv said and that was enough to start them off again.

'You didn't need to do those.' Marianne gestured at the almost empty dishwasher. 'I was going to do them in the morning.'

That would have been a first. 'I had to lock up anyway.'

'I forgot about the curfew.' Marianne yawned.

'Hardly a curfew, the guests all have keys. Although they're actually all in for the night anyway.'

'What about Ethel?'

'I haven't seen her. But the door opened and closed a few times, so she might well have come in and gone straight to her room,' Liv added.

'Don't do that.'

'Do what?'

'Exclude me. If there's a problem – and clearly there is – then I'm involved too. It's bad enough that I had to come home and find out like this.'

Wasn't it just like Marianne to make it all about how she found out. 'What did you tell Ed?'

Marianne flushed. 'Nothing yet. I thought it would be better to wait until tomorrow. He's going to feel bad about inviting her to the pub and buying her drinks. I wanted him to be sober when I tell him.'

There was a logic to that, Liv had to admit.

'What time is Seamus coming down for Shay?' Marianne asked.

'He didn't say. Morning, I suppose. He said something about the girls and a party. I wasn't listening, to be honest.'

'What's the new wife like?'

'Ruth is hardly new. Their daughters are nine or ten, I think.' They were nine since last November, as Liv knew full well from her sleepless nights before their birth, terrified that her half-wish would be granted and Ruth would lose them.

'Did you ever wonder if Shay would be a twin?'

'I was too young,' Liv said. 'I didn't think about him being a person at all. Honestly, I thought it would be a bit like having a puppy.' She deliberately avoided looking at her sister. If Marianne asked her if she regretted it, hand-to-God she would slap her.

'Maybe that's why Ed is so keen,' Marianne said instead. 'He was never allowed a pet as a child.'

Liv busied herself warming handled glasses. If she didn't look directly at her, Marianne might say more. Her confidences were like shooting stars, rare and only visible out of the corner of your eye. 'He's keen, but you're not?'

'I don't think he realises how much his life would change.'

'And you do?'

Marianne looked puzzled. 'Of course I do. Didn't I watch you live it?'

'That put you off, did it?' Liv worked to keep the bitterness from her voice.

'Yes,' Marianne said simply. 'We all know what my patience is like. I don't know if I could put someone else first all the time, the way you do with Shay. All that and running a business…'

'Well, we already know I'm a nicer person than you,' Liv said, shouldering Marianne gently. 'But you always had better instincts. You're right to wait if you're not ready. It's not something you can take back. Although if I'm anything to go by, Ed might be right in thinking that his life wouldn't change that much. Seamus' certainly didn't.'

'That's not true,' Marianne said. 'I'm sure keeping a baby photo of Shay in front of his college ID exponentially increased the odds of him getting into undergrad knickers.'

They collapsed in giggles, quietening at the sound of footsteps overhead, followed by the flush of a toilet.

Liv stirred hot chocolate mix into the milk.

'Do we not have anything stronger?' Marianne asked.

Liv shook her head. 'I stopped keeping spirits in the house. Either Ethel would drink it or I would.'

'When I was upstairs, I felt a great surge of relief at the idea of a hot whiskey to help me sleep,' Marianne said. 'I always thought that alcoholism was a bit like depression. Like, sure it was genetic, but it must be situational too? Then tonight, I found myself wondering if some internal clock had suddenly started ticking.'

'Don't let Ed hear you saying that,' Liv said. 'He would get the wrong idea entirely.'

They shared another little smile. For a moment there was only the sound of the spoon clinking against the glass and the crunch of biscuits.

'I shouldn't have let her come with us,' Marianne said into the silence. 'What kind of person brings an alcoholic to the pub?'

Liv snorted. 'Do you think she was waiting for an invite? Don't take this the wrong way, but whatever you said or didn't say would make little difference.'

Marianne nodded. 'Do you want me to phone Willowbrook in the morning?'

'Thanks, but they won't take her unless she goes voluntarily and we're not quite there yet, I'd say. How was she in the pub earlier?'

'I didn't see much of her, to be honest. She was in and out of the snug, talking to half the parish. And I had my hands full with Ed.'

Liv laughed. 'I bet he didn't know what to make of the place.'

'If only! Three pints in and he was the next best thing to a local. Laughing away with them all like they knew each other.'

'The binding power of alcohol.' Liv nodded. 'Bringing people together when it isn't tearing them apart.'

'Wait till you hear. I came back from the toilet to find him holding court about the famine and *Ireland's incomprehensible relationship with fish.*'

'He didn't!'

'Oh, he did. You should have heard him giving the girl from the Fish Bar and her boyfriend chapter and verse on the diet of the Pacific Islanders. I had to swoop in before someone flattened him.'

'Joely and Damien wouldn't knock a lump out of a duvet,' Liv said comfortingly. 'Did Ed not realise it wasn't the time or place?'

Marianne shook her head. 'He genuinely thought he was being helpful. I should never have taken him in there. I regretted it the minute we opened the door and every head in the place swivelled around for a good gawk.'

'At least he was a novelty. Every time I go in there, people ask me about Seamus as if we're still a thing.'

'You'll have to give them something new to talk about.' Marianne wiggled an eyebrow.

'They'll be a long time waiting. Much like myself,' she added, and was gratified by her sister's giggle. At least one of them saw humour in it. 'They have enough to be going on with, now that you've shown them Ed.'

'The worst thing was that everyone in there knew everything about me. Literally every little thing. Every time someone opened their mouth, they landed me in it.'

'Oh, please. You barely rippled the surface of drama. A bit of public vomiting after a night on the Buckfast hardly counts as sensational news. I'd say Ed was able to give as good as he got in the Marianne stories.'

'Easy for you to say. You never laughed so hard at Mass that you weed in your knickers and had to walk up to receive communion stinking like Pissabed Hanley.'

'He's Paddy Hanley, these days,' Liv corrected her. 'But that's true for you. You were the real scandal in the family. I only got knocked up in a hayshed by the son of the local bigwigs, who hightailed it to university, leaving me with not even a set of school exams to my name and no option but to throw myself on my parents' mercy for the rest of my natural life.'

'Ah, cry me a river. I was Ma-wee-anne for months.'

They laughed until their sides hurt.

'Ed is a good person,' Marianne said suddenly. 'Dependable. Loyal. Don't you think?'

'What would I know about loyal?' Liv said. 'About any of it, really. The lads in the pub have a point.'

'Didn't you watch every episode of *Lost*?' Marianne said. 'The most modern experience of loyalty possible.'

'When the last episode was utter cack, I sat there for a while and wondered if it was me, if I just didn't get it,' Liv agreed gloomily. 'Dependable isn't the worst thing, you know.'

'You've never settled,' Marianne pointed out. 'Don't try and tell me it wasn't because you didn't have the choice.'

'It's true, I did,' Liv conceded. 'Maybe it's us, so.'

'Nature.' Marianne nodded.

'Or nurture,' Liv added.

'Either way, we can blame Dad and Ethel.'

'Dad and Ethel,' Liv said, and they clinked their hot chocolate glasses together.

HOLY SATURDAY

ETHEL

Ethel lay where she was for a few minutes after waking, knowing from experience that the most important information would present itself shortly. There had been a lunch, she remembered. Marianne and that nice, generous husband of hers. No. They weren't married, or she didn't have a memory of any such event. Now there was a man who wasn't afraid to put his hand in his pocket. For all his historical grandstanding, at least he had something to say for himself. While her daughter, who was born and bred to the place, had barely a word to throw to anyone, only boring rawmeish about the company she worked for. As if marketing meant anything to people earning their living with their own two hands. Peter thought she said 'mart' and that was entertaining. 'Viral campaign?' he had asked her. 'Swine flu, is it?' At least she was spared Olive pricking her ears like a terrier every time Seamus' name was mentioned. Martin, God rest him, would turn in his grave at the cut of them.

It wasn't the only thing that would have him turning, she knew. 'Ah, Ethel,' he would tell her. 'Haven't you a grand bed in the home we built?' But it was fine for him to sit in judgement; he was the one gone ahead, not the one left to deal with it on their own. She missed him, in the way that she did sometimes, suddenly and without warning. If he were here, she could pillow her head on his arms instead of on the hard surface of the world.

'Anyone could have found you,' he would tell her. 'Even Shay, imagine.'

But she didn't want to imagine.

From the distant sounds of road and water, she suspected she was in the top corner of Powers' field. She must have wanted to go down to the water last night, but the shortcut undid her. Still, she was dry and not too cold and out of the way of prying eyes. Things weren't too bad. Another minute or two and she would be ready to go on her way. It was early yet; she had a chance of getting into her room before she was seen.

What was it the Powers had in the field this weather? They were mad into the crop rotation since they went organic. It was turnips one year, then potatoes, then corn, then turnips again, then sugar beet. No wonder her head was spinning.

In the distance, the church bell chimed eight. She could chance going down to the snug for a quiet nip before she went home. A quick warmer-upper. That would be the last of it, then. For good and for all.

If she tapped at the back door, Alan would let her in for half an hour. She wouldn't be in anyone's way inside in the snug. She could give it a quick run of a cloth for him, even. Alan always saw her right.

She wasn't the only one to have that idea. She kept her head down walking past a brace of Twomeys – likely Tom and Dan – sitting brazenly at the bar. It wasn't for her to judge. No doubt the bar was warmer than their miserable homeplace. She went there once, looking for the return of a stepladder, and couldn't wait to get out of the dirt of the place. What more would you expect, and the mother only a streel, with no people of her own to set her straight?

'How's Ethel?'

Christ on the cross. If she could gather up certain colloquialisms into a big black sack and drown them in the river. To follow grammatical convention would require her to refer to herself in the third person, like some kind of grandee or small-animal strangler. But just try explaining that in here. Her head pounded. 'I'm grand, thanks. Grand altogether.' Let the sarcasm wash over them, what did she care. She tipped her head at Alan and made the smallest gesture towards her glass.

'I saw your girl in here yesterday,' Peter said from the end of the bar. 'Herself and the husband, is it?'

'You're showing your years there, Peter.' She affected a little laugh. 'Nobody goes in much for husbands any more. Partners, they call it now.'

'I thought "partner" was what we have to say for the gays,' Peter said, looking around for confirmation.

Ethel laughed again. 'Partner is what you say when there's two of them equal in it.'

'Bejaysus, I wouldn't like the sound of that, so. Herself would only be wanting to be perched in here alongside me.'

Ethel doubted it. Peter's long-suffering wife was never gladder than seeing the flat of his arse disappearing down the road. She watched Alan scald the tall glass before pouring in a tot of whiskey and filling it up with hot coffee. Sugar stirred in, whipped cream layered over the cold spoon to create a gorgeous head. A few sprinkles of brown sugar on top. He was an artist in his way was Alan.

'A foreigner, was it?' Dan Twomey piped in. 'Marianne's fella?'

'Fish and teeth,' Dan Twomey added. 'A dentist wasn't it?'

'No doubt but that Marianne would do well for herself.' Peter nodded, as satisfied as if he had reared her by hand.

'No one around here was good enough for her. Nor in the country, even.' Tom Twomey laughed unpleasantly.

Who was he to talk, with his filthy clatch of children? Didn't the whole world know himself and Lily were second cousins that turned to riding each other when no one else would touch them?

'No need for that,' Alan said. 'Plenty of youngsters have no choice but to leave the place. I think we'd all agree—'

But the door of the pub burst open and whatever it was they would all agree on was blown before it.

'Is Dr Nolan here?' Joely was out of breath and frantic.

'We're not open yet,' Alan said. 'Everything all right?'

'There's a body in the water by the rocks. Damien saw it from up on the hill. He's calling the ambulance.'

'Sacred heart,' Peter said, shocked. 'Who is it?'

But Joely was gone, the door swinging behind her.

In the mirror behind the bar, Ethel watched their three hands make three signs of the cross and shivered.

'I wonder did she think to phone the guards?' Peter said.

'I'll give them a call.' Alan disappeared into the back.

The news hung in the air, making the place look seedy somehow. Ethel drained her glass and set it carefully on the counter. Home could wait half an hour while she went to find out what was what.

The whole village had the same idea. The crowd gathered in front of the hotel put the St Patrick's Day parade to shame. Ethel stood at the fringes, watching as the Dempseys made their way through the reeds towards the dark shape in the water.

'I suppose they're sure it's a person?' she asked nobody in particular.

'No doubt about it,' came the reply from one side of her. 'Damien was out with his binoculars – birdwatching – and he saw it clear enough. A body in the water.'

Birdwatching, her eye, Ethel thought. If Damien was twitching by mid-morning, it was because his supplier was out of town. She wondered if Joely bought his spiel or if she was only saving face in front of the parish gossips. Ethel looked across to where Damien was holding court. He had the look of a man missing something. He should man up and say it out, she thought, suddenly. They'd all have a bit more respect for him.

There was an intake of breath as the Dempseys stopped at the lakeshore and began to pull on their waders.

'Fair play to them,' someone said.

'It's like *The Full Monty* in rewind,' someone else said.

'There's plenty would pay the Dempseys to put on more clothes all right.' There was a brief ripple of laughter, then a shamefaced silence.

Into the gap came the hotel Dillons. Sheila with a tray of hot coffees – percolator, Ethel noted, her generosity didn't stretch to the fancy Tassimo machine – and Tiny following behind her with a bottle in each hand, adding a drop to any that wanted it. A wise move. The place would be crawling with guards shortly. With no telling who they would pull the breathalyser on, it was better to have the insurance policy of being able to say you had taken a drop just now for the shock.

'You'll take a drop, Ethel?' Tiny Dillon said when he got to her. 'Whiskey or brandy, ladies' choice?'

'A small nip of brandy, so,' she agreed. 'You're very good, the pair of you,' she added, when it was clear that his notion of small coincided nicely with her own. 'The poor soul.'

'The guards are on their way over from the town,' Sheila Dillon told whoever would listen. 'If we still had our own barracks open, they'd have the whole thing in hand by now.'

There were nods and general murmurs about how the country had let rural Ireland go to the dogs. Nobody had much heart for it though, not with the scene unfolding below them.

Ethel sipped and watched the Dempseys hand one another into the water, the son first, followed by the father. When they reached the shape, each removed his flat cap and pressed it to his breastbone for a respectful minute. Once the caps went back on their heads, Father Mike turned to face the crowd, his eyes closed and his arms held out like a benediction. It put Ethel in mind of that scene from *Titanic*, only he had the water at his back. '*Thou oh Lord wilt open my lips*,' he intoned.

'*And my tongue shall announce thy praise,*' they responded, everyone grateful to have a script to follow.

'*Incline unto my aid, Oh God.*'

'*Oh Lord, make haste to help me.*'

Between the coffee warming her from the inside out and the susurration of familiar words around her, the wait wasn't altogether unpleasant. Her fellow country people would be tolerable, Ethel felt, if they could be kept in a state of perpetual, quietening shock.

HOLY SATURDAY

MARIANNE

'SHAY!'

Marianne woke with a start. Beside her, Ed slept the sweltering sleep of a man whose body was furiously metabolising alcohol.

'SHAY!'

Liv sounded terrified. Marianne stuck her feet into her slippers and her head out of the bedroom door. 'What's wrong?'

'Shay's not in his room.' Liv's eyes were wild.

Marianne didn't understand until she spoke again.

'Joely rang. There's a body in the water.'

Marianne looked at her sister and knew that nothing she could say would make the least bit of difference. 'Give me two minutes to get dressed and we'll go down to the hotel. You need a warm jumper and boots.'

Liv nodded.

'Go and put them on, so.' Marianne gave her sister a little push out the door.

They were in the kitchen tying laces and zipping coats when the back door opened and Shay walked in.

'Where the HELL were you?' Liv flung herself across the kitchen at him.

'I couldn't sleep, so I took Lucky for a walk. Sorry, Mum. My phone is dead, so I came back the minute I heard.' He patted Liv's back and looked over her shoulder at Marianne. 'Where's Gran?'

Liv and Marianne exchanged glances. 'I'll just run down and let her know we're going out,' Marianne said, as casually as she could manage.

When her mother didn't answer the knock on the door, Marianne opened it and went in. There was no sign that Ethel had been home. The bed was neatly made and nothing was out of place. Marianne glanced around, fancying that the room seemed somehow emptier than usual.

'She must have been up with the lark,' she said brightly when she reached the kitchen.

'Stop,' Shay said. 'I know she doesn't always come home.'

'I'm sure that—' Marianne began.

'Don't—' Shay cut her off. 'You didn't even know she was a drunk until a couple of days ago. Didn't stop you taking her out drinking yesterday, though, did it? And now there's someone in the water.'

If asked beforehand, Marianne might have said that Shay angry was a comical prospect. Faced with it, however, it was anything but.

'Shay!' Whatever Liv might have said fell on deaf ears, as Shay stormed out the back door and slammed it behind him. 'He didn't mean it. He's upset,' she told her sister, putting out her hand in useless comfort.

'He's right,' Marianne said, struggling to grasp the zip of her coat. 'I let her stay out all day yesterday and then I left her there, knowing that she doesn't know when to stop.' She gave up on the zip and let her coat hang open. 'A stranger would have done less harm.'

'Nope.' Liv wrapped a scarf around Marianne's neck. 'You can have your pity party later on, but right now we're going down to Dillons.'

They half-walked, half-ran, the blood pounding in

Marianne's ears and a hot stone of guilt in the pit of her stomach. *What if? What if? What if?* Her brain wouldn't let her get any further.

They heard the crowd before they saw it. The low rumble of a community raising its voice in the hope that something was listening. The words of the prayer blinked up to the surface of Marianne's mind.

'Who is it?' Liv asked the first person they came to, a man in a thick waxed jacket and heavy boots.

'They don't know, Liv,' the man said. He nodded hello to Marianne. He looked familiar. Maybe he was in the pub yesterday.

'The Dempseys have done their best and we're waiting for the ambulance,' the man went on, pointing.

Marianne looked down to the water, where two men in oilskins were standing either side of a dark shape laid out on a flat rock. Behind them, incongruously, the bright mocking red of the life ring in its plastic casing.

'They don't know who he is yet. Mightn't be local at all.'

A-tall. It wasn't until she went to college that Marianne realised that Coolaroone had an accent. She would come home at weekends and hate the locals for their pronunciation, then return and hate her new friends for her newfound awareness of how she herself must sound.

'Did you say he, Paddy?' Liv asked, beside her.

'Seems so.'

'It's a man? Only a man?' Marianne had to stop herself grabbing him by the arm.

'Dempsey gave a sign, someone said.'

What kind of a sign? Marianne wondered giddily. She had an image of old Dempsey miming pissing standing up and had a sudden urge to laugh.

'Thanks, Paddy,' Liv said. 'Come on.' She took Marianne's arm and began to thread her way through the throng.

Paddy. Of course. Paddy Hanley from school. Pissabed Hanley.

Marianne saw Ethel a split second before her sister did. Her good wool coat had a smear of mud down one side, but her scarf was knotted just right. Faced with the reality of her, Marianne's fears felt as insubstantial as air.

'Ethel,' she began, but that seemed to be all she had. She turned to Liv, made space for her sister's anger, and was surprised when Liv only hugged their mother. 'I'm glad you're safe,' she said to Ethel. 'But, later on, we're overdue a talk, don't you think?'

'You're the boss,' Ethel said, taking another sip of coffee.

'Ethel. Girls.' Mrs Dillon from the hotel appeared in front of them with a tray. 'Desperate business, isn't it? Will you take a coffee? Dermot is around behind me with a bottle if you fancy a warmer-upper.'

No wonder Ethel was so keen on her coffee, Marianne thought. She watched for Liv's eyes to narrow, for her sister to glance at their mother's cup, but Liv was smiling and accepting a cup. 'You're very good. Thanks, Sheila. Any more since?'

'The Garda water unit are on the way. There's no need for rush here, God rest his soul, whoever he was.' She blessed herself.

It was like a yawn, Marianne thought, as she caught herself reflexively doing the same. A person couldn't help themselves. Once Catholicism was in your blood, there was no escaping it. Like malaria.

The problem with chat in little groups was that unless you were in it, you ended up being edged out. For something to do, Marianne swivelled around as if admiring the hotel. It looked a lot different than it did when they used to come here with Ethel and Dad on Sunday afternoons, at once wishing that the bottle of fizzy-orange-with-a-straw would last forever and impatient for it to be finished so they could go and play catch in the car park with the rest of the children whose parents were taking their time over their ritual pint and glass of Guinness. Back then, the car park was a small patch of ground at the side of the hotel, with a gravel surface guaranteed to lift the skin from errant knees and elbows. That area was now covered with a glass-fronted conservatory, a free-standing woodchip stove and cosy little tables where couples could sit and watch the water. It looked, Marianne thought, like a place drawn from somewhere else.

She turned back to the group to find she hadn't been missed. The chat rose and fell around her as people exchanged the same bits of information over and over. Gaps were ignored or filled with gossip. Coolaroone was never a place for hoarding opinions silently.

'Joely's Damien was the one that saw it,' someone said. 'Out birdwatching, she said.'

There was a general air of amusement around that statement, Marianne noticed.

'He's clean at the moment,' someone offered. 'I see him going in and out to... the community centre on a Tuesday evening.'

'Could be he's having withdrawal,' Ethel said. Her mother was on her third coffee, by Marianne's count, and her speech was taking on an air of belligerence. 'The last time he used to be up on the cliff watching the horizon for invaders, remember? He had us all driven mad about the Russians or the apocalypse or some damn thing. "Sure, let it come," I said to him. "Might as well be looking at it as looking for it."' There was a ripple of laughter.

'Damien is trying,' Liv said quietly. 'He and Joely deserve our support.'

Her words were met with a general shuffling of feet and eyes suddenly finding the ground. 'True for you. She's a good girl, Joely, and she has a lot to put up with,' someone said. 'Please God she'll make a go of the Fish Bar,' someone else added. 'You'd like to see her with something.'

When the siren could be heard in the distance, everyone huddled a little closer and the talk turned solemn.

'We haven't had a drowning since six or seven summers back,' someone said.

'It's never someone local,' someone else said. 'Everyone knows better than to swim in the lake.'

'It's the tourists you have to worry about, ignoring the warning signs and thinking the lake is too pretty to be dangerous.'

There were general nods. 'The lake has a mood and a mind of its own. But try telling that to someone who was reared only to look at it on a postcard.' More nods.

Marianne nodded along with everyone else. She might have been made to feel an outsider in the pub, unaware of the comings and goings of every local Mick and Mary, but no one could grow up here and not be alive to the dangers of the water. Generations of Coolaroone schoolchildren had scared themselves with stories of the fairy queen who stole away those who displeased her and dragged them into the bottomless lake. Even as a grown adult, the truth was the lake had an eerie keep-away power all its own.

Marianne didn't know Ed was there until she felt a hand on her arm.

'I wondered where everyone had come,' Ed said. 'The guests asked and I didn't know.'

'Oh, shit. The guests.' Liv must have forgotten them too. The unheard-of lapse would send her sister into orbit altogether.

'They are fine. I gave everyone breakfast,' Ed said.

'Thanks, Ed.' She swallowed to stop the tears. Lord, how embarrassing to weep over a few sausages lost and then found. 'Someone drowned. We came out…' How foolish it would sound to say they ran out to see if it was Ethel, when she was standing within earshot. 'To see,' she finished, lamely.

'How terrible. Is it someone you know?'

How foreign the question made him seem. As if tragedy required knowing the person involved. Marianne felt a flush of embarrassment at his misunderstanding. At his city boots and ear-flap hat.

She shrugged and turned away to watch the Dempseys. 'We don't know yet.' If it had been Ethel in the water, it would have been as much his fault as her own, as the one who invited her to join them.

Ed put his arms around her. 'You are freezing. Let's go back to the house and I can make a hot breakfast.'

She shook her head. 'That's not how it works.' Seeing his puzzled face, she relented. 'Everyone stays with the body. Anything else is disrespectful.'

The crowd fell silent as the ambulance, followed by a squad car, drove in the gate of the hotel and parked with its doors facing the lake. The two paramedics opened up the back and set off with the stretcher and a resuscitation kitbag. Its bright yellow hopefulness was an admonishment, as if everyone had given up too quickly in favour of standing around with their hands in their pockets.

The woman paramedic reached the rocks first. Off came the Dempsey caps again. Was it chivalry or reflex? Marianne wondered. It didn't matter. Father and son stood back – not so far back that they couldn't see, Marianne noted – while the checking for signs of life began and ended. The body was nudged onto the stretcher and strapped in. No body bags here. Instead, the male paramedic took off his jacket and placed it over the face, tucking the sleeves in to keep it in place. That lasted as far as the low wall, when one side of the stretcher had to be raised to go over first. With hindsight, they should have raised the leg end first, or perhaps gone over in parallel, one-two, like skipping games. In any event, the head was lifted first and the jacket flapped and those nearest the wall got a good look before the paramedics set down on top of the wall and rearranged things.

As they prepared to slide the stretcher into the ambulance, Father Mike walked up with his hand out. Instead of blessing the body – or perhaps in addition to, Marianne was craning to see over the heads in front of her, the crowd having drawn together in a penguin huddle – he was talking to one of the paramedics. After a moment, the woman looked at the man and nodded. Father Mike strode through the crowd, scattering people left and right, savouring his Red Sea moment. He came to a stop in front of them.

'Liv, I think you might be able to help us out here,' he said gently.

For a wild moment, Marianne wondered if it was Ethel after all, if she had really spoken to her mother just now or simply imagined she had.

Ed took Liv's arm. 'Come with me,' he said, and led her to the ambulance.

After a moment, Marianne followed them. It didn't always have to be Liv, as if she herself had no right to the place at all.

His face didn't look any different than it had the last time she had seen him, sitting on the back of the bench, watching the water. She had seen enough television to know that meant he hadn't been in the water very long. Beside her, Liv was frozen and silent.

'Yes,' she heard herself say. 'Fred Stiller. He was with us since Monday.'

She waited for Liv to say something, to set things in motion, but her sister remained mute. After a moment or two, Marianne turned to the woman guard. 'We'll meet you back at the house.'

Acutely aware of the eyes of the parish on her back, she turned to face them. 'Father Mike,' she said, raising her voice so that it rang out clearly across the crowd. 'You might say Mass this morning for the soul of one of our guests, who seems to have misjudged the lake path.'

She didn't wait for a response but turned and led her family along the road towards the village.

HOLY SATURDAY

LIV

Back in her own house, Liv found her voice returned to her. The guards were polite – Liv knew Ellen since their schooldays and she introduced the unknown guard, Fiachra Dunne, who was newly arrived and little use to anyone.

At the threshold of Fred Stiller's room, they stood back while Liv produced the key.

'Are you all right?' Ellen asked. 'Take your time if you need to.'

But Liv could hardly tell her that she had held Ed's arm and for one wild minute been certain she would see Seamus on the stretcher. Seamus too tired to drive but unable to wait to see them. See her.

She shook her head. 'I'm fine, Ellen. It's just weird to think that he left the key on the desk on his way out. You'd wonder what he was thinking.'

'One thing I've learned in this job is that anyone could be thinking anything at any time,' Ellen said.

As philosophies went, Liv thought, it was spectacularly unhelpful. With a small click, the lock gave way and she opened the door.

'You're absolutely sure it was him?' Ellen asked and

waited for Liv to nod before she snapped on a pair of rubber gloves and crossed the threshold.

Liv left them to it and went back downstairs to where everyone important to her waited, safe and well, she reminded herself. Almost everyone. Ethel, being Ethel, had refused to come with them. She was taking a stand, she said grandly. Not letting the guards escort her home like a common criminal or some such horseshit.

In the kitchen, Marianne was hunched over a cup of coffee at one end of the table, while, at the other, Shay was engrossed in his phone. She had a second of deep flooding relief that he was here with her and not in the back of that ambulance on the way to the morgue. If he was gone, she would… what? She would simply disappear. There would be a vast and unconscionable displacement of energy, then a little popping sound, and that would be that. The emotion of it slid away from her, it wouldn't take hold. Not when she had the proof of him, every kind and awkward cell of him, perched in front of her with his mouth full of toast and bacon. There I was, gone, she thought, and had to choke back an alarming giggle.

Ed moved from one cupboard to the next, a pile of dishes and pans accumulating beside him on the worktop. 'French toast,' he explained. 'Sit, sit. Tea and coffee are on the table.'

Relieved, Liv did as she was told. 'You'll go back to the city saying we made you work all weekend,' she said.

'Was that Ellen Ghoul?' Marianne asked, pushing a cup of coffee towards her sister.

Liv rolled her eyes. 'Ellen *Gould*, yes.'

'Between herself and Pissabed Hanley, it's practically a reunion. I thought they were both long gone.'

'Ellen moved back a couple of years ago when the sergeant in town retired. *Paddy* is only back a month or two. His father had a stroke and he came back to take over the practice.'

'People can't stay away,' Marianne said.

At the other end of the table, Shay made a noise that might have been a snort. Liv decided to ignore it.

'What do we tell the other guests?' Marianne asked.

'We can't tell them anything without the guards' say-so,' Liv said, firmly, if only to hide the fact that she hadn't the faintest idea what to tell them. How did a person even go about a thing like that? Knock on their individual doors? Try to catch them in the hall as they returned from sightseeing or rubbernecking or however it was they had passed their morning? Gather them in the breakfast room, à la Poirot? She had no idea but would have to come up with something. Just because Ellen was local didn't mean she had time for hand-holding and breaking news to uninvolved parties, no matter how avid their interest. They would be on their way shortly after rifling through whatever few meagre bits poor Mr Stiller had in his room. She had an image of him, suddenly, his brushed hat and small leather bag. The poor man. His family would no doubt want to visit the scene of his last days. She would keep the room as it was for them. It was the least she could do.

'Should we have insisted Ethel come back with us?' Marianne pushed her toast around the plate, picking off small corners to chew on.

'She would have only left again,' Liv said. 'She's at the stage where she's easily spooked.'

'At the stage of what?' Ed asked, spooning honey neatly onto his toast.

'Gran is an alcoholic,' Shay said through a mouthful of bacon. 'Aunt Mar couldn't have told you, because she didn't know.'

'Shay, that's uncalled for,' Liv said.

He shrugged. 'It's true. You just feel bad now because you didn't tell her.'

'Really?' Ed looked from Liv to Marianne.

'Sometimes Ethel drinks too much,' Marianne said. 'It... we're dealing with it.'

The door opened. 'Morning all,' said Seamus. He glanced

from Shay to Liv. 'Did you know there's a paddy wagon in the drive? What has Ethel been up to?'

Liv shot him a warning look. The last thing she needed was Marianne in a huff that Seamus knew about Ethel when she didn't. She made a great show of clattering plates and cups. 'Hello, Seamus.' How was it that the sight of him always made her heart beat a little faster? It was very irritating. As if she had imprinted on him as a teenager and was doomed to spend the rest of her life feeling slightly breathless in his presence.

She opened her mouth to explain the events of the morning, but Shay got there before her, raising his hand and counting off the points on his fingers. 'Someone drowned in the lake. One of the B&B guests. We just got back from watching from the hotel. The guards are upstairs searching his room for clues.'

Her boy would be wasted on animals, Liv thought. He should be in some line of work that required him to cut through bullshit. Although that was nearly like wishing the dole on him. So many jobs seemed to require the creation of bullshit rather than its excision.

'Fuck.' Seamus whistled. 'Fuck,' he said again. 'What happens now?' This last he addressed to Liv.

Had she missed the meeting, Liv wondered wildly, where they decided that she was the fount of all wisdom on dead guests? Perhaps God – or the other fella, more likely – had appeared to them in the teapot while her back was turned.

'We can't do anything until the guards tell us what's going on,' Shay filled in again.

'Was he here long?' Seamus asked. 'The lad that drowned?'

'He wasn't a lad. He was an older gentleman. Checked in last Monday.'

'Is it Ellen above?' Seamus gestured to the ceiling. 'I'll go up and have a word,' he said when Liv nodded.

'That's hardly your place.'

Marianne looked at Liv for backup. Her raised chin suggested that Seamus knowing all about Ethel hadn't been lost on her. If that was the price of peace, she would happily pay it, Liv thought, and shook her head firmly. 'No, Seamus. No need.'

'Fair enough.' Seamus held up his two hands in a parody of reasonableness. 'I was only trying to help.'

Marianne looked at him, then pointedly looked away.

She had never liked him, Liv reminded herself. It wasn't as if she knew. How could she?

It was almost a relief when Marianne set free the dark thought flapping over all of their heads. 'Do you think it was an accident?'

'I'm sure—' Liv began.

'I don't think so,' Ed said at the same time, stopping her in her tracks.

'Did you speak to him too?' Marianne asked, leaning over the table to him.

If her sister could only see how much she looked like their mother, Liv thought, it would warm her heart. Either that or kill her.

'No.' Ed shook his head. 'It just seems more likely. Out walking early and alone, fully dressed.'

'Of course he would be fully dressed if he was out walking,' Seamus said.

Ed considered for a moment. 'True. Perhaps I meant that it would seem less tragic if he intended it.'

Was there ever, Liv wondered, a less Irish utterance inside these four walls? It was a wonder there wasn't some sort of seismic shift in the foundations of the place, some old Catholic ghosts gasping and keening.

'Do you think so?' Shay asked, interested.

Liv's heart seemed to stop. Was that normal or unseemly interest on his part? She glanced at Marianne, but her sister was looking away.

'At home, we believe in freedom of choice. The right to end your life has been there since I was a child. I know people that chose when and how to go, who they wanted with them.

127

It is sad, of course, when a person decides that they want to draw a line under everything that is possible. But every life and every choice is different.' Ed smiled, a little sadly.

Seamus shook his head. 'I'm afraid I'll have to disagree with you there. No self-respecting Irishman would take his own life in someone else's house. And Easter week, no less. A time for celebration.'

Liv was about to point out that Easter week was chiefly about betrayal, death and a mother's endurance in the face of crippling sorrow, when there was a knock on the kitchen door and a head appeared.

'We're finished upstairs,' Ellen said. 'If we might have a word?'

'Of course, come in.' Liv half-stood.

'It might be best if we could do it individually,' Ellen said, apologetically. 'Only because it's the way it's done. Is there somewhere…?'

'Ellen, how are you?' Seamus was up with his hand out.

'Seamus. Long time no see. I saw your mother at the nursing home last week. She was asking after you.'

He had the grace to look uncomfortable. Ellen was always able to give as good as she got, Liv thought. 'I'll get you set up in the front room, Ellen.'

'We'll want to speak to the other guests as well,' Ellen said as Liv led herself and Fiachra Dunne down the hall past reception and into the front room, Seamus following behind.

'We have only four rooms booked. Three, if you don't count Mr Stiller.' Nobody would count him any more, she supposed. 'They're all out, for the moment.'

'I'll have Shay do a quick recce down the village and round them up,' Seamus said.

'Do you not need to be on your way?' Liv asked, baring her teeth in a smile.

Unfortunately, Fiachra Dunne chimed in at the same moment. 'That would be helpful, Mr O'Callaghan.'

'Lucey,' Liv said. 'He's Lucey. I'm O'Callaghan.'

As she turned to leave, she caught Ellen's sympathetic look and felt herself blush up to the eyeballs.

'Yourself and Shay will be off after that, I suppose?' she said, once they were back out in the hall.

'Actually, I wanted to talk to you about that. I went by the old house to put on the heating before coming here and it wouldn't come on. The boiler must be on the blink. I phoned around, but it'll be Tuesday at the earliest before they can get someone out to look at it. Bank holiday weekend and all that.'

Liv willed him not to say it.

'The house is cold,' he went on. 'A bit damp too, most likely. I haven't been down in a few...'

'You really should rent out the place,' Liv said. 'A house needs to be lived in.'

'You know what Mother is like. She can't bear the idea of anyone in her house.' He shrugged, as if that was all there was to be said. After a lifetime of bowing to her whims, Liv supposed maybe it was.

'I was thinking I would head back late tonight instead. We could reschedule then for another weekend?' He took out his phone and began scrolling through his calendar.

No *fucking* way. Not after eighteen years of dragging his parenting up to an acceptable standard. 'For God's sake, Seamus, just stay here.'

He nodded, thoughtfully. 'It might be better for Shay, I suppose, after the shock.'

Maybe it was for the best, Liv thought.

'Better for you too.' His hand was warm on hers. 'You could do with the support.'

Liv closed the bathroom door and leaned against it, Seamus safely on the other side. The mirror showed her cheeks flushed. Jesus Christ. What she wouldn't give if it was just early menopause. She ran the tap until the hot water came through and steamed up the mirror. It wasn't the shower, but it would have to do. She hadn't time to be weeping herself idly down the plughole. 1. Seamus. 2. Seamus. 3. Seamus. Her whole bloody life.

Don't think about it, she told herself. Think about something else. Think about Ethel. Ethel and the conversation that would have to be had. The thought was as welcome as a drunken stranger's hand up her shirt on New Year's Eve. She considered the third worry. *One foot in front of the other and before you know it, you're there*, her father used to say.

'Unless you're going in a circle,' she told her reflection. 'Then you never get anywhere, only back where you started.'

HOLY SATURDAY/EASTER SUNDAY

ETHEL

Ethel watched them walk away from the ambulance. Olive and Shay, Marianne and Ed. She stayed where she was. *We're overdue a talk.* The body in the water changed everything. One look at her daughters' faces when they saw her made that clear.

They had done this dance before. The apologising, the tears, the whispering, the pretence that Shay was still a heedless child. The thought of it thrummed inside her.

'Should you not be away with them, Ethel?'

Peter nudged her arm and threw his chin in the direction the small, slumped party had taken. Her family. Gone without her. The self-pity was a familiar cardigan settling around her shoulders.

'I'll not have the guards leading me around like a donkey,' Ethel said.

'He was one of yours, all the same,' Peter went on.

Ethel drew herself up a little straighter. 'A night or two in the B&B does not make him "one of ours".' She forced a laugh. 'At that rate, you'd have us responsible for every half-Yank this side of the midlands.'

'Half-Yank was he? Wasn't he the lad you were having a drink with the other night?'

Lord but the man was tiresome. Was she to have no peace at all?

'We had a polite drink, that's all. It would have been rude to leave him sitting there alone.'

'Looked like more than the one to me,' Peter said.

When Ethel glanced over, his face was impassive. He stood with his hands in his pockets, staring out over the sea. 'A word of advice for you, Peter.' She leaned in close. 'Keep your hands in your own pockets.'

'There's no call for that kind of talk,' she heard him say from behind her. 'Martin would turn in his grave to hear you.'

She kept walking. *We're overdue a talk.* Well, it was nothing that couldn't wait an hour. One last hour. For a brief moment she considered walking the lake path or going up to Martin's grave, God rest him. No. She was on the clock now and must take her comfort where she could. Sheila Dillon had run back to the hotel kitchen not five minutes ago to refill the tray of coffees, but with only a few stragglers left, she might decide not to bother. She should go in and offer to give her a hand, Ethel decided.

The lobby of the hotel was cosy after the sharpness of the wind outside. Sheila Dillon was on the phone, miming to Ethel that she would be with her in a minute.

Ethel went and sat on one of the couches pulled up close to the fireplace. The fire was already lit, catching the glass of the sherry bottle – a little welcome they used to offer in the B&B until Olive put the kibosh on it – turning it a kind of deep country orange. They made a nice job of the place, Sheila and Tiny. Sheila, really. Tiny only did what he was told. To look at it now was to remember how shabby it used to be, although they believed it the height of style at the time. It was here herself and Martin, God rest him, came the day of the wedding, after the early morning ceremony. There was only the two of themselves, sitting over their full Irish. Sheila's father, old Mr Dillon, brought them out a bottle of champagne for luck and told them to put it away for their twenty-fifth wedding anniversary. They made the anniversary all right, but the champagne was long gone by then.

'Ethel, what can I do for you?' Sheila Dillon called over when she had put the phone down. 'I thought everyone was gone home now the ambulance has taken him.'

That was the hotel Dillons for you, Ethel thought, all hat and no cowboy.

Ethel got up and walked closer, lowering her voice. She was no common streel to be shouting her business across the floor, reclaimed oak or not. 'I thought I should tell you that the poor man' – Ethel gave a discreet backwards nod, as if the gent himself were behind her – 'was staying with us the last couple of days. I wanted you to hear it from me. One proprietor to another, as it were.' She wondered if she had gone too far with the fellow-feeling. 'God rest his soul,' she added, blessing herself.

Mrs Dillon hastily did the same. 'So Tiny was saying.'

'I had a drink with him only the other night,' Ethel said. Sheila Dillon would know they only came to the hotel for occasions. Before Midnight Mass on Christmas Eve. For the sandwiches after Martin's funeral, God rest him. 'I saw him going into the pub by himself, the poor man,' she added hastily. 'It didn't seem Christian to let him in there with the likes of the Twomeys and Peter Clifford.'

'Is that so?' Sheila Dillon's tone was appreciably warmer.

'He was a most interesting man. Most interesting.' Ethel shook her head sadly.

'Why don't you come in and sit a while?' Sheila Dillon said.

Ethel made a show of thinking for a moment. 'I should be getting back. The guards will be wanting to talk to me about him. You wouldn't know what he might have said that could turn out to be important.'

'They won't miss you for ten minutes. You could do with something for the shock. Did you get any coffee outside?'

'I did,' Ethel said. 'Yourself and Ti... Dermot took good

133

care of us all. Your father, God rest him, would have been rightly proud.'

'Come on over by the fire. You must be cold through after standing out in the cold. That wind would cut you. Easterly, without a doubt. Our Maria does a lovely Irish coffee – a small one will warm you right up.'

Maria did indeed do a lovely Irish coffee, Ethel thought as she made her way home an hour later. Two or three of them, even. She sniggered a little at her own joke, then righted herself against the wall of the nearest house. She was fine to go in and talk to the guards, though. Fine altogether. Nobody would begrudge a soul a small nip after this kind of a morning.

The open front door looked at her sternly, like her mother used to when she had the blackthorn stick in her hand and was doling out slaps. *Crack. Don't be telling everyone our business. Crack.* She stuck her tongue out at it as she walked through.

'Morning, girls. Seamus.' A quick clear of the throat while she waited for the other lad's name to come to her. There it was, merciful and welcome as a twenty euro note forgotten in a pocket. 'Ed. How are things here? I see the squad car is outside. They're still above in the room, I imagine?' She directed her questions towards Ed. Based on the thundery faces around the table, he was the most likely to answer.

'We were wondering where you got to.' Olive's voice was even.

'Sheila Dillon asked a couple of us to give her a hand tidying up. I didn't like to refuse. She was in a bit of a state, truth be told.'

'Mrs Dillon, with her hotel full of staff, asked you to help her to wash a few cups?' Marianne's voice was loud.

'For goodness sake, Marianne, didn't you hear me saying it wasn't about the dishes at all? The woman was upset.'

'What had she to be upset about?'

'We're not all made of stone.' Ethel wasn't quite sure how she ended up defending Sheila Dillon's imaginary feelings, but she was prepared to brazen it out.

'We're to believe you're upset too, are we?' Marianne threw the words out.

'It's a terrible thing,' Seamus said. 'It's fair to say it has us all thrown.'

'I didn't realise you knew him.' Ethel turned to Seamus. Nothing would do Seamus but to be stuck in the middle of whatever was going on, whether he was wanted or not. He was only ever a big thick lug, she thought. She and Martin had been right to put the run on him long ago, Shay or no Shay.

'No matter who it is.' At least Seamus had the grace to flush.

'It is only terrible if it is not what he wanted,' Ed said.

'Not this again, Ed,' Marianne said.

Ethel turned to Ed and stage-whispered, 'Easy, now. Don't set her off.' To the room in general, she added, 'The guards think he did it on purpose, is it?'

'The guards said no such thing,' Olive said, firmly. 'They don't know anything, so we shouldn't be speculating.'

'They don't know anything is right. Ellen Gould would be hard pushed to pick her own arse out of a line-up. The mother was the same. Nothing whistling between the two ears. But you know that already, Seamus.' She rolled her eyes and winked at him.

'I already said that he couldn't have... ki... taken his own life,' Seamus said. 'It's Easter week.'

'Maybe he thought if he killed himself yesterday, he'd rise again tomorrow,' Ethel said, thoughtfully. It was reasonable, as hypotheses went. 'Maybe he was a religious nut. An end-of-days type. They always give off the impression of being meek and mild,' she mused aloud. 'As the days go, Friday is the best of them. If I was going to do away with myself, I might well pick a Friday.'

'Jesus, Gran. Would you just stop!'

She hadn't seen Shay come in from the hall with the two guards.

'Ah, just stop yourself,' she said crossly. 'Am I not allowed an opinion in my own home?' But looking at Shay, she saw he was close to tears and the fight went out of her. 'Don't mind me,' she said, going over and trying to put her arms around him.

He shook her off, a sharp movement that saw Ellen Gould step forward, just in case.

'I'm talking nonsense, that's all.'

'Because you're drunk. Again.' Shay turned on his heel and, a moment later, they heard the thump of his feet on the stairs, the thud of his bedroom door.

Olive threw her a look that would have felled a lesser person and followed him out of the room.

'Children,' Ethel tutted. 'They hardly know their arse from—'

The male guard cleared his throat and cut across her. 'Be that as it may, we'll want a word with you and your husband, Mrs…'

Ethel drew herself up. 'I'm not a Mrs any more. My Martin, God rest him, is dead these ten years. You'd know that if you were any good at all.'

'Ethel,' Marianne cut across her. 'They need to talk to everyone. You can do it now or you can do it later, but it has to be done.'

She should speak to Shay, she knew. Apologise. Explain herself, if he would let her. Explain until that look faded from his face. But if the guards were interviewing everyone, that would keep the girls busy until lunchtime or later. She could slip out for an hour. Gird her loins before battle, as it were. There would be no reasoning with Olive, not until she calmed down.

'You heard the boss, Ellen.' Ethel gave an exaggerated bow – a mistake, the room spun when she straightened up and she had to grab for the sideboard under the pretence of rubbing away a bit of dirt. 'Lead on.'

The Sacred Heart watched her all the way out with his beady red eye. Maybe that was how God was all-seeing, Ethel thought. Hadn't he a spy in every house in Ireland? 'Nobody likes a know-it-all,' she whispered to Jesus in the painting as she passed; he would know she was onto him.

It was a relief to push open the pub door and walk into the warmth. Even the sight of Norah Nolan perched on a bar stool next to her husband couldn't dampen the feeling of homecoming.

'You're looking well, Ethel. Considering,' Mrs Nolan said.

'Doesn't your husband take great care of us all, Norah?' She breathed out hard at the end of it. As if the world and his cat didn't know she was born plain Nora. The 'h' was only an extension built to house her notions. 'Isn't he doing God's own work?'

Dr Nolan twitched briefly beside her, then patted his pocket as if reassuring himself that whatever he was looking for was still there.

'It must be all excitement over your way,' Peter called from his end of the bar.

Did the man ever leave? The smart money said he would die there. They could stuff him, Ethel thought, or bronze him. Was there such a thing as a taxidermist for humans? She must remember to ask Ed. He seemed like a man to hoard those little details.

'Are the guards still there?' Dr Nolan asked.

'They are. I'm only just finished with them myself. Such a grilling as I got. When did he check in and what did he say and what did he have with him and where did he spend his time. "How would I know where he spent his time? We're a B&B," I told them, "not the KGB". That softened their cough for them.'

'How awful to be associated with it,' Norah shuddered.

Yet what had her out today herself, only the excitement of it all? It was better than any television programme. Look at her, fairly panting at the horror. 'It's not association, Norah. It's assistance.'

She sniffed. 'I'm sure that's all very noble, but the very idea of it. I couldn't bear it.'

'Do they know what happened?' Dr Nolan asked.

Ethel shook her head. 'Not that they've said anyway.'

'Trust that shower to play it close to their chest.' Peter nodded. 'The Goulds are mean by nature. The father would peel an orange in his pocket.'

Alan placed a second glass in front of Ethel. 'You'll be needing that,' he said, waving away her proffered tenner.

'You're a gentleman, Alan,' Ethel said. 'My nerves are in flitters.'

Talk turned briefly to other things, returning to the main event every time the door opened to admit another neighbour. Norah Nolan insisted on calling it 'the mishap', as if the man had taken a tumble off a swing in the playground or mistaken one bus for another. Ethel had a mind to spill her drink on her just so she could use the word mishap correctly, but she didn't want to throw Alan's generosity back at him.

When the door opened, a smattering of applause went around the bar.

'The heroes of the hour,' Tom Twomey said, raising his glass to the Dempseys standing in the doorway.

God love them, were they ever in a pub before? Still in their wellington boots and caps, they must have gone home, cooked and eaten the dinner – bacon and turnip, by the smell of them – and come back into town without thinking to change their clothes. Maybe it was true and they only had the one outfit each. Wags had been saying for years they were never seen in town on a Monday because it was washing day and they had nothing to leave the house in.

'You'll be the men for the news, now,' Peter said. 'Tell all.'

Alan placed a pint in front of each of them, waving away

their money as he was doing for everyone today. Dempsey Sr cleared his throat. The designated speaker, evidently.

'We heard there was a body in the water. So down we went in the oils and drug him out.'

Th'iles. That run-on 'th' was something Martin, God rest him, used to do. Over the years it was endearing, then irritating, then invisible. Could a word be invisible? Lord but the Dempseys were rubbing off on her. Listening to them would add years to you.

'And?' It seemed like the whole bar was waiting for the rest of the story. Dempsey Sr looked at Dempsey Jr, who consulted his own feet.

'We waited until th'ambulance came,' Dempsey Sr finished.

'Was he in the water long, John Paul?' someone asked.

Dempsey Sr gave every appearance of thinking hard. 'Took us about forty minutes, I'd say, all told.'

'I meant, what did he look like?'

Beside Ethel, Norah Nolan took a slug out of her brandy-and-port.

'It wouldn't be right to say.' Dempsey Sr scratched his beard. 'But he was fair slippery.'

That was as much as could be got out of either of them. They stood by the bar, drank down four pints apiece and left, the roar of the tractor as it started up drowning out the conversation they left behind them.

Ethel drank her free vodka judiciously. Not for her the unseemly greed of knocking them back one after another simply because they were free. She would give it an hour and then pretend she had a text from the girls with some update from the guards. That would take her through the evening. By now, Olive would know she had left, so she might as well take her time and enjoy it. If Martin, God rest him, were still here, he would tell Olive to leave her alone, a person was entitled to a drink after a hard day's work. Or he might advise letting her work things out for herself. He wouldn't have been one for handing people over to therapists who were only in it to feel better about their own shortcomings. It was just another thing to get through. A phase, like they used to say when the girls were little, and bold. The last time, she managed to make it to day fifteen before hightailing it home in the cab of a bread lorry. Olive was hopping mad over it.

'Serial killers don't drive bread lorries. They wouldn't have the time,' Ethel said. A joke in poor taste, granted, but it held in what she would only have regretted saying. That handing over your authority, your very self, it felt like, to a disinterested party could smother a person. But for all Ethel's bravado, it was a week or more before she could look Shay in the eye.

'Gran! Gran.' Shay's voice woke her.

What was Shay doing in her room? she wondered, before realising that she was outside. She could hear the sea.

'Gran.' He shook her shoulder.

'I'm awake, Shay. Give me a minute.'

She sat up slowly without looking at him. At least she had had the good sense to sleep on the bench. After the heavy showers last night, the ground would have ruined her good coat.

Shay sat down beside her, his white face glowing in the pre-dawn gloom. Rather than look at him, Ethel opened her makeshift pillow-handbag. A little packet of wet wipes and a slightly furry chewing gum did wonders, and she closed the clasp of her bag feeling fresh and recharged. She didn't need any mirror. With Martin gone, God rest him, didn't she know her own face better than anyone? She tightened her coat around her.

'I couldn't sleep, so I came out to look for you,' Shay told her. 'After… you know… Fred Stille.'

'I thought it was Stiller?'

Beside her, she felt Shay shaking his head. 'It was in the register as Stiller, but he only signed himself Fred Stille. No "r".'

That was that, so, Ethel thought. It was no accident. 'Did

I ever tell you that it was my idea to open the B&B? Your Grandad Martin, God rest him, took a bit of convincing. I'm the same age he was when he died. God love him, it was the only thing he was ever first at.'

'Gran—'

Ethel continued as if he hadn't said anything. 'I was convinced we could make it the best little place this side of the Shannon. In my mind's eye, we would have guests from all over Europe, every one of them convinced that they were after finding a little piece of magic in our house. I suppose you think that's silly. You young people now have grander plans.'

'Not—'

Again, she ignored him. 'I wanted to be able to welcome everyone in their own language. It was those little touches that would make the difference. When I was chatting to the guests, I would ask them for little phrases in their own language. German, Dutch, Spanish, Italian, you name it. Not just hello and goodbye, but little wishes that I could confer on future guests that they would know they had found a warm welcome with us. I knew how to say *welcome* and *we hope you enjoy your stay* and *if the weather holds*.'

'I never knew that.'

'One phrase I was especially fond of,' Ethel went on. 'It was "I hope you find peace and quiet here with us". What else were they coming for, after all? They were either looking for God in the statue or looking for the devil in Willowbrook. Peace and quiet was the least I could offer them.' She laughed a little. '*Paix et calme. Pace e tranquillità. Ruhe und Frieden, Fred og stille.*'

'*Fred og stille*?' Shay repeated.

'Danish. That poor man,' she said softly. She felt tired all of a sudden. The way he had sat in the chair with his knees together, taking up as little space as possible. He had wished for beautiful thoughts, had sought out poetry and views to help him to find them. What was it for, any of it? 'I hope he found the peace he wanted.'

Beside her, she could feel Shay bracing himself to speak. 'Gran. I'm sorry for saying it the way I did, but I think you need to get help—'

She thought of the man – Fred, Mr Peace-and-quiet – with his small glass of beer. The dull sound of the ambulance door closing as he left one group of strangers for another.

'I promise I'll try.' She patted Shay's hand. God love him, he was still young enough to be wedded to notions of black or white. Everything was the end of the world. 'I can promise you that.'

She stood. Overhead, the wrens were in full voice and the sun had turned the edges of the sky pink. 'Let's go home first, Shay, pet. Home and then Willowbrook.'

EASTER SUNDAY

MARIANNE

Every time Marianne closed her eyes, she saw his body on the stretcher in the back of the ambulance. His poor face exposed as the paramedics tried to lift him over the wall. Or face down in the water, flanked by the Dempseys. What a way to go. It didn't bear thinking about. Except she couldn't think of anything else. She kept returning to the memory of his gentle interest in fairy lore, his pleasure at the swan. No matter what Ed said, it was hard to imagine someone with his evident capacity for – she searched for the right word – *gladness* – deciding that the world no longer held anything for him. She shivered.

Beside her, Ed slept soundly. She could wake him, she knew, and he would pull her into a sleepy hug and listen or talk, as she needed. She didn't. Somehow it was enough to know she could.

It was a relief to see light appear around the edges of the curtains. To listen to the guests moving in and out of toilets. Yesterday afternoon they had all decided to stay one more night, even after the guards declared them free to leave.

'That's people for you,' Liv said.

Were they afraid they would miss something if they left,

Marianne wondered, or did they think it would make them look guilty to leave town the minute the body was found? She strongly suspected the former, partly because it was what she herself would do in their place and partly because she had met them all the previous day. Liv's surprise at her offer to talk to them had stung. It wasn't as if Ellen Ghoul was the only one who returned home with skills. Seeing her standing there with her notebook, Marianne was reminded of Ellen in school. *Ghoul* because of the way she devoured true crime stories, her sweaty fingers turning the pages of one library book after another while she ate her sandwiches alone in the classroom.

'I was the only person left in my department for a while during the recession,' she reminded Liv. 'I'm used to giving bad news. I'll set up tea and what-have-you in the breakfast room. They can come in there after talking to the guards.'

At Seamus' suggestion, Ed went out for whiskey and brandy. Annoying as it was to admit, it was the right call. The whole thing was, Marianne reflected afterwards, a little like the world's most awkward party. While waiting their turn to see the guards, the two older couples settled comfortably into speculation about what might have happened. They were prosaic about the details, evidently well versed in the vagaries of death. If they mourned anything, it was the lack of interaction with the man in the days prior, and the resulting disappointed absence of distinctive gossipy titbits. There was the strong suggestion that they would like to have spoken to him more, if only to better inform their judgement now. The two younger guests, a bosomy, braless pair – Marianne had to avert her eyes – seemed floored by the news. It was the idea of older people having agency that appeared to upset them most, Marianne thought somewhat uncharitably, as they wondered aloud why anyone hadn't been able to stop him. Their tic of referring to 'the elderly' had a dehumanising effect, like academic articles. Not that she was any stalwart defender-of-rights herself. Beyond the usual human capital reports on the value of the grey brain and the grey pound and how the appearance of valuing the one might generate the other, she really had no interaction with anybody over the age of fifty-five. There was Ethel, of course, but she hardly counted. And Dad hadn't had the chance to get old. That was the virtue in going unexpectedly rather than having the world watch you sicken and die. Getting up as noiselessly as she could, she took her phone into the bathroom and made a note to research the heritability of heart disease.

'Look at you, with breakfast nearly ready to go. Aren't you as handy as a small pot?' Liv said, pouring herself coffee.

Marianne smiled. It was years since she'd heard their father's expression out loud. Thinking it to herself as she cooked and tidied the apartment didn't count somehow. 'Couldn't sleep. You?'

'Like a stone.'

Another thing Liv did better. 'Any sign of Ethel this morning?'

'Her room is empty. She's avoiding me since I told her we need to talk.'

'One of us should have gone in with her to talk to the guards and make sure she didn't disappear.'

Liv shook her head. 'She's a grown woman, Mar. If she wants to go, there's no stopping her.'

Not with that attitude, Marianne wanted to say. 'Is Shay okay?' she said instead. 'He was pretty shook yesterday.'

'Honestly, I don't know. I tried to talk to him – so did Seamus – but he just didn't want to know.'

'A night's sleep will do him the world of good, I'm sure.' Amazing how easily the platitudes came out, even with family, Marianne thought. As if a reviving night's sleep was that easy to come by.

'He stuck a note on my door saying he was gone out for

a walk and not to worry,' Liv said. 'Which reminds me – do you think it would be too much to call Ellen and see if they've contacted the family? I'd feel better if I knew whether to leave the room or not. Knowing that it's just sitting there makes me uneasy.'

'Knowing any room hasn't been cleaned makes you uneasy.' Marianne crossed her eyes at her sister. Then her face fell. 'I can't believe I got his name wrong. How could I have forgotten to ask for ID?'

'It happens,' Liv said.

She was being kind, Marianne knew. It didn't happen to Liv. 'There we were, all calling him Mr Stiller. You'd think he'd have said something.'

'Too polite I suppose.'

'Maybe if I had asked him for ID, he wouldn't have—'

'Marianne. I think we can agree that the tragedy here is that a man chose to die, not that you got the paperwork wrong. It's not always about you.'

The kitchen drew them all, such was the known power of tea in the face of the uncertain. People might not want to be together, but the idea of being alone was worse. Although listening to Seamus banging on about phoning his friend 'in the force' – they all went to school with Ellen, for fuck's sake – was making her teeth itch. Whatever he had going for him back when they were teenagers was long gone, if only Liv would see it.

Marianne was about to suggest that she and Ed might go out for a walk – the thought of fresh air suddenly irresistible – when the back door opened and Shay came in, followed by Ethel.

'I'm prepared to go now,' Ethel declared. She looked at Shay and he nodded encouragingly.

'Mar, will you help Ethel to get a few things together?' Liv said.

'Shouldn't we phone and see—' Marianne began, but Liv shook her head. 'No need. I spoke to them earlier.'

Shay, Seamus and Ed stood in the doorway and waved them off. An unlikely trio, Marianne thought. Throw in the ghost of her father and they could be the barbershop quartet in a museum of curiosities.

'I didn't know cafés opened on Easter Sunday,' Marianne said, for something to say as they drove through the village.

Liv, at the wheel, just nodded. Beside her in the passenger seat, Ethel sat toddler-style, her hands in her lap.

Well, fine. If they weren't going to make an effort, she wouldn't either. Instead, Marianne joined the other two in silent contemplation of the soggy countryside outside the rain-slashed windows. It was odd to think of the Easter traditions dying out here. She would have bet that in a hundred years, people would still be doing the same things. She thought wistfully of Easter dinners past. The traditional slow-cooked roast lamb with mint sauce, baby carrots and garden peas, two kinds of potato. Rhubarb crumble and custard to finish, or, if Ethel was in the mood, rhubarb fool, creamy and delicious. A definite contender for her death-row meal. Fred's last meal might have been in the Fish Bar, she thought suddenly. A bowl of chowder, maybe, or a lonesome seafood salad. Tears welled in her eyes, and she turned her head so Liv wouldn't see. She would only give out to her for being melodramatic.

Ninety minutes later, they were back in the car on the return leg of the journey. Without Ethel, the silence felt more awkward. What would her mother be doing now? *Settling in*, the manager, Judith, had told them, but that could be anything from playing draughts to rocking in a corner or licking the carpet. The set of Judith's mouth had suggested that such questions were best ignored, if a person was so uncouth as to ask them in the first place. Her brisk tone left Marianne feeling like a bold small child.

'Will she be all right?' she asked Liv.

'She'll be fine.' Liv maintained the same crisp tone she had adopted throughout the checking-in process. Even when their mother's belongings were searched, followed by Ethel herself, she had done nothing more than stand there with her arm out so that Ethel could drape coat and cardigan over it.

'Stop the clinical thing, would you? The I've-seen-it-all-before-so-it's-nothing-new attitude.'

'It's not an attitude. It's nothing new because I've seen it all before. Several times.'

'Well, I haven't. And you can blame me all you want, but that doesn't make it any less fucking terrifying. They practically strip-searched her.'

'It's difficult, I know, but it has to be done.' Liv's voice was gentler.

'Could they not just ask her if she had anything on her?' Marianne hated the wheedle in her voice, like a child moaning about unfairness.

'It's their job not to trust her.' Liv glanced over at her sister. 'They do it so we don't have to. Ethel agreeing to go is a step. That's how we do this. Step by step.'

'Thirty days,' Marianne said. By then it would be coming into summer. Everything seemed more manageable on a longer evening. She could take some time off work. Be here for her mother coming home. 'Will she last, do you think?'

'Step by step,' Liv reminded her.

They drove in silence through the village. Outside Naughtons, Alan was washing windows and saluted the car as it drove past. Marianne was surprised to see her sister wave back. Wasn't he half the problem? If he wasn't serving – *supplying* – her mother with alcohol, they mightn't have had to watch her being led away like a calf to mart.

148

When Marianne entered the kitchen and found Ed braising beef, she nearly wept with gratitude.

Seamus and Shay returned shortly afterwards.

'We went to visit Grandma Pauline,' Shay explained. 'You'll never guess—'

Liv turned to Seamus. 'Seriously? Are you going to tell your wife that you missed Easter with her just to spend half an hour with your mother?'

Marianne winced, but Seamus gave a big loud laugh. 'You're gas, Livvie. Listen. I phoned that buddy of mine in the barracks – you remember, Wes? – anyway, I thought he might be able to give us a heads-up on what was going on. Unofficially, you know?'

'It's not a murder inquiry, Seamus. If we have any questions, we can just ask Ellen. There's no big mystery to get to the bottom of.'

'Gran told me Fred Stille was a made-up name,' Shay interrupted.

His face was so animated, Marianne almost smiled.

'How would Ethel know that?' Liv asked.

'She said it was Danish for peace and quiet. So we thought maybe it was, like, an alias, you know?'

Shay looked excitedly from one face to the next. 'We don't know who he really was.'

'We know that he died, Shay.' Liv's voice was almost unbearably gentle. 'Whoever he was doesn't change that.'

'It does increase the likelihood that it was planned,' Ed said. 'I imagine the guards would be interested in Ethel's theory.' He nodded at Shay, who smiled gratefully.

'Dad told them. They're looking into it.'

'Do they need to talk to Ethel?' Marianne asked and was relieved when Seamus shook his head. 'Wes thinks not. I explained the... somewhat unusual situation. He thought it would be enough to verify that the name means what she said it does.'

It was hard to tell whether he was embarrassed for Ethel or by her.

Shay was quiet all evening, picking at his Easter egg with an air of disappointment, as if, having imparted all he knew, he expected more from them. It could have been the weirdness of seeing his parents together, chatting and laughing, telling Ed stories from their schooldays. She didn't realise how much she took for granted that Ethel and Dad were happy. Whether that was because they had made their peace with one another and the choices they'd made, or because theirs was a genuine love, Marianne was no wiser now than she ever was. Maybe Ethel's heart was broken and that was why she drank. Maybe she was a simmering alcoholic all along and it all overflowed without Martin to keep a lid on it. With Ethel, anything was possible.

'Seamus, what have yourself and Shay planned for your boys' evening?' she asked, on an impulse.

Seamus looked at Shay. 'I'm easy. Do you want to head out somewhere for an hour?'

'Driving range?' Shay offered.

'Perfect.'

When they were gone, Liv turned to Marianne. 'What did you do that for?'

Marianne didn't understand why Liv was cross. 'It'll take his mind off things.'

'Shay hates golf.'

'Then why would he suggest it?'

'They watched the Irish Open together once when Shay was sick and it made Seamus so happy that Shay kept it going.'

This was why people shouldn't have children. It was nothing but a minefield of misinterpretation and disappointment. 'Fuck, I'm sorry, Liv. I had no idea.'

Liv sighed and sat back in her chair. 'How would you know when even his own father doesn't?'

They laughed a little at that. 'He's a good kid,' Marianne said, getting up to take a section of the Sunday papers from Ed. 'He's a lot nicer than either of us were, that much I do know.'

'Less of Ethel in him,' Liv said.

This time the laughter was guilty. Marianne opened the paper and turned the pages delicately. On every page there was another story of another foolish young man.

EASTER MONDAY

LIV

Liv woke early. It was hard not to, with Seamus sprawled across all four corners of the bed, radiating heat like a guilty conscience. Where to start with the recriminations? *What was I thinking? He's married. Have I no self-esteem at all?* But she had asked herself all those questions before and the answers never got any more flattering.

She curled her toes hard, one way and then the other, enjoying the tightness, the release. Then the image of Mr Stiller – Stille, she corrected herself – came to her, his toes pointing skyward evermore. She shuddered and crept from the bed to have her shower. There was little need for quiet. Seamus had put away the best part of two bottles of wine last night; little short of an aerial display past the window would wake him.

Fred Stille's presence lingered as she ran the water and stepped in. What was he so ashamed of? What created such despair? She turned the water up as hot as she could stand, letting it sting her skin. 1. Bitter. 2. Adulterous. 3. Die alone. Did it count as adultery if she wasn't the one that was married? How many lapses in judgement did it take for a person to decide that they had had their fill of sunrises and lazy stretches, of hot shower water on the back of their neck, of first-cups-of-the-day?

The bathroom door opened, startling her. She scrambled to wipe away the words, slipping slightly as she did so. 4. Falling and dying in the shower. That was for another list, another day, she thought, as Seamus knocked gently on the glass.

She opened the shower door. 'Not a good idea,' she said.

'It's dark out,' he said, stepping in beside her and closing the two of them into the warmth. 'So it's still technically last night's bad idea.'

There was no sign of Marianne in the kitchen. It was unsettling, seeing Marianne move about the place as if she had never left. She knew that Liv owned half the business, of course. Any assumptions she might have made about what would happen to Ethel's half when she died were not Liv's concern. A day that was – hopefully – many years from now, Liv added hurriedly, in case her thoughts were being beamed to some celestial ticker tape. It was Ethel's business – and thus Ethel's job – to tell Marianne anything she needed to know about her inheritance. Ethel's job to avoid possible misunderstandings and fallings-out. Liv cracked eggs with savagery.

'What did that egg ever do to you?' Marianne stood in the doorway, as if summoned to answer for herself.

'I don't know how they can eat,' Liv said, and was surprised to find tears in her eyes. 'Sitting there fussing over salt and milk as if any of it fucking matters. Fred had toast and eggs too, for all the good it did him.'

Marianne crossed the room and put her arms around her sister. Liv stood where she was, an egg in one hand, a knife in the other.

'They'll be gone later on. And they don't mean anything by it.'

'I know that!' Liv was mortified to hear her voice crack. 'It just seems so...'

'Remember after Dad died,' Marianne's tone was conversational, 'all the food people brought? Not because they thought we couldn't – or shouldn't – make our own dinner, but because it's the most normalising thing in the world. When you don't know what to do with yourself, breaking the day into breakfast-lunch-dinner is a start.'

'It's not functional for them,' Liv felt obliged to point out. 'It's more like… like popcorn at the movies.'

'There was fuck-all functional about the rake of apple tarts we ate the week after Daddy's funeral,' Marianne said. 'I got back home and none of my work clothes fit me. I thought I'd have to take another few days' bereavement leave to spend in the gym.'

They laughed a little at that. She had eaten one of those apple tarts in bed with Seamus, Liv remembered. While his wife was at home carrying his future in her belly. Afraid she would break down and tell her sister, Liv moved her shoulders just enough that Marianne stepped away.

'It's not like you to see the worst in people,' Marianne said. 'Are you sure there's nothing—'

'A man is dead,' Liv snapped. 'What more does there need to be?'

Marianne stiffened. 'I'm aware. I'll go through and serve,' she said.

It wasn't only her father's funeral that had slid her into this particular behavioural spiral. It was the days after Seamus' own father died. And when the recession hit, and she was worried about the business all the time. When Shay started secondary school. That time he was concussed playing hurling. When Pauline first went into the care home. When Shay got his exam results last year. A shameful list of low points lowered still further.

Who was she to criticise those poor holidaymakers for doing their best to move forward, when all she herself could do was go around and around the past like a dog circling shit?

'I'm sorry, Mar,' she said when Marianne came back in

to get fresh juice and water for the young couple. 'I'm a bit all over the place.'

'We all are,' Marianne said. 'Not to worry. We'll get each other through it.' She patted Liv on the back and began to open and close cupboard doors.

'The big jugs are in the dining room,' Liv said. She heard it as soon as she said it.

Marianne's mouth twitched. 'Indeed they are.'

When the last guest pronounced himself stuffed, Liv closed the dining room door and went through to the family kitchen for a coffee. She was jittery still; the caffeine would be kill or cure. Mr Stille had seemed so nice, she thought with a sudden burst of anger, yet he had thought only of himself, leaving his mess for someone else to worry about.

'Coffee and toast?' Ed asked. 'I am baking some eggs, but they will take another—' he looked at his watch, 'four-and-a-half minutes.'

Liv accepted a coffee and sank into her chair.

'Anyone checking in today?' Marianne asked.

'Not unless there's a walk-in.'

'Fred was a walk-in.'

Liv heard the wistful note in her sister's voice.

'Do you think if we didn't have a room, he would have just gone and done it somewhere else?'

It was just like Marianne to squeeze the last drop of gloom out of it. With her sister in this mood, you walked away or you leaned into it. No in-between. 'Is there something about Coolaroone that says "suicide"? Ed, you're a stranger, what do you think?'

Ed thought for a moment. 'Perhaps he knew that it was what he wanted to do and was simply waiting for the right opportunity. If you want to be alone, why not choose a beautiful place?'

'What if they can't find his family?'

Liv wondered if her sister was being deliberately obtuse. Why else would he have given a false name, if not to hide?

'Eggs, lovely. Any coffee to go with them?' Seamus appeared in the kitchen. 'I didn't get much sleep.' He glanced at Liv.

Liv blushed up to her two ears. He might as well take out an ad.

But Ed took him at his word. 'I slept surprisingly well,' he said. 'Although I noticed that my dreams were a little more vivid than usual.'

'That might have been the cheese last night,' Liv said, casting around for anything to divert from Seamus' more pointed comments. 'Or the strange day we had.'

'Are you heading back today?' Marianne asked Seamus.

'I'll hang on a while yet. Wes said he would ring this morning if there was any update on the case.'

'Won't your wife be expecting you back?'

'Ruth knows it's my time with Shay,' Seamus said easily, stirring sugar into his coffee.

Liv flinched at his wife's name and hated herself for feeling the sting of it. Although that seemed to go both ways.

'Where did you learn that little trick?' he had asked last night as they lay together, her head in the crook of his arm. Classic pose of lovers and liars.

His complacency stung, but she was careful to match the lightness of her tone to his. 'Are you put out?' she teased. 'Did you think we had turned all Victorian since you left? Sex only through holes in sheets and that kind of thing?' Perhaps he imagined her pining after him while he went about his life. Just because she didn't parade men around in front of Shay didn't mean she was living like a nun.

'Excuse me,' she muttered now, rising from the breakfast table. 'I need to get ready for check-out.'

Marianne followed her out into reception. 'What's with you and Seamus this morning? Did you have a fight?'

Liv cut that conversation off at the pass. 'I thought he'd

156

be on the road by now. Actually, can you do me a favour? Can you phone Ellen and see if they are any closer to finding out Fred Stille's real name? That would be really helpful. I'd like to be prepared in case we get a call from a family member or something.'

'If Seamus' friend is going to phone, then there's hardly any point in me pestering Ellen. If we haven't heard anything by lunchtime, I'll call her then. Okay?'

'Whatever you think.'

Left alone, Liv leaned against the desk and waited for the day to come and sweep her away. When it became clear that if she wanted any such transportation, she would have to do it herself, she switched on the computer and dived into the accounts, soothed by their black-and-whiteness. If the columns balanced, you moved on. If they didn't, you started over. What could be clearer?

When she returned to the kitchen, Ed was about to go for a walk and asked if she wanted to accompany him. She agreed, if only to avoid Seamus for a while longer.

Ed was pleasant company, Liv decided. They had already walked the length of the lake path and he had said no more than a handful of words. There was an openness to his silence, a lack of watchfulness that felt nearly as warm as chat. Her headache began to lift. When they reached the fork that would take them back towards home or further out of the village, she glanced at him and he nodded. 'Lead on.'

'You must think us strange,' she said. 'Fred. Ethel. Seamus. Everything. I'm sure you think it's no wonder Mar left and never wanted to come back.' Even as she said it, she felt foolish. Wasn't the answer in the question: Ethel was the way she was and Marianne never came home. There was no great mystery in it.

'It is not that she does not want to come back,' he said. 'It is that she is afraid if she comes back, she will never leave.'

On someone else, that would have sounded like a judgement of her own life, Liv thought. Yet, for Ed, it was simply a fact about Marianne. How did he manage that separation of truth from feelings? There was a knack to it. If he could bottle and sell it, he would make a fortune.

'When we go to dinner with new people – work colleagues or new neighbours, that sort of thing – at some point in the evening, Marianne always talks about Coolaroone and what it was like to grow up here. She has a story she tells about a time it snowed and all the children took—'

'Fertiliser bags and spent the day sliding down the hill and under the electric fence at the bottom,' Liv finished, laughing. 'I haven't thought about that in years.'

'It sounds idyllic the way she tells it,' Ed said.

'When Dad gave guests directions to *Gaofar*, he used to start off with "Keep your back to the water",' she said, smiling at the memory. 'Me and Marianne used to laugh until we nearly had to hold onto one another or fall down. "They're hardly going to go face-first into it," Marianne would tell him. He made a point then of raising his voice when he said it. He got such a kick out of hearing us laugh together.'

They walked on, the sun warm on their backs one minute and cowering behind a cloud the next, like a kitten skittering around a ball of lint.

'It was beautiful here, growing up,' she told him. 'It was wilder then. The village was smaller, that was part of it. But once the statue moved, the tourists started coming and...' she finished with a shrug.

'Is the statue nearby?'

'Don't tell me you've never seen the statue!' Liv pretended outrage. 'I'll have to have a word with Mar about her hospitality.'

He already knew the story, but, as they walked, she told him again. The young girls who first noticed the Virgin Mary swaying and weeping, then the fever spreading to the grotto regulars, then devotees in their droves coming to witness the same thing. 'It was quite the media event,' she said. 'They had to widen the road to accommodate the tour buses. It was the fastest bit of road maintenance ever seen in the public sector.'

'Do you believe that it really moved?'

Something about the directness of his question called for a direct reply. Liv took a moment to sort through her feelings about it all, dusty though they were. 'If you're asking did I ever see it move, then no. I was afraid of it, to be honest, so I couldn't imagine anybody making it up for fun. At the time, I really believed it moved. Or, rather, I had no reason to believe it didn't. I wouldn't have understood that distinction back then.'

He smiled. 'Does it still move?'

'If it does, nobody mentions it.'

He raised an eyebrow. 'If a statue moves and nobody sees it, has it really moved?'

Liv laughed. 'Exactly.'

At the grotto, she knelt for a moment out of habit. Ed pottered around the railing, putting his nose to various flowers and inhaling vigorously. Liv smothered a smile. For some reason, she had him pegged as the allergies type.

She wasn't praying exactly – it had been a long time since that particular habit had held sway with her – but still there was something about the place that prompted thoughtfulness. Taking a moment. The hippies would have a word for it. Or the Germans. Some useful verb that encompassed both the action and the accompanying feeling. If not counting her blessings, exactly, then letting the gratitude seep into her awareness. Acknowledging, for a moment, her extraordinary luck in wanting what she had.

They walked back the long way, which took them past the old school, long fallen into disrepair. 'We went to school here,' Liv said.

'Marianne told me. Two classrooms, two teachers, every-one learning everything together.'

It was nice – if surprising – to hear that Marianne remembered it as fondly as she did herself. 'People imagine that it was backward, but it was really the opposite.'

'My father had a similar experience as a boy growing up. One small village school. He remembers it as very collaborative.' He smiled. 'Quite modern, if you think about it. Necessity rather than theory, of course, but essentially the same result.'

He had a point, Liv thought. Certainly, they had lacked no grounding when they entered secondary school in the town. Before starting, she would have said her greatest fear was being asked a question in front of everyone, but by the end of the first week she was confident there was little that would give her trouble. If anything, the Coolaroone bunch were that bit more independent than the town kids. She had carried it with her, that sense of her own ability, right through secondary school.

'I wanted to be a doctor, you know,' she told him suddenly, surprising herself. 'Seamus and I both did. That was the plan. Before Shay came along.'

Funny how she could think of it now, those dreams she held so dear for so long, and not feel the helpless rage that had been her companion in the early years of Shay's childhood, before she copped on and remembered to be grateful for what she had. It was a long time since she had blown out her birthday candles, pictured Seamus and thought: *May you have a long career in your lab and die on a weekend only to be found by the cleaners on a Monday morning.*

Further on, she pointed to the hill where the outline of a Celtic cross could just about be seen if a person knew what they were looking for. 'They say that during penal times, the hill was blessed in the dead of night by a priest that was being hidden locally. People were buried there then, so that they could get to heaven.' She stopped, suddenly self-conscious about the religious seep in their walk. Ed hadn't knelt with her at the grotto; she was probably boring him rigid. 'Or so the story goes anyway. It's no wonder we are the way we are. A village of relics and…'

'And?' Ed questioned.

Liv smiled. 'I was trying to think of something else beginning with "r" but nothing fit. I thought "rascals", but it sounded a bit light-hearted for us, as if there was no badness around the place.' Jesus, listen to her go on. He would never want to come back. Would her sister be cross or grateful if she scared him off? she wondered.

'Roués,' he suggested.

Liv shook her head. 'Too fancy, I'm afraid. The lads around here wouldn't know a roué from a rack of lamb.' She was grateful for his laughter.

As they crested the hill, nearing home, the house came into view. Liv thought, as she did every time, that the pale buttercream of its walls was worth the curse of having to repaint every two years. The extension curled low to the left, part-hidden behind the cherry blossoms, their delicate petals giving her a burst of ridiculous, giddy joy, heightened by a sudden gust of wind that pushed her forward as if hurrying her home.

'Ethel used to tell the guests that *Gaofar* meant breezy,' Liv told Ed. 'It wasn't lying, she said, it was just poetic licence.'

This morning, Ethel was waking up in Willowbrook, parched and half-wild, her daughters' names dirt on her lips. No poetic licence could change that fact.

Liv had a sudden urge to be a child again, on winter nights, with Marianne's comfortable warmth beside her.

EASTER MONDAY

ETHEL

She was restless. Rest. Less. Pacing back and forth. She had a hole worn in the carpet, they joked. Probably a joke. Probably. She couldn't see any hole. Could she?

They left her just inside the door. Was it today or yesterday? Dropped like a bag of dirty washing. The whiff of stale embarrassment. Worse if they hung around. But still. In and out. Other things to do.

Over and back. Window and door. Door and window. Twelve steps. Ironic or instructive? The answer might make all the difference. Survival, that was the thing.

A list, they said. Of what? she said. Of anything, they said. Open the notebook. *A list of things I could list.* Wrist aching already.
    Reasons to be here. Reasons. Always reasons. Shay. His name pinned to the paper like a butterfly to a board. Scratch it out. Set him free.

Reasons not to be here. The world falling down around our ears. When she could be out doing.

But: the body in the water.

But: Shay.

Raise a glass to action.

Maybe Fred Stille was blind drunk when he did it. Gin, delicious in his breakfast orange, then a nice walk into the water.

They said he was wearing his clothes but: in her mind's eye he is naked as a jay bird.

Daytime. Why was she in her pyjamas?

The only meaningful sleep is in pyjamas. The rest is just naps. Like the walking dead. The winter ones were too warm and she itched like the devil himself was running his fingers over her skin.

She signed whatever it was they gave her. If she died, she wouldn't haunt them. That, maybe.

Her pyjamas had no pocket to put the biro in. No. How was she to do the crossword with no biro? It upset her and then it didn't. The itch was back and her pyjamas, her pockets, her mind, were no longer important.

EASTER MONDAY

MARIANNE

'How was your walk?' Marianne asked Ed.

He crossed the kitchen to kiss her. 'You should have come. Everything is very beautiful here. Wild and peaceful.'

He wasn't actually mansplaining her homeplace to her, Marianne reminded herself. He genuinely liked it. 'Wild and peaceful. Isn't that an oxymoron?'

'Is that the one that explains itself?' Ed asked.

'That's a tautology. An oxymoron is something that seems to contradict itself.' Marianne thought for a moment. 'Like family holiday.'

'I think a family Christmas here would be okay actually.' He drew her into a hug. 'You, me, your family.' He ran his hands down her sides. 'Our family.'

'Definitely maybe,' Marianne said lightly, moving backwards just enough that he had to drop his hands or stretch further than was advisable. Ed was nothing if not a stickler for osteo health. 'What time are you planning to get on the road?' she asked.

He frowned. 'Are you not coming home with me?'

She shook her head. 'I thought I would stay another few days. Liv shouldn't be on her own with all of this.'

'I think she will be glad to hear you are staying,' Ed said.

'Did she say something?'

'I had the impression that she is… lonely. Worried. It will be good for her if you stay. Good for you both.'

'Aren't you quite the expert on my family all of a sudden?'

Ed smiled. 'It is the easiest thing in the world to comment on other people's families. You do the same when it is the other foot and we visit my parents.'

He was so determined to find the positive. Pollyanna, but in khakis. It couldn't but be endearing. 'Do you want me to make you something to eat before you leave?'

'Later is fine. First, I promised to help Liv with some research into our mysterious guest.'

The 'our' landed, wobbled a moment, settled.

'Ed says you're staying,' Liv said when Marianne found her.

'For a few days. If that's okay?' Marianne wasn't sure why she was asking; it was her home too.

'Whatever you like.'

Could she not, this once, admit that she was glad of the help, the company? 'I thought you could do with a hand,' she prompted.

Liv glanced up from the computer. 'Does Ed not want you to go back with him?'

'I think it's better if I stay. I have some holiday time to use up anyway.'

Liv looked at her for a moment. 'Don't fuck it up,' she said lightly. 'Ed's a good guy.'

Which made her the bad guy, Marianne thought. 'So you're on his side?'

'There can be two good guys, you know,' Liv said mildly.

'Like who?'

Liv thought for a long moment. 'Bert and Ernie?'

'The fucking lobsters? Jesus.'

'You're lucky to have him,' Liv said.

She sounded wistful, Marianne thought. When was the last time she had heard Liv talking about anyone? 'What about you? Is there…' Marianne stopped, unsure what exactly she was asking. 'Are you… lucky?'

'I don't deserve luck,' Liv said, and before Marianne could jump in with a demurral, she added, 'I slept with Seamus.'

'Oh.' That explained a whole lot about the atmosphere this morning and her sister's odd mood. Stranger still was Liv choosing to confide in her. Some other response was clearly called for, but she could hardly ask her sister what the hell she thought she was doing. 'Are you okay?'

'No. Definitely not okay. I know he's married and I did it anyway. In cold blood. Fairly monstrous really.'

'You were upset about Fred, and Seamus was here. He caught you in a vulnerable moment. If anyone is the monster, it's him.'

Liv shook her head. 'Upset, yes. Vulnerable, no. I knew exactly what I was doing.'

Typical Liv. She could have her head in the guillotine and she would be instructing them on sharpening the blade and how to clean up afterwards. 'What are you going to do?'

'Nothing! Absolutely nothing. It was a one-time thing.' She paused. 'A two-time thing. Two-and-a-half, maybe.'

Marianne giggled. 'A half? What are you, seventeen?'

'That's exactly it! He knocks every adult thought out of my head. Like some kind of poor decision time-warp hellhole.'

Marianne watched her sister rub her eyes. Maybe she was trying to erase the image of Seamus in the altogether. His might have been the body they all giggled over twenty years ago, but time stood still for no man. Fun though it would be to play into Liv's guilt and feel – for once – like the functional one, the truth was that this was only a big deal if her sister turned it into one. Like almost everything, it wasn't actually the end of the world.

'You need to just let it go. You're a free agent—' Marianne was about to press the point further when the door opened.

'What's that about a free agent?' Seamus enquired. 'Are the guards sending someone else to investigate?'

'I thought you were going to go and visit your mother,' Liv said.

'I left a message for Wes – I was going to hang on a while, see if he calls back.'

'You don't need to do that. Ellen has it in hand.'

Marianne resisted the temptation to snigger at the idea of Ellen Ghoul having anything more complex than a Snickers bar in hand. She was a guard in a small rural town. Her wheelhouse was speeding tickets, drink-driving and small-scale vandalism from children who wore tracksuits no matter the event or the weather.

'You should call to see your mother,' Liv was saying. 'She would appreciate it, especially since yesterday was such a flying visit. You can phone Shay if Wes has any update.'

'You're the boss.' Seamus sketched a mock salute. 'I'll take Shay with me over to Mother.'

'She sees him plenty. I'm sure she'd rather have the time with you.'

Marianne watched them, fascinated. Ed would have cut through the passive-aggressive tone with a single statement. *I think you should leave now*, he would say. *I would like if you left now*. And that would be that.

After Seamus left, Marianne could hear him calling up the stairs to Shay, then Shay's feet thumping down the stairs. Her sister's mouth grew so small it all but disappeared.

Shay stuck his head in the door. 'I'm going to see Grandma Pauline,' he said. 'Back in a bit.'

'What about—' Liv began, but he was gone.

'Fucking Seamus,' Liv swore softly.

'Indeed,' Marianne said in her best *Carry On* tone, but Liv didn't reply, leaving her feeling foolish.

Liv closed her computer with a snap and tucked it under her arm. 'I need a coffee.'

In the kitchen, Ed was tapping on his laptop.

'Any luck?' Liv asked.

Marianne watched her sister shake the kettle to see if there was enough water in it, as if there wasn't a perfectly functional gauge on the outside for exactly that purpose. She must have seen her do the same thing a thousand times. The thought was smothering and she had a sudden memory of arriving at college on her own and feeling like someone had opened a window. Like she was filling her lungs with air that hadn't already been cycled through someone else's body.

'There is nothing on the main English news site for Denmark,' Ed was saying. 'I have been looking to see if there is anything posted on their noticeboard,' he explained to Marianne. '*Please come home, Papa.* That sort of thing. But it seems nobody is looking for him.'

'Maybe he had no family,' Liv said. 'Or they think he is still enjoying his holiday somewhere.'

That idea was somehow less bearable. 'Poor Fred.'

Neither answered her. She had a momentary horrible thought that she and Liv were somehow sharing Ed. She thought of Seamus. Evidently, Liv liked sharing other people's people. The thought was a hard nugget of spite in her throat.

'There's nothing on the Danish missing persons website either,' Liv said. 'I've gone back about a year so far.'

'I'm going through the photos on the website to see if any of them are him. Some just have a text description, so I'm doing my best with Google Translate. Of course, he might not ever have lived in Denmark.'

'Even if he didn't live there, his family would post it on this Danish site, surely?' Marianne said. 'In case he came back. Got confused or whatever?'

Even as she said it, she knew how unlikely it was. Fred Stille was precise in his speech. Ordered and careful. Whoever else he might have been, whatever he may have been trying to hide, confusion had played no part in it.

'We don't even know for sure that he is Danish. It might be as simple as him liking a particular book or TV show and choosing a name based on that.' Liv spooned coffee into the pot. 'We have only Ethel's notion to go on.'

'The guards seem to be taking it seriously,' Marianne pointed out. She felt oddly cheated at the idea that he might not be Danish after all. Despite having never been, she had a feeling of order, of naturalness, when she thought of Denmark, of his being from there. Surely that sense of logic would imply a certainty to what he had done, if not a beauty exactly. Had he been Irish, there would have been something more shambolic in it, the prospect that, drunk, he had simply stumbled into the water, into the idea of ending it all. She understood, suddenly, what Ed meant when he said it would be less sad if it was something Fred had chosen.

'The guards don't know Ethel like we do,' Liv said.

Marianne had had enough of being written off and talked over. 'I'm going for a walk. If you're gone when I get back, I'll give you a ring later.' She had to press past her sister to land a kiss on Ed's cheek.

It was quiet by the water. People generally had better things to do on a Bank Holiday Monday than trace the paths they took every other day. How conditioned they all were to take it for granted. Marianne stopped to sit for a while, pulling the pack of cigarettes from her pocket and looking both ways before lighting up. Smoking outdoors felt healthy, somehow, as if, along with the chemicals, she was dragging nature itself into her lungs. Another oxymoron for Ed.

Every so often a fish would appear – although so small and so fleet, it was more the suggestion of a fish – and she watched as the water rippled and then stilled in its wake. In a hundred years, fish would still jump for their own fish reasons, even if people no longer sat and watched. The thought didn't so much make her feel sad as disconnected. Was that how Fred Stille felt? That the world and everything in it was happening beside rather than around him? Such self-indulgence, she scolded herself. Her fingers reflexively sought out the wood of the bench, solid beneath her fingers as she knocked once, twice, three times. Whether they liked it or not, in a hundred years they would all be dead and gone. She circled the idea, poking at it a little bit. She would be – where? In the churchyard here, beside her parents. Or somewhere else, as yet unknown? A stone carved with her name. Hers and Ed's, maybe. She closed her eyes and tried to see if there were any names beneath theirs. Would seeing names in that space mean that she could picture having children or losing them? Did one make her a better candidate for parenthood than another? All that came to mind was a tree. A tree nourished by whatever organic magic lay in broken-down teeth and bones.

Which of them would go first, herself or Liv? Liv, of course. She was never one to follow behind. Marianne's mind skittered past the swell of panic at the thought of a world without Liv. Her sister would have a better tree too, no doubt. Marianne smiled at her own irrational crossness. Imagine going back home and telling Liv she was annoyed because her body would make better fertiliser. She would be in Willowbrook alongside Ethel before you could say *the DTs*.

They don't know Ethel like we do, Liv had said, and it was true, they didn't.

They had never seen her kindness. The dozen eggs sent regularly to Mrs Twomey to make sure there was food in the house after the birth of yet another child of dubious welcome. Nor her composure when Mr Twomey, on learning of the gift, came spitting and swinging into their kitchen. We had them to spare, Ethel said, calm as you please. I'm sure you want her strength up, ready for the next one. *You jumped up little cunt*, he said, then. *You wouldn't know a good Catholic family if it bit you in the hole. Didn't your fella only manage to put it in the once, wasn't it?* You can be on your way, Ethel said then, opening the door so that he could shuffle out. When he was gone, Marianne ran to throw her arms around her mother. 'Were you scared?' she asked her. Ethel took a

170

long moment before answering. 'A man like that is little better than an animal,' she said, at last.

It was years before Marianne realised that that had been her mother's way of saying 'yes'. She was horrified to feel the tears rising in her throat.

She hopped off the bench before the tears could take hold. Further along the path, the Dempseys were sitting side by side on matching folding plastic stools, their rods in front of them. 'Morning, Missus,' the father said, while the son squinted off into the sun.

Missus? Did they not know who she was?

'You've your good deed done for the week anyway,' she said. 'Finding our Mr Stille like that. You have my family's thanks.'

'Nothing good about it.' Mr Dempsey cleared his throat and hawked a mighty gob of sputum into the water, where it would, no doubt, choke a shoal of fish. Maybe that was his method, she thought, but the light-heartedness had withered inside her.

'I'll leave you to it,' Marianne said. She sounded foolish to her own ears. It wasn't as if they had initiated a conversation with her. She had merely interrupted them, that was all.

She ducked under the fence to walk up towards the main street. It wasn't her; it was them. Living in a house that silent must change a person. Their words were drying up, little by little, like a rusty spigot. When a social response was called for, all they brought up was brackish and unpalatable. She pushed away the thought that if Liv had been the one to disturb them, there would have been chat a-plenty.

'Marianne!'

She heard her name being called and turned to see a hippyish woman come flying out of a doorway.

'Sorry to shout after you. You'll think I'm awful. I saw you crossing and waved from the window, but you didn't see me.' The woman registered Marianne's uncomprehending look. 'Joely. From the Fish Bar? And the… um… the drowning?'

'I know. Hi.'

Joely beamed. 'How are things at home?'

'We're all okay, thanks. How are you and—' Marianne cast around for the name of the feckless boyfriend who had spotted the body in the lake. 'How are you both?'

'Damien is very shook. He's not himself at all. I'm worried it might cause a setback.' Joely dropped her voice. 'He's had his troubles in the past.'

Was she to pretend to know or not know? Marianne opted for generalities, the Coolaroone staple. 'A fright like that would knock anybody for six,' she said.

'That's what I keep saying, too,' Joely said gratefully. 'But it's like he doesn't hear me, you know? Liv says I should just give him time.'

'Well, if *Liv* said so…' Marianne said. She resisted the urge to add that Liv's life advice had seen her playing musical beds with her married ex and was thus slightly less than gold-plated.

Joely smiled uncertainly. 'I wanted to ask about Ethel. I heard that she was… under the weather.'

'Is that right?'

Joely clutched her arm. 'Oh, God. I didn't mean to… I hope I haven't offended you. We're all very fond of Ethel. She's the life and soul of the place. It's just that I thought she hadn't been herself for a while now, so it's good to hear that she's… going to feel better soon.'

Which version of Ethel was she so fond of? Marianne wondered as she pushed open the café door. More to the point, who exactly were the 'we' that were so invested in her mother's well-being? Queuing, she realised that Shay and Seamus were sitting at a small table in the back. She waved. Seamus was talking, talking, talking, as ever. She could see his head wagging as he talked, and Shay nodded along. They didn't see her and she dithered for a moment before ordering her coffee to go. The teenager at the counter was mercifully uninterested in chat, meaning Marianne's ignorance of her name lay undiscovered.

This fucking family, with its rules and secrets. Wasn't home supposed to be the place where you came to reconnect with your real self? If that was the case, then Marianne was clearly a nobody, with nothing to offer that anyone else might want. Better to be like Ethel, who, once gone, never returned to her homeplace. Everyone there was dead, she said, when the girls questioned her. They died when she was a young woman, before she met Martin. There was nothing there to go back to. This was her home now. Young Marianne felt safer for her mother's words. At the idea that this place could take such deep hold in a person that it created them anew.

Little fooleen that she was.

Her anger lasted the walk home. Ed had waited to say goodbye, but she gave him only the barest attention as he hugged her and told her to take care of herself.

'I'm going to clean Fred Stille's room,' she told Liv, who had come out onto the front steps to wave Ed off. 'I rang the guards and they said it's fine.' Let Ellen fucking *Gould* sort out any mess the lie created.

Upstairs, she stripped the sheets from the bed. The small rowan branch was under the pillow, and she snapped it in two, tearing up the cheery little accompanying information leaflet for good measure. What more bad luck could come?

Finished with the bed, she pulled open doors and drawers, only to find them empty. She dragged a chair over to the window and began to take down the curtains, resisting the urge to rip them out directly. Who even had curtain hooks any more for fuck's sake, when the whole world had moved on to eyelets and tab-tops? No doubt there was some reason for it, a reason that only *real* locals would know.

'Aunt Marianne?'

She turned to see Shay in the doorway.

'I saw you leaving the café and I… can you not tell Mum that you saw me and Dad in town?' His words came out all in a rush.

Marianne shrugged as much as she could with an armload of curtains. 'It's none of my business.'

'It's just that she would have wanted Dad to spend longer with Grandma Pauline,' Shay said. 'But it's hard when she… is… the way she is.'

The words were so clearly Seamus', he might as well have been standing there. Marianne couldn't let it pass. 'What way is she, exactly?'

Shay glanced over his shoulder and shuffled a bit further into the room. 'She complains about Mum. How she doesn't visit enough.'

'Doesn't she go every week?' And Liv wondered why Seamus assumed he still had a free pass into her knickers, Marianne thought sourly.

'I think Grandma Pauline forgets. She keeps telling me how great Dad is and how… well, she's not very nice about Mum.' Shay flushed. 'I know she's lonely – I do – but…'

'It's hard to listen to,' Marianne finished for him, and he nodded. 'Does your dad not say anything? Tell her to stop, or defend Liv?'

'We… it's best to pretend not to hear her.'

I bet it is, Marianne thought. For Seamus, anyway. What was he about, letting his mother bad-mouth Liv when he was barely out of her bed? Just the previous night, imagine. The shitbox.

'Here.' Shay took the curtains from her, crumpled them on the bed and began to remove the curtain hooks. 'Did you already take away all his things?'

'No. I started with the curtains.'

Shay frowned. 'He doesn't have any stuff?'

Marianne considered it. 'He checked in with very little. As I understand it, the Scandinavians think differently about stuff than we do. Maybe that's it. Once they start to get old, they clear out everything they don't need any more. Death-cleaning, they call it.'

'That's a bit depressing.'

'If I remember correctly, it's more about treating your possessions with respect. Giving them away the way you would want.' She remembered the elderly woman who lived a few doors down from her and Ed. The thin crowd that appeared one day, bowed and black, followed the next day by a skip and an impatient relative. 'It's kind of sweet, I think. Although it does imply a failure to trust your family to do what you want when you're gone.'

'You'd never know anyway,' Shay said.

'*Why, if the dead are immortal, do insurance companies pay out?*' Marianne quoted.

'*Moby Dick*,' Shay said, with surprising certainty.

'Look at you!' Marianne said, and he ducked his head with pleasure. 'Are you sure you shouldn't be thinking about doing English in college instead of science?' Too late, she remembered they weren't supposed to bring up last year and the Great Failure To Get Enough Points For University.

'If I go.'

Something in his tone made her glance over at him. 'Do you not want to go?' For a second, she thought he was simply going to shrug in response.

'I'm not sure I see the point any more. I might be better doing something more practical.'

His effort to sound casual betrayed him.

'Like a trade, you mean?'

He nodded. 'Or just, you know, work. Something.'

Hardly a plan, Marianne thought, but said nothing. He must be so sick of people trying to pin him down. She pushed aside thoughts of what Liv would want her to do here. 'If you want me to see if I know anyone that's looking, just let me know.'

He nodded. 'I can always go to college later on. Just because I don't go now doesn't mean I can't ever change my mind. Look at Gran. She never went to college, but she can speak fourteen languages.'

Being able to say hi-how-are-you-nice-weather hardly counted as speaking a language, Marianne thought. 'It's true that plenty of people go back as mature students.'

'Do you think you would have done something different if you had waited?'

'I didn't want to wait, though,' Marianne said, gently. 'What I wanted, more than anything else, was to leave.'

'You didn't want both? To stay and to go?'

Her heart broke at how hopeful he sounded. 'Not back then.'

'Aunt Mar?' he turned in the doorway. 'Thanks for… you know.'

If she had a child, it would share genes with that lovely boy. She gathered towels from the bathroom and threw them in a pile by the door, all the while wondering when her mother's affinity for languages had stopped being impressive.

TUESDAY

LIV

'Ethel is doing all right,' Liv said, ending the call. 'The first couple of days are always a bit intense, but she's still there anyway.'

Marianne's head snapped up. 'Did you talk to her?'

Not everything had to be a competition. Liv kept her tone even. 'We're not allowed to talk to Ethel for the first seven days.'

'I'm sure there's a way around that. It probably just takes a word with the manager. Judith, wasn't it?' Marianne was saying now. 'I might give her a call later.'

A *wrong-side morning*, their dad used to call it, when Marianne was in a huff this early in the day. But he wasn't here to make excuses and they weren't children any more. 'Actually, it's part of the detox. It takes that long for the confusion-hallucination-agitation stages to pass.' She turned on her heel and went out to the reception area. Let Marianne flex her moods somewhere else; she was damned if she was going to sit around and absorb it.

Liv often found paperwork a series of dull jobs. If an alien landed on the street outside and trotted in to chat, she would find it hard to explain the point. There should be a collective noun for it. A boredom, maybe. *A boredom of admin tasks.* Today, she would have settled for boring. Instead, there was a litany of phone calls and emails, apologetic or brisk, all with the same message: booking cancelled. The morning passed and on they piled, a third, fifth, eighth. Even her regulars, the backbone of the business. The couples who had come to see the statue back in the day and who returned for a week every year to pay their respects or to relive a time when potential still fizzed within them. Some had even travelled for Martin's funeral. Over the years, of course, their trips became less about the statue and more about the pace of the place. Tiny Dillon gave guided walks around the lake on Saturday mornings, pointing out the dainty wagtails and starlings and holding out the hope of a white-tailed sea eagle. The Dempseys did two fishing trips a week: 'pike, perch and peace', it was called locally, which got the point across nicely. People came back from those days out raving about finding themselves. Mindfulness in human form, that was the Dempseys. Liv once heard Sheila Dillon describe them as 'the next best thing to a vow of silence'.

Gaofar's frequent flyers were mostly kind enough to lie. One American couple, whose cheerful conflation of truth with tactlessness had always amused her in person, told her bluntly, 'Honey, we're too old to be getting mixed up in any funny business. Better safe than sorry.' Another favourite regular – a live-forever pensioner from the North who had told Liv that her holidays in Coolaroone were like drinking the elixir of her own youth – said, 'I'd never hear the end of it from my own children. Maybe later in the year, Liv, pet.'

Where were they getting their information? Liv wondered, cutting and pasting their names into her standard cheery reply. What exactly did they think was going on here? She flipped through booking screens. They were now at half-capacity or less right through until June. Not shut-down bad, but it certainly meant that her plans to overhaul some of the rooms would have to wait. Maybe it was time to think seriously about a cancellation policy. Her father would turn in his grave, she thought, as she opened a search engine and typed *Coolaroone – death.*

They were the third item on the search results. *Investigation into unexplained death at popular B&B* screamed the headline. 'It wasn't at the B&B,' she muttered, clicking into the article. It got worse as she read on; the characterisation of Mr Stille as an 'unknown guest despite the existence of regulations requiring all guests to show proof of ID on arrival' made them sound like the worst kind of chancers. Ellen had been philosophical about Marianne's oversight in forgetting to ask for his ID. 'He likely would have given some story to avoid it anyway,' she said. 'He sounds like a planner.'

Further clicks found several more articles, but they were largely repetitive and she suspected that the first had simply been picked up by the others. She scanned back to the top of the article for the writer's name and began to compose an email. She wasn't foolish enough to get angry in an email. Instead, she explained that she was the B&B owner and included her phone number in the hopes that the prospect of an insider's account of events would excite a callback. It took less than twenty minutes for the phone to ring. The voice on the other end was Midlands-flat and unapologetic.

'Is there something in it that's inaccurate?' he asked.

'His death wasn't "unexplained" for a start. He drowned in the lake. Nowhere near my business.' Liv tried not to think about the forgotten ID. 'Not to mention the insinuation that we are not a legitimate business—'

'It's not libel,' he pointed out quickly. 'The man was staying at your establishment, that's not in dispute.'

Even the way he said it – *establishment* – was somehow seedy. 'Libel is one thing, morality is quite another. Do you know how many cancellations I've had since you wrote your scurrilous piece of so-called journalism? Care to hazard a guess?'

'I'm sure they'll all rebook later—'

'Eleven this morning alone. You're going to close my business for the sake of a clickbait headline.'

'That's business, sweetheart. No need to get hysterical about it.'

Liv would have sacrificed her right arm to reach down the phone and slap the little prick. 'Have you ever owned a business? Been responsible for the lives of those around you? If you had, maybe you wouldn't be so casual about destroying people's livelihoods. You might have stopped short of accusing us of killing the man, but you certainly did your best to make it sound as though something nefarious was going on here.'

He gave a great bark of laughter. 'Nefarious. There's an underused word.'

She hung up. Smug bastard. She picked up the pen holder on the desk and hurled it at the floor.

'Good morning, Liv.'

She started. 'Jesus Christ!'

'Jesus Christ to you too,' Father Mike said with a broad smile. 'It doesn't sound as good in English as "*Dia dhuit*" but sure we'll take it.'

He rocked back on his heels as if he had all the time in the world. Maybe he did. Priests might still have a hold on birth and death, but people had the internet for pretty much everything in between. 'What can I do for you, Father?'

'Might we have a word in private?'

'There are few enough guests left, Father. We're nothing but private these days.'

'They'll be back again, I have no doubt. A place as fine as this won't be overlooked for long,' he said.

The unexpected kindness made her remember her manners. 'Come on through and have a cup of something.'

'I won't say no to a coffee,' he said. 'I was with an elderly parishioner all morning and it would be no word of a lie to say that I don't think the poor woman ever heard of coffee.'

When the coffee was half-drunk and the plate of biscuits nearly gone, Marianne appeared.

Liv made the introductions, hoping that Marianne would, at a minimum, be polite.

'I remember you from the hotel,' Father Mike said as he shook her hand.

'Is there coffee in the pot?' Marianne asked. She poured a cup and reached for the milk jug, set out neatly beside the rarely used sugar bowl. 'What is it with you priests and your ability to put away sugar, does it get soaked up by all the prayer or what?'

'Actually, they train us for it in the seminary,' Father Mike said with a wink. 'It's everyone's favourite module. They run it just before Lent.'

Marianne laughed and sat down. 'I took a call there, Liv,' she said, sounding almost natural. 'Someone cancelling for the June weekend. I said it was grand, but you'd call back if there was a problem.'

'Not another one!' Liv thought better of swearing. 'People have been phoning all morning to cancel their bookings. We made the online news sites, it seems. Not everyone likes the idea of holidaying in the B&B where the dead man was staying.'

'People are so ready to make it all about them. The poor man lost his life and there they are, fretting about their bloody holidays.' Marianne tapped her spoon sharply against the side of her mug.

'Has there been any further development in identifying the gentleman?' Father Mike asked. 'I didn't like to phone the station again today. They have enough to do without me annoying them.'

'They are still trying to figure out who he was so they can trace his family,' Liv said.

'That's what I wanted to talk to you about,' Father Mike said. 'There are no funeral plans—'

'Ellen said they can't bury him before the post-mortem,' Liv said.

'They can't bury him.' Marianne enunciated every word as if they were slow.

'Quite. In the meantime, I thought we might go ahead and offer a rosary for the repose of his soul.'

'We don't know that he was Catholic,' Marianne said. 'Most Danes are Lutheran.'

'I'm sure our Lutheran brethren would agree that a few prayers are better than nothing,' Father Mike observed. 'I thought we could have it this evening in the grotto. The weather is to be fair all day – although it will turn tomorrow – and he liked the outdoors, by all accounts. Plenty of people have told me that they saw him out walking.'

The whole village turned out at the grotto. Close your eyes and it could be 1985, Liv thought. Except without Dad. Pull yourself together, she told herself sternly. It's not the time or place.

'Anyone driving through will think the statue is having another go-around,' Gen echoed as she passed.

Liv waited for a snide remark from her sister, but Marianne only turned to Shay to ask, 'How does everyone know it's on? He hardly went to every house to tell them?'

'Facebook,' Shay said. 'There's a "Love your Parish" page where everything is posted.'

'Really? I didn't know that,' Marianne said.

'It's a closed group,' Shay explained, 'so it's really only locals that see it. Father Mike is on Twitter though and that's open to everyone.'

'His handle is @FrMikelovesyou,' Liv chimed in, trying to catch her sister's eye. It worked. Marianne smiled and Liv reached out to squeeze her hand.

'You must be delighted with the turnout,' Peter said from behind her shoulder.

'It's hardly our turnout, Peter.'

'It is until we find his family,' Marianne said, letting go of Liv's hand. 'We're his people until they find his own.'

Were there tears in her sister's voice? Marianne was gazing off to one side and she couldn't see her face.

'How's business? Ye must have people running out of the place after reading that article on the internet. Leaving their bags behind them in the rush to get out, I'd say.'

For a split second, Liv wondered if Peter was the unnamed source in that cruel news article. No, she decided. Peter's reach was local, he had no interest in the world outside Coolaroone. 'You needn't worry about us, Peter,' she said gaily. 'Our regulars are our stock-in-trade.'

'They'd want to be some hardy boys not to be put off by a dead body, all the same. No sign of identifying him yet, I hear. You'd think ye'd have the right name on the fella at least. There wouldn't have been any carry-on like that when your father was alive—'

Before he could get any further, however, Paddy Hanley joined them. 'Excuse me for interrupting, but the priest is looking for you, Peter,' he said. 'How are you, Liv? Shay, Marianne.'

'Looking for me, is it?' Surprised, Peter hurried away.

'What on earth would anybody want with him?' Marianne muttered.

'It's hard to imagine,' Paddy agreed. 'But I'll let Father Mike tell him that himself. It's what we pay him for, after all.' He turned to Liv. 'How are you all doing? It must have been a fair shock.'

Just then, Father Mike cleared his throat and tapped on the microphone to begin.

Paddy leaned in and said quietly, 'Listen, I know you had a bit of support over the weekend, but if there's anything you need, you know where I am.'

'Thanks,' Liv mouthed as he walked away and the rosary began.

The words to the prayers flowed automatically and, with them, the memories. Liv closed her eyes and let them take her back.

It was all anyone at school could talk about. Three of the girls were down at the grotto on Sunday evening and saw the statue moving. 'Not so much moving,' Bernadine Burke said, her tone low and mysterious, 'but sort of *swaying*. Like she was humming along to music only she could hear.' It didn't surprise Liv that Bernadine Burke would know what was going on in the Virgin Mary's head – she knew everything else that was going on, after all. That time that Mrs Lynch was caught kissing someone who wasn't Mr Lynch, Bernadine had the whole story within the hour. The three girls who had the vision were not in school that day, of course ('traumatised,' Bernadine said, sagely), but by the time they came back on the Wednesday, the story had only grown in size and scale. Two more people – adults and therefore unassailable – swore they had seen the Virgin moving on the Monday afternoon. In broad daylight, no less. Such was the faith in their story that the school principal, Sister Eucharia, held a special assembly, calling the girls up in front of the whole school to lead them in a rosary for special intentions. Liv was mortified for them. Imagine having to stand up there with everyone gawping at you while you hoped you didn't count the wrong number of Hail Marys! She would rather poke out her own eyes. Liv peeked through her fingers at the three of them standing there, as ordinary as anything. Mags picked her nose in the yard, Cathy would pinch you as soon as look at you and Louise was rumoured to wear the same knickers for two days at a time. The vision suddenly began to seem less miraculous and more like something that could impose itself, terrifyingly, on the least of them. The surest way not to see the statue move, Liv decided, was not to see the statue at all.

Luckily, Ethel was of the same mind. 'Hysterical nonsense,' was all she said whenever the topic came up. Liv was grateful for her mother's oddness. It was almost worth the teasing she usually got for what the others called – in not so pale imitations of their parents' voices – her mother's *notions*. Like the fact that she didn't have family on that side. Her mother could be anyone, Bernadine Burke informed her. How would they know, with no people of her own to examine? She could be – this last whispered – a *tinker*.

It helped that Marianne was mad to go. Ethel and Marianne never thought the same about anything. 'You ask her,' Marianne pleaded and Liv pretended she had. Mar would only cry again if she refused outright.

But Ethel gave in one evening. About two weeks after it had all started, when the tour buses were stopping nightly at their gate so that people could ask if they had any rooms free. Marianne was jubilant. 'Told you Dad would talk her into it,' she hissed as they ran upstairs to brush their hair and put on their Sunday clothes. Liv didn't think he had. As far as she could see, nobody ever talked her mother into anything she didn't want to do. Least of all her gentle father.

Down at the grotto, it was like being at a carnival. Liv held tight to her father's hand as they pushed their way to a spot by the wall. While they waited, she swung from his hand, making sure to keep her back to the statue. Beside her, she heard an older boy tell his younger brother that he wouldn't see anything because he hadn't made his First Holy Communion yet. 'Jesus doesn't know you exist until then,' he said with certainty. Was it true? Liv wondered. She and Marianne had made their First Communion two short months earlier. The white dresses and little handbags containing their prayer books and rosary beads. The wafer melting on her tongue. She closed her eyes and wished with all her might that Jesus hadn't told Holy Mary where she lived.

When the prayers started, her mother poked her to turn around and she did, keeping her eyes so tightly shut that she saw black behind her eyelids. Every Hail Mary was, she told herself, one closer to going home without seeing anything. Afterwards, she began to walk to the car, with her eyes still closed and her arms held straight out in front of her. 'Liv, would you ever stop looking for attention,' Ethel snapped, and Liv's eyes watered at the unfairness of it. Attention was the last thing she wanted. Her parents wanted to stay, they said. 'Why?' she cried. It wasn't as if they would talk to anyone but each other and they could do that at home. She begged and pleaded and said she had a pain in her stomach. Eventually, their neighbour, Tadhg Hayes, overheard and offered to drive her home. Liv held her breath until they agreed. Oh, the relief! Even though Tadhg Hayes' car smelled of cat pee and Tadhg himself had a habit of putting his hand on your knee when he drove. It was still better than seeing Our Lady sway to invisible music and having to describe it to the whole town.

'I am now following @FrMikelovesyou,' Marianne said, waving her phone. 'Oops.' She righted her wine glass, which had waggled along with the phone.

'Begging to be trolled, isn't it?' Liv agreed.

'If he follows me back, I can slide into his DMs,' Marianne said.

Beside them, Shay groaned. 'Please stop. It's excruciating.'

'Why?' Marianne pounced on him. 'What should we say instead?'

'Nothing. You should say and do nothing.'

'D'you hear your man?' Marianne said to Liv. 'He thinks we're only good for… knitting and… and library books!'

'Don't knock library books,' Liv said. 'Although, on the knitting, I concede you may have a point.'

'So, if we can't slide into DMs.' Marianne held up a hand to Shay. 'Hear me out. If we can't… do that, what else is off limits? Swiping right? Mofo? ROFLing?'

Marianne sounded it out – rowfling – and Liv had to squint to work it out.

'I think I prefer it when you're not getting along,' Shay said. 'It's less embarrassing.'

'We get along just fine,' Marianne insisted. 'Sisters fight. If you had one, you'd know.' She heard her mistake even as it left her mouth. 'Sorry. A sister you live with all the time, I meant.'

Liv shuddered. 'This shop is closed for business.'

'That's it, I'm taking Lucky out,' Shay said.

'Has he any girl?' Marianne asked when the door closed behind him.

'I don't know. A whole bunch of them used to hang around together last year, so it's probably one of them. If he wants me to know, he'll tell me.'

'Very modern, I'm sure.' Marianne swirled the wine in her glass. 'In a place this size, come on. You must know who she is.'

'I assure you I don't.' Liv could feel annoyance, temporarily at bay in light of the rosary or the wine, creeping back into the room. 'What does it matter?'

'Of course it matters. You of all people should know that it matters.'

'What's that supposed to mean?' Liv asked, despite being fairly certain that she knew full well what Marianne meant. She just wanted to see if her sister had the balls to come out and say it.

'You were his age when you had him. Things happen. People's lives can change at this age.'

'People's lives are *supposed* to change at this age. That's exactly what they're supposed to do.'

'That's right, I forgot you subscribed to the theory that who you are at twenty is who you are forty.' Marianne wagged her finger at Liv. 'No more change allowed!'

'I happen to like my life the way it is. I don't have to justify that to you. Or change it to make you feel better.'

'Why would I need to feel better?' Marianne snapped. 'Maybe I like my life too.'

'Sure you do. That's why you ran back here last week. Because you were so happy with how your life was going.'

'I didn't realise there were conditions on my visits.'

Marianne's tone was icy. 'From now on, I'll be sure to only come back when I'm full of the joys.'

That wasn't what she meant. Somehow Marianne always managed to twist her words into the worst possible version of her thoughts.

'Perhaps Shay will feel the same when he leaves,' Marianne continued. 'Although, wait a minute. He doesn't want to leave, does he?'

Liv looked at her sister. 'What do you mean? Of course he wants to leave. He has to, for college.'

'Except he doesn't want to go to college. Told me himself. Knew he'd get a more rounded response, let's say, from someone who's seen a bit of the world and knows what's what.'

Afterwards, Liv would have time to slow the scene down in her mind. To think about all the wrong turns that the conversation took, to replay what she should have said instead. She would have time to focus on the content of her sister's words rather than the tone. In the moment, however, she had only blind rage and the one thing she had promised herself never to say. 'That's funny,' she said, surprised at how steady her voice was. 'How you claim to know the world, but you don't know your own place.' She looked at Marianne's puzzled face and said, with exaggerated care, 'This place is no longer yours, not a single brick of it. Ethel cut you out and left it to me and Shay. Lock, stock and barrel.'

Marianne's face, bloodless and moon-white with shock, hung between them, even after she had stumbled from the room.

WEDNESDAY

ETHEL

Mealtimes at the trough were all slurping and elbows. People who nudged others should be taken outside and shot. The sun was a bastard in her eyes. Not fair to bastards. Shay didn't do too badly for himself.

Without the garden, there was work to be found in the peeling of an orange. Quietening the hands. Creasing the newspaper to the crossword page.

Mornings, it was the tiny things that kept a body together.

An easy one to start. One across: A bug might settle into a rug (6). *Snugly.* Two across: The Battle of Britain arena (3,3). *Mid air.* One down: One may be warranted (6). The word danced in the dust-covered sunlight. The cleaner should be fired. (*One may be warranted.*)

Evenings, it was the tiny things that broke a body. What there was before and what there might be after and how to live through it. Mouthfuls of bread and panic. (*One may be warranted.*) The door to the garden locked at five-thirty. The curtains keeping the tears inside.

The people who had everything came home. So too did the people who had nothing. What about the people that never went home, what did they have, only the search? Home was home was home. That first guest, years earlier, alone and anxious for chat. Following her to the church to do the flowers and staying for Mass after, God love her. Everyone wanting to be seen. Martin always saw her.

If all else perished and he remained. Ghosts can show you the way home, he said. The handsome man carries maps in his head, of all the places he hasn't been. Was that a song, was it? (*One may be warranted.*)

Eeny-meeny-miny-moe. The girls and their games. Pinafores and knee socks, there and gone in the blink of an eye. Like Martin. Holding hands while the stone woman wept and swayed. Didn't half the country see her, and why would they lie? The Holy Mother never moved for them. Eeny-meeny-miny-moe. And into dust we shall return.

The day was nothing but a torment of weather. Red sky at night, they said, and now look at it. They'd be playing hide-and-seek tomorrow with the rain and the sheets on the line.

One may be warranted.

No sleep for Ethel.

No sleep until she had the answer.

WEDNESDAY

MARIANNE

When Marianne woke, she was half-sitting across the pillows, the laptop on the bed beside her. She stretched carefully, mindful of the kink in her neck. When had caution replaced the feeling of luxury that used to accompany a full-body stretch in the morning? The movement of the quilt brought the screen back to life, showing her a series of windows on how to challenge a will.

When she stormed upstairs to her room the previous night, reeling from Liv's revelation, it was so that she could cry privately. Throwing herself across the bed – aware that there was just a little part of her wondering what she looked like – she waited for the tears to come. They took a little bit of coaxing. She thought about her father, what he would say if he were here. How disappointed he would be that they were cutting her out. His girl. His favourite, not that they were ever allowed to say so. 'Shame on them,' she hissed into her hands. That got her going properly, at last.

When she was in danger of flagging, she imagined Liv and Ethel going together to the solicitor, their steps purposeful and in tandem. Laughing together over lunch afterwards. Clinking glasses and toasting their future. It didn't take much for the anger to flicker and flare into life. If an underling at work were to tell her the story, she would crisply tell them to first identify the problem, then shortlist solutions until the best one presented itself. The problem was simple enough: she was being stripped of her birthright. Her options, as she saw them, were to accept, to plead or to fight.

The latter seemed the straightforward answer, Marianne had felt, in the clarifying aftermath of her storm of weeping. Trawling through websites, however, revealed that while they were long on shysters eager to take her money and tell her what she wanted to hear, they were short on actual advice. There was a brief moment of hope sometime around midnight when an online noticeboard seemed peopled with like-minded wronged souls, but a bit more poking yielded issues on a spectrum from optimistic (*there's a patch of unclaimed land next to my garden wall. Nobody seems to own it. Can I include it in my will?*) to outright delusional (*my married boyfriend died and left everything to his wife and children. Can I sue? I only want his car. For sentimental reasons, let's say*).

Marianne closed down her screen. She wasn't up for another deep dive through other people's crazy. A real library was what she needed. Bricks and mortar and life experience. True, in books people were always having houses unexpectedly gifted rather than taken away from them, but perhaps that was genre-specific. A librarian would know. A sympathetic older lady – no, an older gentleman – who would guide her to the right information. Marianne could almost picture her kindly bearded guide, a kind of cross between Gandalf the Grey and Charlie Bucket's Grandpa Joe. She blinked and he vanished. The useless fucker. Her father would have made two of him.

She should phone Ed, or risk him seeing her failure to do so as yet another sign of her ambivalence about his place in her life. But he was just here, chatting and helping and fitting in. How could she explain that the place that was so welcoming to him had rejected her so roundly? That her own home no longer wanted her? How mortifying. And, besides, he would have questions she couldn't answer. Questions that made her foolishness real. Marianne pulled the quilt over her head. She was a fool, that was the truth of it. Coming back here as if she belonged. For all she knew, everyone in the village was apprised of the situation and talked about it among themselves as soon as she had passed by. Mortification, like wind, drove her back out from under the covers.

She dragged the quilt over to the window seat and tucked herself in. She might as well enjoy the view while she could. No doubt Liv would shortly be charging her to stay. She waited a moment to see what the self-pity might yield, but it appeared that she was all cried out. Marianne turned her attention out the window. It was early enough that the birds were only gathering on the wires, arriving in twos and threes as if they were families. Blackbirds were her father's favourites. He would stand by the kitchen window, tea in hand, and listen to them chattering. 'The gossips are at it again,' he would say, beckoning her over to stand with him. She had a sudden surge of anger. This was her father's place too. A place he wanted to share with her. It was only Ethel who never wanted Marianne to be happy. Ethel who was impossible to please. Nothing was ever good enough for her. Herself and Liv used to joke that their father died in his sleep so as not to put anyone to any trouble, but maybe there was some truth in it.

She dressed quickly, grateful at last for having the foresight to pack her power cardigan. Although it was more of a general impression of crispness she had envisioned. Chic even while pushing a shopping trolley kind of thing. Not that Liv had let her do the supermarket run. Well, now she knew why, didn't she? For God's sake, she had done *nothing wrong*. Leaving for university and then to work wasn't some terrible transgression that should see her exiled like some kind of Greek tragedy. She wasn't like the crazy people online. She had a right to be here. And Ethel needed to be reminded of that fact.

'You can't see her,' Judith said. To underline her point, she lifted her hand like a traffic warden.

'Ten minutes. That's all I need. Just to be sure she's okay,' Marianne said. She needed a damn sight more than that, but she hadn't left a trail of rubber all the way here only to be turned away by an officious little tinpot.

'You can't see her. Not for five minutes, not for ten minutes, not for fifteen minutes. I can't be any plainer than that.'

'This isn't a prison, for heaven's sake. She came of her own free will. Surely she should be allowed to see whoever she wants?'

'Indeed. But I think you'll find that it is you who wishes to see her, rather than the other way around. At the moment, seeing family could… disrupt Ethel's progress.'

Marianne exhaled. Inhaled (disinfectant, artificial lavender). Exhaled again. Quietly. Anger made no impression on the Judiths of this world. Starved of any real power, they were the kind that would observe the rules to a T and if they broke as much as one – inadvertently, of course – they would duly fine themselves.

It took an effort to smile. 'I appreciate you taking such a personal interest in my mother's care, Judith. I just want to see her for a minute, to reassure her that we haven't forgotten her. After all, isn't rehab about remembering and revaluing that connection with family?'

'You will be able to see her in a few days' time. Wouldn't you rather she is fit to hear whatever blame you want to lay on her?'

'How do you know it's blame?' Marianne snapped. 'For all you know, I'm here to tell her I'm pregnant after years of trying and you're depriving her of the chance for a few extra days of happiness.'

'Marianne.' Judith put down the file she was holding. 'It's clear that you're angry and you have things to say to Ethel. But if you want her to have a shot at recovery, then you need to accept that we know what we're doing. What she is looking for right now is an excuse to drink and you want to come in and hand it to her? That might not have been your intention, but that is exactly how Ethel will spin it to herself.'

'Shouldn't you be encouraging her to take responsibility for her own decisions? Isn't that the first rule of rehab, admitting you have a problem?'

'Admitting it the first time is the easy part. When you wake in a strange gutter in a pool of your own vomit, with your pants on backwards and your child's birthday present in the dirt beside you,' Judith said softly. 'It's admitting it again the next day and the day after and the day after that, when you're washed and clean and strong and the gutter feels like a bad dream you once had. That's the tough bit.'

Marianne swallowed. 'I wasn't… I didn't…'

'Marianne. I'll tell you what I tell everyone that crosses my threshold: anger solves nothing. Not in life and certainly not in recovery. You will be welcome to visit at the right time. When you're calm enough to realise that this is about her, not you.'

Walking to the car, it occurred to Marianne to wonder what the place cost. Whatever it was, Judith seemed worth it. She made a mental note to ask Liv for a bill for her half. She wouldn't give it to her sister to say that she hadn't paid her share. Especially not now. She earned a salary that was nearly embarrassing when she was talking to Coolaroone folk the likes of Joely and Pissabed Hanley, and she had been renting out her own apartment since moving in with Ed. She told him it was her pension fund, but the truth was she couldn't bear the idea of letting it go. Even if Willowbrook cost her all she had, it would be worth it not to cede the moral high ground to her sister.

With Judith's words ringing in her ears, she felt soft enough to confide in Ed. Locked into her car was as good a place as any.

'What do you want to do?' Ed said when she finished speaking.

'A few minutes ago, I wanted to break something,' Marianne said. In front of her, Willowbrook's windows glinted. 'I think I just want answers.'

'What can I do to help?'

She sighed. 'If you really want to help, tell me what to do.'

'Talk to Liv, of course.'

Marianne snorted. 'She got you on her side with that little nature walk, did she? Spun some sob story about being left to pick up the pieces at home?'

'You asked me what to do and that is what you need to do. Talk to her. Maybe she said it out of anger—'

'She most certainly did,' Marianne interrupted.

'Or maybe she is wrong.'

'She might be wrong,' Marianne said slowly. 'You're absolutely right. I should talk to the solicitor.'

'That's not what I said.'

Marianne hardly heard him. How had she not considered that Liv – perfect, accurate Liv-the-almighty – could simply be wrong? She could have kissed him! 'The solicitor will know. There might be nothing to worry about at all.'

'What is it that you are worried about?'

This time, his words got through. 'What do you mean? It's my home.'

'Our apartment is not home for you?' His voice was even.

'It's not a competition, Ed. Home can be both. You know that. When you're going to visit your parents, you tell me you're going home for the weekend or whatever. Don't make it into a thing.'

'I'm not trying to make it into a thing. I just want to understand if you're feeling… untied.'

'Untethered,' Marianne corrected him. 'I'm not a dog attached to a post.'

'Should we get married? Would that make a difference?'

Marianne rolled her eyes. The question was so prosaic, so… *Ed*. Not that she was the kind of person to need the down-on-one-knee bullshit. So it didn't matter really. It shouldn't matter. She watched shadows move behind the windows of the treatment centre and wondered if Ethel was in there looking out at her daughter being half-proposed to in the car park.

An old memory jogged loose in Marianne's mind. 'The morning of our confirmation – that's the one where you accept the Holy Spirit as your guide to life,' she explained before Ed could ask, 'Ethel had a face on her like thunder because Dad was admiring our outfits but never mentioned hers. When we got to the church it was raining and he handed her a brand-new umbrella in that exact shade of blue. He must have gone into the city especially to get it.' Marianne stopped and cleared her throat. 'There was no online shopping in those days.'

They sat in silence for a moment or two.

'I'm going to ring the solicitor,' she said. 'I know you think I don't need the place. But there's a world of difference between not wanting something and being told you can't have it.'

Thinking about it afterwards, Marianne would have to concede that she had worked herself up a bit on the drive home. The solicitor's secretary, when she phoned, had refused to let her talk to him or to give her any information about overturning wills. She could make an appointment if she sought advice, she was told stiffly. Marianne stalled the car in the drive while trying to reverse into one of the spaces. Her father would turn in his grave if he saw her. Stalling the car was high on his list of driver offences. *If you haven't control of the clutch, you haven't control of the car.*

'Sorry, Dad,' she muttered again now.

'I was just making a fresh pot of coffee if you want a cup?' Liv offered.

She could take it and fling it in her face, Marianne supposed. Scar Liv's face in a way that no careful skin care routine could fix. No. With her luck, Liv would need a skin graft and she would have to be the bloody donor. 'I think you owe me a little more than coffee.'

Liv sighed. 'If we're going to do this, let's actually do it. No passive-aggressive crap. Sit down and I'll tell you everything I know.'

Marianne sat.

'Before Dad died, they signed over half the business to me—'

'I know. He told me.' At least one of her parents had had her back.

'A couple of years ago, she told me she had left me the rest as well. For Shay, she said. She didn't say any more about it and I didn't know whether or not to even believe her. If anything, I thought it might just be guilt after one of her early benders. But then I went to the solicitor to make my own will and even though he obviously couldn't come right out and say it, he sort of implied it.'

Marianne watched her sister as she spoke. Liv twisted her cup with one hand and refused to look at her. That alone told Marianne that her sister believed it to be true. She could understand Ethel wanting to make sure that Shay was protected, but it rankled to have that protection come at her expense. Had it even crossed Ethel's mind that to firmly embed Shay in the place would rip Marianne out of it. Maybe that was the point, she thought sourly.

'I'm officially homeless then.' She tried for a little laugh, but it wouldn't come. She should be ashamed of herself, she knew, for her extraordinary selfishness in laying claim to the word homeless, but it wasn't her fault the word had been made to mean something else. She might not be 'houseless', but 'homeless' was exactly what she felt.

'Of course not,' Liv said. 'I would never do that to you. When... when the time comes, of course, we'll... sort something out.'

'Based on your charity, though, rather than because it's what Ethel wanted. What Dad wanted.' Marianne was horrified to hear her voice crack.

'Who knows what Ethel wants? That's why I never said anything. I assumed it was a fit of pique, that at some point she would change her mind and undo it again. You know how she is.'

'So you think she lied when she said it was for Shay? That her real intention was to punish me for something?'

'That's not what I—'

'Because Ethel does grudges better than anyone, we both know that.'

'I thought she would change her mind,' Liv pleaded. She tried to take Marianne's hand, but Marianne twitched away from her.

'This is the woman who has never once been back to her homeplace since leaving, despite it being two hours' drive away. She's not known for softening over time.'

'This is your home. It will always be your home. The paperwork doesn't matter. We can fix it. I can—'

'You can do what? Do you think so little of me that you believe I would take the bite out of Shay's mouth?'

There was a sharp rap on the door and Ellen Gould appeared.

'Hello, Ellen.' Liv gave her eyes a quick swipe with her sleeve and turned to the door. 'We didn't hear you there.'

'The front door was open.' Ellen put down her bag and looked from Liv to Marianne. 'Everything all right in here?'

'We were just...' Marianne trailed off, feeling foolish. She cleared her throat. 'Is there news? Did you find Fred's family?'

'Not yet. We've been in touch with Interpol—'

'He's not on the Yellow Notices,' Marianne said. When

Liv and Ellen looked at her with curiosity, she flushed. 'Did you think you were the only one who could do a Google search?'

'No harm in that. This isn't an official visit as such. I wanted to tell you we found some clothes that we think might have belonged to Mr Stille.'

'I thought you found his clothes on the beach already?' Marianne said.

'We did. These were found in a number of bins in the village.'

Bins. Marianne's throat contracted. He had walked through the village, casting himself off, bit by bit. It seemed, suddenly, the saddest thing she had ever heard.

'Did he appear to have a change of clothes?' Ellen asked.

'He did,' Marianne said. 'I saw him wearing two different jumpers and shirts. One was brown – sort of fawn-coloured, you'd say – and the other was a dark red. It might have been the same jacket and trousers, but the rest was definitely different.'

Ellen nodded and opened the bag out, a clear plastic bag containing a red jumper and pale blue shirt. Marianne felt the tears spring to her eyes. Jesus, she would want to get a grip. It wasn't like Ellen had thrown his body onto the table. She cleared her throat. 'Will you be able to find him from his clothes?'

'The tags were snipped out,' Ellen said. 'Even the care label. It could have been bought anywhere.'

'Where did you find them?' Liv asked.

'Some of the local CCTV footage showed Mr Stille walking through the village and pausing at the bins, so we took a closer look.'

'Little enough doubt that it was deliberate, so,' Liv said. 'You know, I think Ed was right when he said that it was less tragic if it was intentional. There's some comfort in thinking that he went on his own terms, hard though it might be for us to understand.'

'True,' Ellen said. 'Nobody goes to the trouble of divesting themselves – almost literally – of every possible means of identification without some forethought.'

Did he really want to be forgotten, Marianne wondered, or was he simply finishing the job the world had started? She turned to Ellen. 'Where is he? Can I see him?'

'Marianne! Why in the name of God would you want to do that?' Liv said.

Ellen ignored her. 'Do you really want to?' she asked Marianne.

When Marianne nodded, Ellen did too. 'Come on, so.'

Ellen was a very considerate convoy leader. She was probably used to it, with her job. One of those strange, unremarked skills that separate the real adults from the frauds. Marianne followed, with Lyric FM on low.

She had a right to feel sad, no matter what Liv said. A right to grief, even, despite what Madame Heartless thought. And what about Fred himself? He had a right to be regretted, truly, for who he wanted to be thought of in his final days. She put on her indicator and turned left, behind Ellen. Whatever his reasons, he deserved to have that choice respected. Ethel's wishes didn't trump Martin's just because he wasn't there to argue for himself. Her dad had wanted her to have her home. He wanted her to be happy. Whether or not a life in Coolaroone was part of that happiness was immaterial; it was having the choice that mattered. The choice should be hers.

They drove into the grounds of the small county hospital, following the discreet sign to the mortuary. They knew they were coming, Ellen explained in the car park. Marianne followed the white-coated figure down the corridor. She had expected something out of the movies, all shiny steel and white walls, but this looked more like the storage unit for Gen's café.

'It's colder than I expected,' she said to Ellen as they looked down at Fred.

'People sometimes want to spend time with the body,' Ellen said diplomatically.

'Will he be here until they find his people?' Marianne

asked. It seemed manageable, somehow, the idea of him here, waiting to be claimed. The doctors and technicians would be in and out every day, a bit of company for him.

'I'll ask.' Ellen disappeared.

Fred didn't look like he was asleep. He looked, Marianne thought, a little like a waxwork, with his face smooth and unlined. To look at him now was to understand the depth of the burden he carried. She allowed herself a series of brief fantasies: a beloved partner buried. A terminal illness. A crime unconfessed. Everyone he loved gone before him. Living taking more effort than he had in him. Whatever it was that had created the lines of pain that had been on his face until so recently. Now, he looked calm. As if the effort was no longer taking it out of him.

'They'll keep him for a while anyway, under the circumstances.' Ellen arrived on quiet feet behind her, making Marianne jump.

'Until the inquest?'

'The cause of death is clear,' Ellen said gently. 'That means there's no need for a legal ruling.'

Fred looked different than Marianne remembered. Smaller and less familiar. 'He curated his own death,' she said. 'Do you think he knew about this part?'

'Maybe he didn't care what happened afterwards. He might have thought he would be gone on somewhere else. Or into the void. Whatever you're having yourself.'

When standing there began to feel foolish, Marianne indicated she was ready to leave. It seemed disrespectful to just walk away, so she waited while the white-coated figure pushed Fred back into the refrigerated wall and closed the door on him.

'Thanks,' she said to Ellen in the car park. 'I was… That felt important.'

'No bother. I was curious to have a look myself. Coming to meet the lads here was on my list of things to do when I moved back, so this was as good a time as any.'

'It's like one of your true crime stories come to life,' Marianne said.

'How well you remembered!' Ellen looked delighted. 'I'll have to tell my mother. She'll get a kick out of you remembering. She always used to say to me: "Ellen, you'll need a job that makes a virtue of your nosiness!" Speaking of mothers, I was in Willowbrook earlier on the off chance that anyone had a connection to our man. I saw Ethel while I was there,' she said. 'How are you doing with that?'

'They won't let me see her.' Then, without knowing she was going to, she blurted, 'I didn't even know she had been there before.'

If Ellen was uncomfortable, she hid it well. 'That's people for you. There's a lot we hide from one another.'

'I suppose you see it all in your job.'

'It would put hairs on your chest,' Ellen agreed. She opened the door of her car and sat in, the weight causing the car to groan. 'For what it's worth, Ethel was out in the garden, pottering around.' She winked at Marianne. 'In case you were having visions of padded cells. I might have been into the crime novels, but I seem to remember you were fond of the drama.'

Marianne opened her mouth to retort, then recognised the gentle teasing and smiled instead.

Somewhere, she thought, were people who remembered things about Fred Stille's schooldays. His scabby knees or weird sandwiches. His loneliness or his potential.

Try though he might, he wasn't completely erased.

THURSDAY

LIV

It took Liv a minute of fumbling around on her nightstand to realise that it wasn't her alarm that was ringing but the phone itself. The dread was instantaneous. Shay? Seamus? Marianne? Ethel? Later, Liv would think that Sophie's choice would have been a lot simpler if she was woken out of her sleep to make it.

'Mam's had another stroke.' Seamus' voice was heavy. 'The nursing home rang a few minutes ago.'

'I'm sorry, Seamus. Is she…?' There was no kind way to finish the sentence. Liv found herself wondering if Ed would simply have asked, 'Is she dying?' Of course, Ed could get away with that sort of thing.

'She's in hospital. Stable for now, but they advised me to come.' Seamus sounded awkward and Liv knew what was coming before he asked. She gave herself credit for making him say it. For affording herself that much dignity. 'I won't be able to get there before lunchtime. Is there any way yourself and Shay could head over for a bit? I hate to think of her on her own.'

There were many possible questions Liv could have asked: Why can't you get there yourself? What about your wife?

Do you think I have nothing else to do? To ask any of them would be to open an argument that was years in the making. She looked at the generic B&B duvet set on her bed. After sleeping with Seamus, she had put her favourite set into the charity bag and forgone new ones: she didn't deserve them. 'Tell them we'll be there in three-quarters of an hour.'

'Do you think you could ring them? I have an early meeting and Ruth is already—'

Liv closed her eyes. She could already feel the fingers of a headache creeping around the sides of her skull. 'No problem,' she said. 'That's no problem at all.'

The hospital was hot and noisy. Liv wished she could have stayed outside in the cool hushed fog. 'Let's find Grandma Pauline,' she told Shay, marching off purposefully. Old people in varying states of distress wallpapered both sides of the corridor while staff rushed here and there. Whatever wrongs people committed in their lifetimes, Liv thought, age exacted a hefty price for having survived them.

Things were quieter on the wards, away from Accident & Emergency. 'Pauline Lucey?' Liv asked at the desk. 'We're her family.' Explaining the complexities of their relationship would create unnecessary hassle and Shay was old enough to be sensible about it.

He was not, however, old enough for the patience required by hospitals. After ten or fifteen minutes of slouching in a chair beside his grandmother's bed, he announced that he was hungry. 'Do you want anything?'

'I'll take a coffee if you find a machine or something,' Liv said. 'Do you need change?'

Shay shook his head and sloped off. Two grandmothers in various stages of disintegration. She could erase 'Shay = scarred' from her shower door as many times as she liked; the world had its own ideas about damage. She stood at the door and watched him walk away. Her beautiful boy. How many times had she told him to stand up straight? Not enough to reach the magic number where it worked, evidently. A product she had seen advertised online flitted briefly through her mind, some kind of posture-improving vest that was worn while sitting at a desk. At the time, she had dismissed it as a random cookie misfire, but now she wondered what her laptop knew that she didn't.

Pauline lay unmoving in the bed. The machines monitoring her emitted the occasional beep. First one, then another quickly, then nothing for a long time again. They were simply checking vitals on a set schedule, Liv knew, but she preferred to think they were asking and answering one another. Still okay? Okay.

In a room not unlike this one, Ethel lay or – Liv checked her watch – sat, doing who knew what. Less than a week in, it was likely she was fuming at her daughter. Daughters, this time, Liv reminded herself, as if it made a difference. Past form suggested that after her early acquiescence, Ethel would move into a phase of seeing herself as having been taken advantage of in a vulnerable moment, before coming to rest on a more palatable idea, that her treatment was something she was doing for the family rather than for herself. Having thus convinced herself that that was motivation enough, she would leave Willowbrook and embark on a sobriety that began as martyr-like and thinned week by week until it snapped.

Liv sighed. This was why she tried not to think about Ethel. Thinking about Ethel meant worrying about Ethel, with no appreciable control over the outcome. She could cut up Ethel's bank cards and sleep with the car keys under her pillow, she could plead with Alan to water down her drinks and leave blankets on the front step, she could keep Ethel away from the guests and take every effort to reduce the consequences of her mother's actions to encompass only themselves. But the long and the short of it was that she could take her to the doorway over and over and over, but there was no going through it for her. For all the self-indulgent bullshit she heard in Al Anon every time she tried it, they had that much right at least. Was this what it would be like from now on? Just her and an old lady in a room until Liv herself was the one in the hospital bed? After the will debacle, Marianne could decide to stay away for good and it would be hard to blame her if she did. If they were closer, Marianne would know it instinctively. If they were closer, Liv reminded herself, she would have told her sister the first night Ethel didn't come home. Or the moment she mentioned the will at all. It was sudden and wounding, the realisation that that was what her behaviour must look like to Marianne. What exactly was she punishing her for? For making her choices, the way they were raised to? She would do well, Liv knew, to think about why she was so quick to take offence at the idea that Marianne saw Coolaroone as merely a fallback, when Liv had made it her whole life. She needed to own her own choices. Punishing her sister only left them both lonely.

The way things were going, there might be nothing to fight over. There were still more cancellations than bookings. Liv got up and walked to the window, tapping on the glass for something to do. Memories were short. They had seen out worse during the recession and would do it again. If she didn't believe that, she wouldn't be able to sleep at night. The B&B was more than a storehouse of memories, more than a roof over her head. If it was her past, it was also her future. The only thing she had to gift her child. The irony was not lost on her. She needed it – deserved it – more than Marianne did, just not at any price.

'I brought you coffee, I think,' Shay said from the doorway. 'The labels on the machine were worn away.' He handed her the cup and sat down. 'What happens now?'

'We wait and see,' Liv said simply.

'Either she gets better or she dies?' Shay asked with studied casualness.

'It's not that simple when people are older. It might be

that she just stays like this for a while. With strokes it can be hard to predict.'

Shay just nodded and took out his phone.

Liv could have done the same but chose not to. Ever since reading an article about how people had lost the art of sitting still with their thoughts, she made a conscious effort not to reach for distraction any time she found herself on her own. It would be a long life if she were to get into that habit now, before Shay was even out the door. Or a short life, maybe, if the tinfoil hats were to be believed and they were all bathing in radiation morning, noon and night.

She must have dozed off, waking only when the door opened to admit the doctor and her team. Liv wiped her mouth hastily and hoped she hadn't been snoring.

'Pauline Lucey, seventy-nine, ischemic stroke…'

Liv admired the doctor's composure, the way she looked at Pauline rather than at her notes. She herself might have learned the same trick in medical school, how to appear engaged while mentally planning her dinner or a dirty weekend away.

'Mrs Lucey, as you know, this isn't your mother-in-law's first stroke. Based on her history, I'm reluctant to say what exactly we might expect when she wakes up, if indeed she does return to us. It's not simply her age that's a factor here but her overall condition, which has declined considerably since the last event, I understand.'

She talked on for a minute or two while Liv did her best to take mental notes to share with Seamus. 'Her son is driving down. He should be here in a few hours. Is that… does he need to come sooner?'

The doctor looked at Pauline speculatively. 'Unless she has another attack – and we're not seeing any signs of anything imminent – then I think you're all better served by him taking it easy on the road.' She smiled and shook Liv's hand before leaving.

'Scary,' Shay remarked when she was gone.

'Efficient,' Liv corrected him. 'I wanted to be a doctor when I was your age, you know.'

He looked up from his phone. 'Is this your subtle way of having the "what-are-my-plans-for-the-future" conversation?'

She wanted to tell him that not everything was about him, only he wouldn't believe her. At nearly nineteen, who would?

'I knew Aunt Mar would tell you.' Shay sounded defeated.

'She didn't mean to. I sort of surprised it out of her. We were arguing and it just… came out. You could say I provoked her.'

'Arguing about what?' Shay asked with interest.

'Just… sister stuff. Baggage, I guess.'

She waited for him to press. Instead, he asked, 'Do you wish you had gone?'

There were so many possible answers. All the lives she had once dreamt of. She pushed away the memory of her earlier envy of the doctor. 'I had you by then, so I just wanted you to be happy and healthy.' She caught sight of him rolling his eyes and laughed. 'All right then. Apart from that… I wanted to be my own boss.'

'Like you are now?'

Liv thought about all the days she dragged herself from bed and wished she had a job she could leave behind. That was the thing about working at home: other people only ever saw the not-going-to-work part of the day. They never thought about the fact that she never left work to go home. She looked at Shay, thrown sideways in his chair. The vulnerability of his bare neck, his ears. All that mattered was that he felt safe. That he knew he had a home always, unchanged and unchanging. Liv thought of Marianne and sighed. Fuck. What have you done, Ethel? What have you done?

'I wouldn't change a thing,' she said and smiled at her son. 'Whatever you want to do, whenever and wherever you want to do it, we'll figure it out. "Life is long", your Grandad Martin used to say.'

THURSDAY

ETHEL

Write a story from childhood, they told her. Fine. She would.

But the spring sun was weak and insistent. It showed up everything, the dust and streaks. Her skin itched with the memory of her summer garden and late-onset sunburn.

A story from childhood. First this and then the crossword. One down: *Grace period (4)*. The world was cute and no mistake. *Amen* to that, indeed.

Her notebook was too new looking. There was something judgemental about its pristine cover. Something smug. She bought Shay a notebook a few years back. She hadn't gone out looking for it, just stumbled across it in a shop somewhere. The idea was to do things with the book rather than writing in it. The notebook itself recorded the experience. Poor Shay. He handled it like a bomb, gingerly showing her where he had left his shoe print in dirt or carefully pressed in a small stick. Given the chance to put a stick into a book, who wouldn't turn it into a flag? She sighed. Imagine that being the limit of his imagination. But, then, Seamus contributed fifty per cent of the child's DNA, which was enough to snuff the *joie de vivre* out of anyone. *Take it into the shower* was another instruction, she remembered, and looked at her shiny notebook speculatively. It wouldn't be worth the effort of pretending to have done it by accident.

She tapped the pencil against the page. *Peann luaidhe.* A lead pen. No matter that there hadn't been lead in them for donkey's years. Young people, with their directness, had the right idea. Take *féinín* for example. If there was a neater little word, she'd pay to hear it. 'Little self' rather than selfie. You couldn't deny Irish had an elegance all its own. She wondered if the Indians – the native Americans – had a similar expression. There was some affinity there, wasn't there, between them and the Irish. Hadn't they sent money over during the worst of the Great Famine, despite themselves having hardly a pot to piss in? She would have to look it up when they gave her iPad access privileges. There was a monument somewhere, she was sure of it. Some class of a thing with leaves. The power of nature to support us or break us, she supposed. A message along those lines.

Outside the window, the garden was still suffering a winter hangover. What she wouldn't give to get out there with her shears and a bucket – a bit of pruning would leave grand space for the new flowers to bud. She could start the garden again soon, Judith said. Once they were sure she wouldn't suck the weedkiller out of the soil.

Around her was the scratching of pencils on paper, the heavy breathing of the tongue-protruders. How obedient they all were, pressing themselves neatly into the little white squares, like flowers into an album. She used to do that as a girl, take a flower and press it into the middle of the family Bible – the heaviest book in the house – and then sit on it.

A story from childhood. When she was in school, they had learned the story of Fionn and the Fianna by heart. There was only one story, it seemed, that of Ireland's legendary warriors and their leader. *Lá breá samhradh a bhí ann. Bhí Fionn agus gasra do na Fianna amuigh ag fiach. It was a fine summer's day, Fionn and some of the Fianna were out hunting.* She couldn't remember how the rest of it went, what else Fionn and his band of warriors got up to. Likely the sun led them astray one way or the other, into a thunderstorm or a fight or adultery. A lot of the old Irish legends seemed to feature one or another.

Funny how some details stuck. The story of Fionn. The look your husband gave you the night before he died. The fondness in it.

Ethel put down her pencil. What would Fionn the legendary leader make of the place now, she wondered. His spear would be no good to him in a modern age. He would have to rely on his wits, like the rest of them. He would be less of a giant than a bewildered oul' lad. Rather than feasting and slaying men in their hundreds, his idea of a grand night out would be a few pints of stout with the Dempseys. Wasn't it a wonder he was still remembered? You couldn't throw a stone now without hitting a dozen Fionns and Oisíns, Diarmuids and Oscars. Everywhere you turned, there was another Irish warrior. They had a good story, *Na Fianna*. That was the trick to being remembered: a good story.

FRIDAY

MARIANNE

Marianne woke when Liv climbed into the bed beside her in the darkness.

'I know you're still cross with me, but I had an awful dream and there isn't anyone else,' Liv said simply.

Marianne heard the catch in her sister's throat. Liv was always prone to nightmares. When they were children, it seemed every second morning she would wake to Liv's cold feet wrapping around her calves. 'What was it?'

'We were at Mass, and I was cutting people's throats. I had a big knife and I was walking up and down the aisle of the church, up one side and down the other, slitting the throats of the people on the outsides of the seats. The weirdest thing was that they were all sitting waiting for me to do it, as if… as if we all knew they deserved it.'

'You hardly ever go to Mass any more. Surely that tipped you off to the fact it was only a dream.'

'It felt real,' Liv whispered.

'Fuck's sake. Tell me you at least took out a few of the Twomeys.' But she drew her sister's cold feet in against the warmth of her own pyjama legs.

'I was wearing mittens,' Liv said.

'Very Tarantino touch, the mittens,' Marianne repeated, and the bed shook with their laughter.

'Last night I dreamt I was buying new cutlery,' Marianne said. 'Talk about depressing. I'm one *Coronation Street* omnibus away from peak middle age.'

She felt Liv smile against her shoulder. 'I understand the weird-and-shaky feeling,' she said. 'When Ellen took me to the mortuary and I saw him all by himself in the cold, it was the loneliest thing in the world.' With something like horror, she heard her voice crack.

Liv reached out and draped a hand across her shoulder. 'They'll find his family, Mar,' she said.

'What if they don't? They have so many other things to do. He seemed so nice, and he'll end up buried in a strange place with nothing to his name. And that's not even his!'

'What do you want to do?' Liv asked.

That was the very question that had gone around and around Marianne's head since leaving Fred's body behind. 'Promise you won't laugh?'

'Let me remind you: a meat cleaver *and mittens*. I won't laugh, trust me.'

'I'm going to go to the Danish embassy.'

Liv sat up and swung her legs out of the bed.

'What are you doing?'

'There's a train at six-thirty. If we skip breakfast, we can be on it. What are you waiting for? It's not like we have any guests to worry about.'

'What will we say when we get there?'

'We'll have three hours on the train to figure it out.'

It was a long time since they had spent so much time alone, without other people, other talk. Marianne looked out the window at the countryside going past while Liv read the paper. Every time she tried to imagine what she would say at the door of the embassy, her brain skittered away from the words like an anxious foal.

'What do you think Dad would say if he were here?' she asked Liv when the tea trolley had deposited coffee and Danish pastries, sweaty in their plastic wrapping.

'About Fred or Ethel?'

'Either.'

'It's hard to imagine things with Ethel would have got this far,' Liv said, stirring milk into her cup. 'He probably would have been supportive. Driven her to Willowbrook and hoped for the best. What else is there?'

'We all have our cross to bear.' Marianne imitated Martin's voice. 'Do you think he would have gone to the pub and had it out with Alan for continuing to serve her?'

Liv shook her head. 'It's not Alan's fault. If he didn't sell it to her, she'd be drinking in the fields. Or worse, the playground.'

Marianne didn't see how that was worse, but then she had never pushed a child on the swings there, so it felt less like desecration and more like teenage bad behaviour. The kind her father had no truck with when they were growing up. 'Do you think she drinks because Dad died and she can't cope without him?'

'I don't think it's that simple. When she's not drinking, she has a lot going on. Between the business and the local committees for this and that, she has a fuller life than I do. But then,' Liv shrugged. 'Who's to say what makes people feel lonely?'

Marianne looked closely at her sister. 'Is that why you keep going back to Seamus?'

Liv drank her coffee, and for a moment, Marianne thought she wasn't going to answer.

'It's not loneliness. It's… hard to explain.'

'He snaps his fingers and you come running,' Marianne said, and immediately regretted it.

'I know that's what it looks like,' Liv agreed.

'Are you sure it isn't something simpler, like a brain tumour?' Marianne asked hopefully. 'It'd be such a relief. I could shave my head in solidarity.'

Liv laughed. 'Not a brain tumour. I'm sorry to disappoint you.' She took another drink of her coffee. 'I had such plans, you know? Then I had Shay and it felt like everything got… smaller, somehow. Seamus knows me. Who I am. Who I was.'

'If you're looking for people you've known for years, surely Coolaroone is the best place for options?'

'I'm going to regret telling you this, but… for a while there, I had a bit of a casual thing going with Paddy Hanley,' Liv said.

'You and Pissabed?' Marianne couldn't have been more surprised if Liv had said she was bedding Father Mike. 'He doesn't even live here!'

'He was home every weekend to help his dad with the practice,' Liv shrugged. 'He started going out with someone else before he came back, but I think that's over now.'

'You make it sound like a turn-off that he's available.'

Liv reddened. 'That's not fair.'

'Lots of things aren't fair.'

'You chose to leave,' Liv reminded her tightly. 'To live your life somewhere else.'

'True. If only I'd known there was a penalty. A hidden clause, as it were.' Marianne tried to laugh, but it wouldn't come out. No more tears, she told herself. It was hardly daylight yet.

'It's not like that.' Liv looked at Marianne. 'Sometimes I think *this is my place.* No matter its faults, it's the only place I fit.'

'You could fit in anywhere. You could go to college if you feel you missed out first time round. Plenty of people go back as mature students.'

Liv shuddered. 'Be there at the same time as Shay? Talk about ruining it for him. If he goes.' She shook her head. 'No.

If I wanted to, I would have. I tried a night course in business a while back, but, sure, I could have practically given the class.'

'There's a million things you could do,' Marianne said, impatient with her sister's lack of enthusiasm. Life might have been small when she had a newborn baby and few resources, but those excuses sat poorly on a grown woman. If she didn't like her life, there was nothing stopping her from changing it. Make a decision. Move on.

'You don't need to pity me, you know,' Liv said suddenly, as if she had read Marianne's mind. 'Most days, I have my life exactly the way I like it.'

'Most days,' Marianne repeated. She sank back in her seat and looked out the window at the trees flashing past. 'I suppose that's not so bad.'

The taxi dropped them off at an incongruously modern building, all steel and glass. It wasn't until she saw it that Marianne realised she was expecting stone walls and wrought-iron gates. Something a little more courtly and old-fashioned. In short, she wanted Fred the man, embodied in warm brick building form.

The staff at the embassy – the one bemused receptionist and kind diplomat they were eventually ushered in to see – were faultlessly polite. Their accents, echoes of Fred Stille himself, reduced Marianne to shameful tears, so that it was some time before they grasped that he was not, in fact, either a relative or friend. They were given tea in warming mugs while the diplomat listened and took notes, before excusing herself to make a phone call.

Left alone with her sister and a box of tissues, Marianne braced herself for mockery. For Liv to remind her that she had no entitlement to such grief for a stranger, wrapped up in her particular brand of brisk cop-on-to-yourself-ness. But Liv just took Marianne's hand and held it tightly between both of her own until the woman came back to explain, again, about the missing persons website, about the number they should phone if any information came to light.

They made the midday train, running the fifty yards from the barrier to the door while the train guard shouted encouragement. Liv had suggested lunch, or even a spot of shopping, but the sight of people hurrying about their business made Marianne feel nauseous and faintly dizzy, like being in overheated shops on Christmas Eve with her coat still on.

'I'll get us something to eat,' Liv said, disappearing in the direction of the dining car.

While she was gone, Marianne logged on to the missing persons website and scrolled through to see if anything had been added. The woman at the embassy had promised she would post some information about Fred, but there was nothing yet. For the tenth time, she googled 'Fred Stille', only to find the same businessmen smiling out at her, the same gravestones with long-dead Freds, forever remembered by their loving families. Did he google the name before choosing it? Marianne wondered. Did he look at these same faces and think that he could slip in amongst them and vanish unnoticed? Or did he simply choose a name that he found meaningful, a name that, perhaps, he wished to have in death, if not in life? Looking at the non-Fred Freds on the screen, she felt a flash of anger that the internet had pushed him so far to be forgotten, even from those who wanted only to bury him well.

She snapped her phone shut, then reopened it and googled *Gaofar*. The first link was their own website – that was something – then the local business directory. The third link down appeared to be a news item about Fred's disappearance. She clicked into it and read with an increasing sense of irritation.

'Have you seen this?' she demanded when Liv came back, bearing a paper bag of white bread sandwiches, crisps and cans of Coke. Jesus, it was like being on a picnic in the 1980s.

'Have I seen what?' Liv glanced at the screen. 'Oh, that. Yes. I phoned the journalist and asked him to consider his words a little more carefully, but he pretty much laughed me out of it.'

'Prick,' Marianne muttered, snapping open her drink. 'You should rebrand the business. Not just because of this, although...' she waved her phone at her sister, 'it certainly doesn't help.'

'Rebrand how? Change the name?'

'No!' Marianne was horrified. 'The name was Dad's. I mean something a bit more directional. Call it a guesthouse rather than a B&B. Honestly, Airbnb has pretty much ruined people's expectations of B&B pricing anyway, so it wouldn't hurt to get a bit of distance from that particular term.'

'A bit of rebranding?' Liv raised her eyebrows. 'To a hammer, everything looks like a nail.'

Marianne stuck out her tongue. 'Actually, I was thinking again about the retreat idea. There's still some land—'

'The one thing we have going for us is that we don't have a mortgage on the place. Thanks to Holy Mary and the economic miracle she wrought in Coolaroone.'

'Will you ever let me finish? I've decided to sell the apartment.'

'You don't need to—'

'I want to. And don't worry, I'm not doing it to make a point. Ed and I have been dithering for a while about a bigger place.' Marianne shrugged. 'Maybe now's the time. Besides, you won't need to build much. An outdoor room – you know the kind of thing, like a big garden shed, but warm? – and rent it for a fortnight at a time to artists, writers, that kind of thing. Solitary, in touch with nature, meals with the family or on a tray in the studio. You know.'

'Meals with Ethel? We'd have to pay them, not the other way around.'

'They'd be delighted to have a dipso around the place. She'd give us artistic credibility.' Would laughter ever again not feel guilty? Marianne wondered.

'I half-want to say I couldn't possibly and half-want to take the hand off you,' Liv said. 'It might just work.'

Marianne's eyes filled with tears. 'Christ,' she said. 'I don't know what's going on with me today. I'm all over the place. Do you honestly think it might work? You're not just humouring me?'

'Honestly. The rest of the day was about humouring you, all right. But this idea might be one to explore.' She snapped the lid of her drink and raised it to her sister. 'You know, I think Dad would have liked the idea. Can you imagine all the random questions he would have for them? Why that name and where is that character going and did they ever consider setting it on a farm?'

'The research on their behalf that they had to be polite about,' Marianne joined in.

'His name in the acknowledgements,' Liv said. She raised her can. 'Cheers.'

'Cheers,' Marianne echoed, before reaching – again – for the packet of tissues tucked into her handbag.

FRIDAY

LIV

Through the window on the corridor, Liv could see Seamus asleep in the chair beside his mother's bed. Sleeping, he looked as innocent as a puppy. *A puppy sitting in a puddle of its own wee*, Liv reminded herself before she opened the door.

She advanced towards the bed, keeping up a steady stream of what would kindly be called meaningless prattle, the sort her mother-in-law drew out of her like pus out of a boil.

'Hi Pauline. It's Liv. No, you're not dreaming, it's Friday. I thought I'd forgo our usual schedule and pop in this evening to see how you're doing after the little fright you gave us yesterday. How is she?' She addressed this last to Seamus, who was stretching and scratching. Why wouldn't he? she thought suddenly. He had no need to impress her, hadn't she been making that clear for the last twenty years?

'The nurses were around earlier. They said she is holding her own, but they couldn't say much more until the doctor comes around later.'

'I always found that to be a bit of an odd expression,' Liv said. 'Holding your own.'

'It's only odd if you're holding someone else's,' Seamus

said. But he yawned rather than winked, which took the flirty edge off it.

'Myself and Shay waited as late as we could yesterday,' she said, careful to keep her voice neutral.

'My meeting ran over and then traffic was bound to be a bastard, so I waited until late in the evening. Every time I drive down here I wonder why they haven't built a better road and then I get here, and I remember.'

'Easy there,' Liv said. 'Some of us still live here you know.'

He held up his two hands. Whether implying an apology or inviting acquiescence, Liv wasn't sure. Nor did she want to find out. With herself and Marianne mending fences, she was in – if not a good mood, exactly, then a solid seven.

'Thanks for being here. Although it was handy it was a Thursday, you would have been visiting her anyway.'

Typical Seamus to issue a thank you with all the good taken out of it. 'I did it for Shay.' *Not as penance for opening my legs to you not a week ago*, she added to herself.

'Are Ruth and the girls not with you?' she asked.

'They're coming down shortly,' Seamus said. 'Ruth didn't want the girls to miss school. Gracie's been struggling a bit.'

Ruth would kill him for the casual way he told her, Liv thought. No mother wanted her child's shortcomings paraded in front of strangers.

'Pauline will appreciate that,' Liv said. It seemed the polite thing not to acknowledge that the only things Pauline might conceivably appreciate would be better drugs or a speedy delivery into her eternal rest. Not that she would rest much there. The sky would be too blue, the music too soft, Jesus suspiciously kind. She nearly wished she believed it all – she'd pay to see Pauline Lucey try to put manners on heaven.

'Shay was in earlier,' Seamus said. 'He said you were gone to Dublin. Something to do with your mysterious guest, he said.'

'Marianne wanted to go to the embassy, just in case there was anything more we could do,' Liv said. She was reluctant to say more. Marianne's face had been so sad and there was something unbearable about the idea that Seamus might laugh at her sister's upset. Or worse, that she herself might laugh along with him, betraying poor Mar.

'Did you hear anything from your friend Wes?'

'I meant to give him a call and check in, but things just got away from me.'

Liv was just filling him in on the discovery of the clothes in the public bins when the door opened to admit Ruth and the girls. Ruth was immaculately turned out, as always – Pauline was a great one for leaving photographs lying around where she knew Liv would see them. Why did she have to be wearing her walking jacket? Liv groaned to herself. As if she hadn't a perfectly decent coat at home in the wardrobe. It was false shame, she knew, to cover the little thrill that shuddered through her at noticing that Seamus and Ruth no longer kissed one another hello.

'Ruth. How are you?'

To her surprise, Ruth gave her a quick hug. 'Thanks for being here yesterday. It was a comfort to know Pauline had family with her.'

'It was nothing,' Liv said.

Ruth shook her head firmly. 'Both of my parents died in hospital. I would hate to think of anyone being alone here when there's any risk... You were very good to do it.'

The rounds of chat began again. What the doctors said and didn't say, this time veiled in a layer of thesaurus-speak, presumably so the children wouldn't understand too much. Liv wondered at the subterfuge. They were nine, after all, not toddlers. Turn on a news bulletin and they would hear far worse. The two little girls were dressed in close to identical outfits and shadowed one another around the room. One would go to look out the window and the other would drift after her. One opened the door to the bathroom and the other followed to look too. Liv wasn't sure which was which, although instinct suggested that the one who stood up straighter might be Tessa, while the one half a step behind might be Gracie. Names chosen because Ruth liked them, no doubt. One look at her told you she wasn't one for pushing around. She was inwardly smirking at Ruth for dressing them alike at nine years old when she realised that it was likely their own choice.

Tessa stood with one leg crossed over the other and Gracie did the same after a minute. Tessa sat on the arm of Seamus' chair and Gracie crossed to perch on the other side. Liv watched them and wondered if herself and Marianne would have been closer if they were identical.

'We were up at the house,' Ruth said to Seamus. 'It's freezing. There's no way we can stay there, not with Gracie's asthma. What was the name of that hotel you mentioned? The Dillon, was it?'

Liv recognised the tone. Hard and bright. As if Seamus were a hapless student on work experience. She had heard it a lot out of her own mouth those first few months of Shay's life. It was soothing to hear it from Ruth; it gave Liv a rush of fellow feeling. At least, that was what she later blamed for her impulsive offer.

'You're welcome to stay with us if you like?'

'Thank you, but we couldn't possibly impose,' Ruth said.

It was a clear opportunity to undo her rash offer. But there was Ruth being so damn *nice.* And those two little girls. 'No imposition at all,' Liv said, waving her hand as if to invite her ex and his new family to stay were the most normal thing in the world. 'We have the space, as it happens.'

'That's very kind of you,' Ruth said. 'We'd love to.'

She didn't even pretend to look towards Seamus for approval.

Out in the corridor, Liv leaned against the wall and wondered if she was sadistic or masochistic. Marianne would know.

When she got down to the hospital lobby, Seamus was

there before her. His face was pink, and he was out of breath, as if he had run down the four flights of stairs from his mother's room.

'What the fuck, Livvie?'

'Excuse me?'

'You can't tell her. It would ruin everything.'

Liv looked at him. Did he really think so little of her? 'I have no intention of telling Ruth anything. I prefer to keep my private life private.'

'Thank you.' He was so relieved he took a step towards her before thinking better of it. 'You're a star, Liv. You've always been my... well, I don't have to tell you.'

He would never change, Liv reflected, as she walked to the car park. She had the strangest feeling that she could have told Ruth everything and she wouldn't even blink. The woman happily accepted her offer of room and board; she clearly didn't see Liv as any kind of threat. Liv didn't know whether to laugh or cry.

'What on earth possessed you?' Marianne said when Liv told her.

'That is exactly the word for it. It was like I was possessed.'

'Couldn't be.' Marianne shook her head. 'Ethel put the rowan branch under both our pillows. This is all you, you eejit.'

'It seemed like the right thing to do!'

'Was it the right thing or you trying to make up for a wrong thing? For yourself and Seamus still—' she made an 'o' with her finger and thumb and Liv reached to grab her hand before she could go any further. 'Making the beast with two backs?'

'There's something about hospital rooms. Some kind of voodoo that suspends normal social rules. It must be to do with the way time slows down there—'

'Stop trying to turn it into a sociology lecture,' Marianne said. 'That won't undo the fact that you slept with her husband not a wet week ago and now you're installing her down the hall, like something out of a French farce.'

'He's in my life, Mar. We share a child.'

'Don't give me that,' Marianne scoffed. 'Why on earth did he agree to it?'

'He didn't really have a say. I asked her and she answered. We sort of bypassed him.'

'I bet he loved that,' Marianne snorted.

Liv felt a giggle bubbling up her throat. 'What am I going to do?'

'Whatever you're going to do, you'd better start doing it,' Marianne said unsympathetically. 'There's the doorbell now.'

Liv opened the front door with her warmest smile, nearly blinding Paddy Hanley with the force of it.

'Liv. It's a long time since anyone looked that happy to see me.' He patted the old collie by his side. 'Other than old Buddy here.'

'Paddy Hanley,' Marianne said, appearing behind Liv. 'We were only talking about you earlier.'

'Is that right? Should we be worried, Buddy? What do you think?' The dog grunted and sat down on the doorstep.

'We were talking about everyone who moved away,' Marianne continued easily. 'Liv mentioned you came back at weekends to help your father.'

'I'm back for good, actually. Dad is pushing on a bit. He finds the night-time callouts hard going, but sure you can't ask a calving cow to wait for morning.'

'Did I hear you were engaged?' Marianne asked, tilting her head to one side.

It was her own fault for telling Marianne anything, Liv decided. First and last time she would make that mistake.

'Not any more,' Paddy said. 'We tried it, but she didn't take to the place.' He glanced at Liv.

'There's no pleasing some people,' Marianne agreed. 'Will

you come in for tea? Or something stronger?' She paused, then added, 'Or do you still avoid liquids after lunchtime?'

Liv wondered what the odds were that the floor would open up and swallow her. Sinkholes left and right, the world over, but none when you needed one.

Paddy laughed. 'Do you hear them, Buddy? If you were a few years younger, you'd be defending my honour, wouldn't you, boy? Poor old fella, he isn't able for much of a walk, but he likes to pretend he's keeping an eye on things.'

He hardly had one foot in the door when Seamus' car swung into the drive.

'Paddy Hanley. Long time no see.' The two men exchanged that sort of handshake, shoulder slap thing that men did. To see them, anyone would think they were friends. 'What has you all the way over here?'

The cheek of him, Liv thought. As if he had any say in who came and went from her home. With a sinking feeling, she realised that if he believed he did, it was only because she let him think he still had a stake here.

'Seamus and his—' she began, but Paddy cut across her.

'I was looking for Shay, actually,' he said. 'I'm looking for someone to do a few hours at weekends and I heard he was good with animals.'

Liv was taken aback. 'That's very kind, Paddy. I'm sure he'd love it. He's out at the moment, I'm afraid, but I'd say he would take the hand off you for experience like that.'

'What about his exams?' Seamus reminded her.

'The exams are not the be-all and end-all,' Liv snapped. 'It would be good for him to do something he loves.'

'He can give me a ring when he gets in. Or have him drop down to the practice – I'm there most evenings. I'm late now, as it happens. Come on, old fella, let's leave these people to their evening.'

'I'll grab the bags and follow you in, Livvie,' Seamus said.

Liv slumped against the door.

'So that's Paddy Hanley 2.0,' Marianne said, watching

him walk down the drive at Buddy's slow pace. 'You could do worse.' She nudged Liv and gestured towards Seamus. 'You have done worse.'

'Same room as last time?' Seamus asked as Liv followed him into the hall. 'You mean my room?' she said.

Seamus caught her arm and pulled her into the front room, closing the door so they couldn't be heard. 'Is this some kind of trap? You said you wouldn't tell her.'

Liv looked at him. 'Tell her what, Seamus? What would I be telling her, exactly?'

'Don't give me that. You know—'

She held up a hand. 'That's it exactly. I know. The question is whether *you* know. What am I to you, Seamus?'

He looked at her, his mouth open in fright. 'You know what you mean to me. We're hardly dewy-eyed teenagers that need to…'

'I'll tell you, shall I? I'm a comfort. I'm a memory of who you used to be.' *When you were younger, thinner, fitter*, she didn't add. Seamus visiting her on his weekends home from university. Sitting in this very room – she could weep at the sad symmetry of it – telling her stories about freshers' week, his new digs. Lectures and new friends. Each of them more interesting than her, Liv thought miserably, as she shuffled Shay from one enormous breast to the other, feeling bovine and stupid. She said little. What new experiences had she worth sharing? Shay drank and slept and shat. What was there in that to interest someone living in the city? 'We outgrew each other a long time ago, only we hadn't the sense to realise it.'

'That's not… We're Shay's parents,' he said.

'We are,' she agreed warmly. It cost her nothing to be kind now. 'Shay's parents. That's exactly what we are. That's all we are.'

FRIDAY

ETHEL

She had to do the therapy, they told her. Or what? she said, but they had no answer to that. Other than the one she already knew.

She returned to her crossword. *Salt, dry or smoke (4)*. Even the fucking crossword was against her.

They couldn't hold her longer than the month, that was the truth. In fact, when it came down to it, they couldn't hold her at all, not without her say-so. That little reminder put manners on them. No matter that the girls delivered her here, she was free to walk out on her own two legs any time she pleased. They didn't need to know that any time she was on the verge of doing it, the thought of Shay's little face stopped her. She had given him enough lectures on persistence down the years. *Growth mindset*, Olive corrected her, when really it was just persistence, the same as it ever was.

He was a quiet one, Shay was, but deep with it. He reminded her of Martin, God rest him. He had that same way of observing things. In her first week here, when sleep was hard to come by, Judith appeared in her room one afternoon, holding the copy of *Moby Dick* she had given Shay last year when he failed the Leaving. She wasn't supposed to say it like that, she knew, but in the privacy of her own head, who was there to give out to her? She had given it to the girls as teenagers, but neither of them took to it. There was something in that, if she had a mind to think it through. It wasn't to be a lesson in perseverance, she told Shay – she was barely out the door of Willowbrook after a particularly short stint, so she was sensitive to the perceived value of sticking with it – but rather about how there was a lot of world out there to see if a person had a mind to see it.

It was a long time since anyone had given her a book. As a child, there was neither money for books nor interest in them. The occasional *Reader's Digest* appeared in the house, whenever the priest called to her mother's sick bed. Saintly, he called her, his face somehow greedy for the yellow glow of her suffering. He had no time for her father, walking past him where he sat by the range with his two hands tight around the glass. Afterwards, Ethel used to wonder what might have happened if things were the other way around. If her father's liver had been the one to sicken and her mother the one to decide life was no longer worth living. There would have been no unconsecrated grave for her mother, she was sure of it. Priests had affections like anyone else.

The *Reader's Digest*s were typical of the man. Mean-spirited and dry. Young Ethel could never shake the feeling that all the good bits were taken out. They seemed to be all moral and not enough world. When she and Martin returned from their honeymoon, after carrying her over the threshold, he carried her right back out again and into town to sign up for a library card. She signed her new name and swore to herself she would never go back. Christmas and birthdays, there was always a new book propped beside her breakfast. Later on, she got cute and had a chat with Noeleen in the bookshop, giving her a list of things she wanted to read so that the woman could gently steer Martin when he came in.

At Noeleen's funeral, the local councillors hoisted the coffin onto their shoulders as if she was an election winner, before lowering her beneath a dry Bible quote the woman would have hated. They had laughed together, once, about a headstone in a book that said the person had lived 'A quiet life of extensive usefulness'. Wouldn't it have tickled Noeleen to be looking up at that?

But people starved and drowned in the gulf between what they deserved and what they got.

She opened the cover of the book to find a note stuck into it. *'Gran. Sometimes it is about perseverance after all. Sorry it's a bit messy. Love, Shay.'* For a minute she thought he meant her being in Willowbrook, but it turned out he had underlined bits as he went along. It made her heart thrill a little whenever she turned a page to find his pencilled lines. These, then, were the things that mattered to him. *The interesting ones are like islands, he said; you don't bump into them on the street or at a party, you have to know where they are and go to them by arrangement.* Where would he seek out interest, she wondered. If he was leaving, where would he go?

Away from the house where she, succubus that she was, had traded his freedom for her own. There was only so much bad behaviour one house could hold, and she had hoarded it for herself. That was an end to it now, she told herself. Her go was over. It was Shay's turn now, to do with what he would.

Inevitably, some of them broke her heart. *That is always a dangerous moment, he said, to make a big decision, when you are not sure of what you deserve.* You deserve the world, she wanted to tell him. Sure he was too old to believe that fairy tale any more.

She sighed and returned to her crossword as the others filed out of one room only to go and sit in another. She could hardly leave it unfinished.

C-U-R-E.

SATURDAY

MARIANNE

All day, Marianne felt odd little shivers and the urge to look over her shoulder. Someone was walking over her grave, she thought. It should be easy to pass it off as superstitious silliness. But. But. It wasn't like she thought Fred Stille was haunting her, that would be ridiculous. Just because he spoke to her, really spoke to her, in life didn't mean he had anything to add in death. Google offered no help at all. All it offered her was so-called Confucian wisdom: *respect ghosts and gods but keep away from both*. 'I'm fucking trying,' Marianne muttered.

'Do you believe in ghosts?' she asked Ed when he picked up the phone. Several unhelpful minutes later, she hung up. Alive is alive and dead is dead. No in-between. That was comfort in Ed's world. To be fair, he had offered to come down for the weekend – a generous suggestion, given that this was his rostered Saturday to work. Anyone but Ed would have had their arse in the car the minute they heard Seamus and the new family had descended on the place, but gawping at others was never Ed's style.

The previous evening, having expected to be fascinated by the Liv-Seamus-Ruth triad, Marianne was surprised to find her attention drawn to the two little girls. How ironic that Seamus should be the one to copy their family, when he had run a mile from being any part of it. The truth, of course, was that the twins were exactly as self-centred and dull as all little girls, except in duplicate. Looking at them, she wondered if people had thought the same about herself and Marianne at that age. But, she reasoned, Ethel had had more sense than to dress them alike. The appearance of Shay, however, lit them up like sparklers.

'This is our brother Shay,' Tessa told Marianne solemnly.

'I know, pet,' she said and felt like crying at the simple truth of it. He took them seriously, listening to their questions and nonsense, before producing a deck of cards and teaching them to play Patience.

Ruth herself was brisk and warm, like Liv. Unlike Liv in that she let Seamus away with nothing. She spoke to him kindly, as if his efforts were the best that could be hoped for rather than anything of value in themselves. Marianne observed them and wondered, as she did with all couples, if that was what herself and Ed sounded like to other people.

Liv seemed lighter in herself, moving from here to there, brewing tea, pressing coffee, keeping the chat going whenever it threatened to flag. Maybe her sister meant what she said and she really was finished with Seamus, finally.

Marianne yawned and stretched, fiddling with her phone and hoping the conversation around her would shift her thoughts in another direction. Pauline, schools, ace of spades, vaccinations, the weather, black seven on red eight, carbon tax, Pauline, hospital, trolley crisis, king starts a new column, Pauline again. She scrolled idly through her contacts, pausing, as she often did, at her dad's phone number. Ten years later, she still transcribed it carefully into each upgraded phone. A tiny written record of him, even if it no longer worked. For the first few weeks after his death, she called it regularly to hear his voice. Not so much a message as his voice saying 'Martin' and then the beep. Whenever she tried to phone it now, an automated voice simply told her that the number was no longer in service. It was a relief, every time, to know that his number was not still out in the world, having a whole new life without him.

Ethel phoned rarely, although she made a point of calling Marianne first thing on the morning of their birthday, before she left her room or saw Liv. It was touching that her mother remembered how those three extra minutes were a source of glee to Liv, as the older of the two, and how much Marianne hated them.

Gracie glanced at her and smiled shyly. That same chill stole over her. Somewhere there was a family or stepfamily – what the Scandinavians, bless their jumper-loving hearts, called a 'bonus family' – sitting around a table, drinking tea and waiting for Fred Stille's real name to appear on their mobile screens. For his trilby to appear around the lip of the door. For his gentle wisdom. The thought was unbearable.

It wasn't so much the idea that life was short that drove her to her feet, as the certainty that life was shitty and people had no business making it worse. 'No business at all,' she said aloud.

Liv glanced up at the sudden parting of chair and table.

'I need to go and see Ethel,' Marianne said, breathless as if she had been running. Please, she begged her sister silently. Please don't offer to make a call, to intercede on my behalf so that I can see her. Don't make a power play out of it. Just this once, let me be a local too.

Liv nodded. 'I'll keep a plate for you,' was all she said.

'I'm making a break for it, Judith,' Marianne heard her mother say as she followed the nurse down the hall to where Marianne waited for her in the lobby.

Judith smiled. 'Break all you want as long as you know you'll pay for it.'

'In blood, I suppose,' Ethel said and wiggled her eyebrows at Judith.

There was an ease to it that surprised Marianne.

An ease that vanished when it was just the two of them.

Ethel seemed thin and a little impatient. Marianne told herself that it wasn't unwelcome. Anger meant that things could just fly out of mouths. Ethel in polite mode would have required subjects to actually be broached, and Lord knew that wasn't either of their strong suits.

Ethel hummed under her breath as they circled the front garden, then the slightly larger back garden. No wonder they died young in Victorian times, Marianne thought, if this was the extent of their cardio. She drew in a breath and let it out, over and over, until she was nearly dizzy. At this rate she would be climbing back into her car with an earful of Leonard Cohen and everything important left unsaid.

'I need to talk to you about something.' There, it was said. There was no going back now.

Ethel kept walking.

'Are you not going to ask what it is?'

Ethel sighed. 'You're not a child, Marianne. If you have something to say that you believe is worth disturbing the peace, then I can't stop you.'

Without having said a word yet, Marianne felt she was already on the back foot.

'Liv told me about the B&B,' she began. 'That you're leaving it all to her.'

Ethel said nothing, just continued to look into the distance.

The calmness was unnerving. 'Why did you cut me out?' Marianne was forced to ask at last.

Ethel nodded slowly. 'I can see it might look like that.'

'How else would it look?' Anger stirred now, stretched and rolled over.

Ethel crouched and deadheaded an unsuspecting flower. 'Do you remember your father's funeral?'

'Of course.'

'For the few days you were at home you were like a hunted rabbit, forever looking for a hole in the ditch to scramble through. I sat and listened to you arguing that we should roll the rosary and removal in together to shorten the whole thing. Don't get me wrong.' She rose suddenly and put her hand on Marianne's arm. 'It's not a criticism. God knows it was a hard few days. But I carried it with me afterwards, the scared little face on you. How trapped you felt here.'

Marianne didn't come home much after the funeral, it was true. 'I couldn't bear seeing the spaces he used to fill,' she said.

'None of us could,' Ethel said.

How had she never considered that her mother and Liv had to confront those spaces every morning, every day? But, surely, then, they should understand exactly what the place meant to her.

'Let me guess: you thought that the best way not to "trap me" was to "set me free"?' Marianne found herself doing air quotes. Shay would cringe on her behalf if he saw her.

'Don't be trite,' Ethel said sharply. 'I knew if I willed it to you both, then it would be sold. You don't want to live here and Liv will never afford to buy you out. It would have split the two of you for good. That's every mother's nightmare. Happiness for one at the expense of the other.'

Not this again. Her mother was always overly invested in her and Liv being friends. As an only child – and thus with no benchmark – she misunderstood the vital point that siblings were a different category entirely. But surely even her mother had to see that this decision would fracture them just as badly.

'That's convenient,' Marianne said. 'If it was all out of some sort of good wish for me, why didn't you discuss it with me?'

'It was none of your concern until after I was gone,' Ethel said smartly.

'Or you were drunk when you decided,' Marianne shot back.

Ethel crushed the deadheads in her hand, rubbing the

pieces between finger and thumb and letting them fall to the ground. For a moment, Marianne thought she would deny it. Or turn away and refuse to say anything at all.

'Do you want me to say that anger might have been part of it? All right, it might have been,' Ethel said at last.

'I knew it!'

'It shouldn't have been. I didn't think it was at first. I told myself I didn't expect you to stay any longer after the funeral. You had a life to get back to. We all did. Wouldn't I have been the hypocrite to be running around after guests myself but expecting you to put everything on hold.' There was no trace of humour in Ethel's laugh. 'Without Martin, we were a man down, already at half mast. The two of you only have each other, but you refuse to see it. The minute you hit fifteen, that was it, you were like two north poles on a magnet. So you can ask: was I angry? Of course I was. It was a waste… a criminal waste. What I wouldn't have given for a sister to…' Ethel let whatever else she might have said tail away on the breeze.

'We might be closer than you think.' Marianne was surprised at the depth of truth she felt in it.

Ethel shook her head. In the light, she looked tired and Marianne wondered if her mother was getting any sleep.

'I'll change the will,' Ethel said. 'You can fight it out between you after I'm gone.'

'You don't have to—'

'Sacred heart of Jesus. You were the same ever. Always wanting what you didn't have and having what you didn't want.'

The criticism stung. 'You'd want to think hard about telling anyone else how to live their life,' Marianne said.

'Enough.' Ethel held up a hand. 'We'll say nothing of any use now.'

They walked to the door in silence and buzzed to be let in.

'Back so soon?' Judith enquired. 'We can't be all bad, so.'

'I heard there was lemon meringue pie tonight,' Ethel said. 'I couldn't have it on my conscience to let you eat my share.'

'Your conscience has more to worry about than my waistline.'

Marianne listened to the warmth of their laughter as she made her way back out to the car. Whatever she herself was doing with Ethel, she was clearly doing it wrong.

'How are you, Marianne?' Alan said, looking up as the door opened.

'Spare me the hypocritical pleasantries.' Marianne placed her hand on the bar counter and was surprised to see that it was trembling. Out of the corner of her eye she saw the man at the end of the bar swivel to look at her.

'Something I can do for you?'

His measured tone was a red rag to a bull. If he thought he could humour her, he had another thing coming.

'I'm more interested in what you've already done,' Marianne said through clenched teeth.

'I don't follow you.' Alan stopped, the cloth in his hand.

'*I don't follow you,*' Marianne imitated him. 'Let me spell it out: you're a vulture. You prey on vulnerable people. People with problems. You promise them... what? Solutions? Peace? Forgetting? They sell their souls to you, *and you let them.* You make me sick.'

Alan waited until she was finished. 'I understand that it's difficult to see someone you love in a tough spot.' He leaned forward, his voice low. 'But this bar is my business. What people choose to do with their own lives isn't.'

'Are you pretending you think it's that simple?'

'It is that simple. People are responsible for their own choices. It might be a nanny state out there.' Alan pointed to the door. 'But not in here.'

'Tell yourself whatever you need to be able to sleep at night,' Marianne said, with less conviction. She was starting to have an uncomfortable prickle of recognition that Alan's argument was one she herself frequently made.

'People make their own choices,' Alan repeated.

Marianne stumbled back to the car, her eyes filling with tears. She drove fast, back out of the village, one hand drumming the steering wheel. Was her mother right? Was this who she had chosen to be? Someone perennially dissatisfied with her life, with her family, with Ed? What had her choices given her, after all, compared to what they had taken away?

The car was too small to hold that realisation. Marianne pulled in to the verge and got out, walking a careful hundred yards back the way she had come, then hunkering down in the grass. Anyone driving past would think she was having a piss on the side of the road. Let them. She had bigger things to worry about. She had spent years, it suddenly felt like, simply being glad that she hadn't ended up like her sister. Every decision subconsciously weighed to make sure it differed from the one Liv would make. Leaving. Travelling. A career trajectory. The morning-after pill any time there was any doubt. That one time there was a missed period, then, after two weeks of freezing fear, an unusually clumpy one. What if her body had been telling her – back when there was still time – that this was not for her? What if she tried to get pregnant now and the same thing happened? Atheist though she was, she sometimes couldn't shake the thought that God not only existed but also was designed in the mould of the meanest kind of uncle. The kind that laughed at you rather than with you. The kind of too-late-tough-luck merchant you were expected to be a good sport about, to give a wry shrug and accept it as your due.

A carload of teenage boys drove by, blaring the horn and leering. Mercifully, their suggestions were blown away by the wind. No good decision was ever made on the side of the road. Marianne walked slowly back to her car, climbed in and drove home.

SATURDAY

ETHEL

What's your story? Share your story. A story told is a burden shared.

The story this, the story that. Jesus wept. Or he would have if he had to sit in therapy sessions. Ethel had no choice but to walk out. They'd want to have a think about their obsessive interest in the past, she told them. If it was the roots of the thing they were after, they could find her in the garden. Burying her daughter's words, not that there was any need to tell them that. 'We'll say nothing of any use now,' she had told Marianne, sending her back into the world without a tot of comfort. She had better not die on the road home, Ethel thought and crossed herself quickly lest the thought find a rogue angel to carry it out.

Judith let her rant for a minute or two before unlocking the door to the cleaning supplies press. There it all was, the bucket, gloves and trowel, just as she left it. The man that came once a week to tend the grounds had his own tools. These were Ethel's.

A garden was a life's story. When the girls were small, she had tried to interest them in the *Gaofar* garden, but neither of them had time for it. Marianne would start with enthusiasm and plans greater than whatever she was asked to do, only to wander away after five minutes to go and join her father. (*Or you were drunk when you decided.*) Olive would stick with it, even when it was increasingly clear that any interest she had was gone and she was only doing it to please. She put up a half-hearted battle when Ethel told her she could go on and play. That was nearly the most thankless part, having to talk her into stopping.

It was a pleasure to tend to the garden alone. To put her hands into the soil and know that it promised nothing and hid nothing. You got out of it what you put in, simple as that. It was, she often thought, the only honest place left. Everywhere else, time played tricks, frightening people with its stretching and contraction. Its steely intent. Perhaps that was where humans had gone wrong. When they turned time into God and imagined themselves under its immovable thumb day upon day. Where had that led, only to stress and Botox and engineering dogs so as to have to hoover less. Sometimes at night, Ethel lay in bed listening to her roommate snoring and wished for a blast of holy light and a bit of irritable smiting. A God who was appalled at how far out of hand things had got, now that was a God she could get behind.

She sat back on her haunches and looked at the bucket of weeds. It was only half-full, her punishment for lollygagging. That was her mother's word, the emphasis always on the second syllable, making the word more peculiar in her mouth. If it was a story they wanted, she had plenty of tales of nights counting her mother's breaths, of bloody washcloths and worse, of watching her body, a strange hot flag of yellow and red. The husk and the empty gasp of her. But Ethel didn't care to relive it.

Besides, a story – a real story – was nothing without a little flair, a soupçon of drama. The slow drop-by-drop death of one country woman didn't hold up in story terms.

She could tell them about the summer of the moving statues, a time that seemed to consist solely of long evenings and limitless possibility. The B&B was open two years by then. Without the internet, they were dependent on word of mouth and she wasn't sure there were enough mouths to talk about *Gaofar*. But even if they weren't ever full, it was clear after the first few months that there was enough demand to keep them going. Willowbrook drew people from far and near, their relatives anxious to stay a night or two nearby to check them in or out. Or to accommodate the duty visits. It was doing well enough for Martin to settle into the leisurely afternoons reading the paper, for the creases to disappear from his forehead. Well enough that he stopped sighing after his farm and went back to patting her on the behind when they passed one another in the hall.

The week after the first sighting of the statue moving, every room was booked, with as many squeezed in as each family could bear. Nobody believed a word of it, of course. Rumour had it one poor woman, Patsy – one of the Mullinses, three girls and none of them ever married – was reduced to tears more than once by questions about what she might or might not have been drinking on the night in question. By the second week, even the hard-core naysayers were keeping their mouths shut and their pockets open.

She held out for a few days, withstanding Marianne's pleas and then Liv's. 'I don't care what everyone else is doing,' she told them. 'I'm not racing over to the grotto on the say-so of some poor gligeen.'

Eventually, though, Martin pointed out that if they went once, that would be an end to it and life could go back to normal.

The whole village was out. It reminded her of the annual threshing festival at home, when her parents still had the farm.

'You'd think the novelty would have worn off by now,' she said to Martin as they passed bus after bus parked with their left-hand wheels tight into the grassy bank so that things didn't grind to a halt altogether.

He laughed and tucked her arm into his. 'A moving statue

never grows old. In twenty years' time, we'll still be talking about it, you wait and see.'

As buses continued to spill out their mixes of the hopeless and the hopeful, the girls grew restless. Marianne asked several times to go and join the group of children loitering on the edges of the crowd, who showed every sign of looking for any devilment that was going. 'I'll be just over there,' she kept insisting, until Martin gave in and said yes. Olive, by contrast – and was there any other way with twins, Ethel wondered – was pettish, taking hold of Martin's two hands to swing from them, causing him to let go of Ethel's own hand. He let them walk all over him.

Sheila Dillon came over, towing a little fellow in shiny shoes, who turned out to be her fiancé.

'This is Dermot,' she said, pulling him forward.

She all but put his hand out for him, Ethel thought, making a mental note to say it to Martin later.

'Martin, Ethel. I see ye've met Tiny,' old Mr Dillon boomed, coming over to join them.

'Dad,' Sheila hissed. 'His name is Dermot.'

'Great crowd out,' Martin observed, glossing over the awkwardness.

'Business is booming, right enough,' said Mr Dillon.

'We're booked out,' Sheila said grandly. 'In fact, I meant to phone to say that we'd be pleased to send some clients your way any time we're full.'

'We're full as well, as it happens,' Ethel said. 'Right through into next month, actually.'

'No room at the inn,' Martin added. 'Not even for herself.' He nodded at the statue of Mary.

'Isn't that something! You might recommend us for a bite to eat if anyone asks,' Mr Dillon said. 'Us local entrepreneurs have to stick together.'

'He was a gentleman ever,' Martin said when the Dillons had moved on to the next group.

'Tiny is right,' Ethel said. 'He's hardly five foot in his socks. And timid, to boot. She'll eat him without salt.'

'Some men like that.' Martin nudged her gently to let her know he was joking.

Father T raised his hands for quiet and, once the hush fell, began to roar out the rosary.

When he finished – without hide nor hair of any movement from the Virgin – the crowd was inclined to linger. Johnjoe threw up the shutters of the chip van and a shout of approval went up. It was like a wedding, Ethel thought, only without the speeches and tight shoes. As the smell of hot grease began to pump out the back of the van, Ethel was glad when Martin suggested they buy burgers and make a picnic of their tea. Olive pulled at him, half-crying and wanting to go home. Ethel was annoyed. She had no intention of coming to the spectacle a second time and wanted to make the most of this one occasion.

'Could we let her run on home by herself?' she asked. 'She's nearly nine, sure.' Nearby, Tadhg Hayes overheard and offered Olive a lift home. He had a reputation for being handsy, but there was little enough harm in him, Ethel decided. 'You're very good, Tadhg, thanks. Off you go, Olive. We'll be on behind you in ten minutes.'

After half-eating her burger, Marianne ran off to play with the other children. While the little girls stood in gossipy groups, Marianne was busy jumping off the bridge wall with the boys. Ethel sighed. It wouldn't surprise her one bit if Marianne came home pregnant in another few years' time. She was altogether too interested in how much people liked her – that was never a good start for a girl. The trick was not to care. That was what kept a person out of trouble.

Beside her, Martin opened two cans of Coke and handed her one.

'Have you anything to liven it up?' he asked, nodding at her handbag.

Using his back as a screen, she added a shot of whiskey to each can.

'She's an awful woman, Martin,' a voice said behind her and she nearly jumped out of her skin.

Beside her, Martin laughed easily. 'Dr Nolan, Norah. Do you fancy a little drop yourselves?'

'A drop, so, thanks. To keep the wolf from the door.'

Ethel poured for them both. She could feel the doctor's eyes on her the entire time. The shamelessness of the man, with his brand-new wife standing beside him!

'Only a small one,' she said. 'The squad cars will be out in force tonight.'

'Don't mind them,' Dr Nolan said. 'They won't be stopping anyone tonight. They'll be too busy keeping the traffic moving to worry about a few sips of whiskey.'

'It would be a miracle itself if they bagged the doctor,' Martin added, and the two men laughed.

Ethel got up slowly, her knees stiff from kneeling, and emptied her bucket of weeds over the low wall that ran around the edge of the Willowbrook garden. It all felt so long ago now. Coolaroone's fifteen minutes of fame. It had driven poor Patsy Mullins around the bend. If she wasn't drinking at the start of that statue summer, she was surely drinking by the end of it. She could be seen weaving down the streets, accosting anyone who would listen to her worn-out story. Ethel met her a time or two here in Willowbrook, but she couldn't say she knew her as such. Like everyone else, she avoided poor Patsy. There wasn't enough patience in the world to listen to that every day. Last year, someone shopping in the city saw her queueing for the homeless shelter and, shortly after, her death notice appeared in the paper and on rip.ie. Did the Virgin Mary come to meet her at the gates of heaven? Ethel wondered. Did she stretch out her hand and say, *I was only waiting to meet you again, Patsy*? At the funeral, Ethel waited for the priest to say it, or something like it. The congregation would have lapped up that sort of sentimentality. But he missed his chance. It was hard to respect a priest that lacked a sense of occasion; there was so little else to the job.

The opposite could be just as bad. Her mother's funeral had been quite the display. The casual observer would have thought the priest was going to climb into the coffin himself, so extreme was his grief. Ethel's face darkened at the memory. And no drop of pity left over for her poor father. Him not even buried with her mother, after giving up his life for her, but out beyond the wall of the graveyard with the rest of the hidden. If Ethel were a man, she would have dug him up and moved him herself.

Was that what Fred Stille was about? she wondered. Maybe he just wanted to spare his family the shame of wanting to end things on his own terms. But to read the papers, it seemed that other countries had no such hang-ups. Human failings were simply another thing to be grieved and mourned, like every other loss. She should ask whatchamacallit, Marianne's fellow. He would know the lie of the land, being European himself. 'Himstregims,' she said out loud, for the pleasure the word gave her. A Danish traveller said it once as he tried and failed to remember the name for a travel iron. 'Contraption,' she told him. 'You know – a thingamajig.' And the pair of them stood and smiled at each other like eejits, delighted with their exchange.

The light was starting to fade. The afternoon had got away from her. The present swallowed up by the past, greedy little bugger that it was. Her stomach rumbled. Merciful hour, what she wouldn't give to be in front of Connie's chipper, queueing for a burger for herself and Martin. Connie shouting out the hatch, 'And was she dancing?' and throwing in an extra shovel of chips to anyone that said yes, yes, they had seen her move. Then, snapping open the can of Coke, adding the little drop. The sheer festivalness of it.

'Did it really happen?' was all the younger generation

wanted to know. Everything had to be about truth. As if what people saw wasn't a holy thing between them and their God. There were plenty of times in her life she saw inexplicable things. Sometimes it was the drink, sometimes it was just a feeling, call it loneliness or longing or need. If naming it calmed a person, then what of it. If it comforted a person, whose business was it.

'You've a fine job made of the rockery.' Judith had come out to call her in for supper. 'The place goes to rack and ruin without you.'

'Sure, why else would I keep coming back?' Ethel agreed, walking slowly up the path and back into the light of the hallway.

SATURDAY

LIV

If she were to die today – flip her car, say, or suffer a brain aneurysm, just go to sleep and never wake up – would Shay spend his holidays with Seamus and Ruth? Playing happy families with these little girls as if that was the way it was meant to be all along. If she was erased in the morning, what had she done, really, since that one shining decision nearly twenty years ago? If she was to stand alone in front of St Peter at the pearly gates, would she be nervous while he consulted his clipboard? As if it was once again lunchtime in primary school on a day that Marianne was at home on the couch, lapping up attention and flat 7Up.

'Liv?'

Ruth's voice startled her. 'I was miles away,' Liv said as brightly as she could.

'Are you all right?'

'I should be asking you that, with Mrs Lucey in hospital.'

Ruth raised an eyebrow and said in a low voice, 'You and I both know that if the shoe was on the other foot, she wouldn't spare a thought for me.'

'She always seems so fond of you,' Liv said. 'She talks about you a lot.'

'She does exactly the same thing to me. It's all Liv-this and Liv-that. *Isn't it a shame you don't have a more flexible job, like Liv?*' Ruth gave a shrug and a smile. 'She was wasted as a housewife. She could have been running a small country somewhere.'

Liv snorted a laugh. Of course she would let herself down in front of Ruth.

'Seamus told me about the guest you had that took his own life,' Ruth continued. 'What a terrible situation. Do you think he had family?'

Liv admired the crisp way she said it straight out. None of this *tragic situation* or *passed away* bullshit. She glanced at where Seamus and Shay sat playing Snap with the girls. 'I wish I knew. I'd like to tell them that it wasn't awful. That he seemed happy in his last few days.'

'Do you think maybe he was sick? Terminally ill or something?'

'That would certainly make it easier for the rest of us,' Liv agreed.

'Time does its own damn thing,' Ruth said, her eyes drifting to her girls.

Liv watched Ruth watch the girls. They had met several times over the years, of course. Short polite meetings with Shay at their centre. Looking at her now, it was hard to imagine that this was the woman whose death she wished, over and over, in ways both savage and unremarkable, for more years than she cared to admit.

'What is it like, being a twin?' Ruth asked suddenly.

Liv thought for a moment. About the closeness of their childhood. The drift in their teenage years. The loneliness of her father's funeral. *Marianne = gone*, written over and over on her shower door. All of it too private to share. 'As a child it was both comforting and frustrating. Marianne was always there, but she was *always there.* As an adult it's easier and trickier at the same time. People expect us to be closer than we are.' She turned to Ruth. 'That's not very helpful, sorry. I've never been anything else, I suppose, so I have no gauge.'

'I worry about them,' Ruth said simply.

Liv squeezed her shoulder in sympathy. 'I don't suppose you fancy something a bit stronger than tea?' she asked.

'I will if you will. Anything at all is grand. I'm not fussy,' Ruth said.

Ruth was lively company. Quick with an opinion – she spent a lot of time in the car listening to talk radio she said, drily, there was nothing she couldn't comment on, given the chance – but equally quick to laugh. They were halfway down the bottle when Marianne appeared, taking down an extra glass and pushing it towards Liv with an unsteady hand.

Shay disappeared with the girls to take Lucky for a walk and Marianne got up to open another bottle, pouring a good third of it into her glass and downing a large gulp. Liv frowned.

'Aren't you going to ask how it went with Ethel?' Marianne asked.

Liv noted the white of her knuckles on the glass, her glittering eyes. 'How is Ethel?' she asked, trying to keep her tone neutral. Nice though Ruth was, she would prefer not to look like a family straight out of some dysfunctional courtroom show.

'She's just fine and dandy.' Marianne drained her glass and reached for the bottle, emptying it into her glass and draining it again. 'She had a lot of interesting things to say, as it happens.'

'I'm sure she did.'

Marianne picked up the empty bottle. 'There's more, right? Now we've Ethel tidied away?'

'I think you might have had enough,' Liv said.

'She's afraid I'll turn into our mother,' Marianne said, turning to Ruth, her voice slurring slightly. 'Fuck you. Just because I had a drink in the playground doesn't mean I'm anything like her.'

'I didn't say—'

'You said nothing. But she said... SHE said...' Marianne wagged her finger in Liv's face. 'She said she didn't want me to be like her. That she was trapped. And you were trapped. Because of Shay and—'

'You know, I think we should head over to see Pauline again. Since we're here,' Ruth said loudly, waking Seamus from his doze. 'Liv, thanks for the chat.'

'You're very gracious. She's very gracious,' Marianne announced to Liv. 'Not cold at all, considering.'

If Marianne wasn't clearly past the point of feeling it, Liv thought, she would hit her over the head with her glass. It didn't help that Seamus was now smiling openly, clearly enjoying the spectacle. He wouldn't be so slow to get moving if he knew she had told Marianne about them.

'My pleasure,' Liv said, smiling through her teeth.

'My pleasure,' Marianne mimicked.

When the door was barely closed behind Ruth and Seamus, Marianne reached for Ruth's half-drunk glass of wine. 'You need to let her know that this is *your* house.'

'Are you making the point that it's not *her* house or that it's not *yours*?' Liv asked.

'Of the two of us, I think it's fair to say I have a clearer grasp on what is and isn't hers. Is that what you're doing? Opening your house to her because you opened your—'

'Don't,' Liv hissed. 'If all you're going to do is sit around in judgement—'

'*Me* judge people? Are you fucking joking? You sit here, doing the same thing day in, day out, never changing anything in case it doesn't all work out perfectly. What is it that you're so afraid of, Liv? It can't be life, because you haven't seen any of it.'

Marianne's words too closely echoed Liv's own fears of the previous day and she saw red. 'I've raised a fine man. I run a business. I am part of this community. *I* haven't seen any of life? You're a fine one to talk. Taking an obscene pay cheque for a job that adds nothing to the world and that you couldn't care less about. Stringing poor Ed along while you decide if you want him or not. But go ahead, oh wise one. Tell me all about the big bad world.'

The noise of the door stopped her in her tracks, and she sat down across from her sister, breathing hard.

'They're gone to see Grandma Pauline,' Shay said, coming into the room. 'Hi, Aunt Mar.'

'Shay. The very man. Do you want to run this place?'

'What?' Shay looked at his mother, confused.

'Mar,' Liv said sharply. 'That's enough. Shay, can you make a pot of coffee?'

'Let him answer. Ethel is giving him the place so I don't get it. It's a fair question.'

'What is she talking about?' Shay asked his mother.

Liv followed him over to the sink and began to fill the kettle. 'She went to see Ethel and there was some discussion about whether or not she should come home to run the place with me.' It was a truth of sorts, she told herself. She was hardly going to tell him the rest of it. What child could cope with that burden? It was one thing to read about children blaming themselves for their parents' unhappiness, quite another to have the proof of it sitting in front of you, as drunk as a lord.

'Is Marianne thinking of doing that, coming back here? Because that would be good, wouldn't it? For you, I mean?'

Jesus, he was planning on doing a runner the minute his exams were over. Liv tried not to panic. 'I'm fine with the way things are,' she said. 'I mean, I know that things will change once you finish school but otherwise…'

'I'll be like him,' Marianne announced from the table.

'Like who?' Shay asked.

'I'll be like Fred. Dead in a ditch where nobody knows me.'

'He wasn't dead in a ditch,' Liv said crisply. 'He made a

252

decision to end his life and he must have had a good reason for doing so. Just because we don't know what that reason is doesn't mean we can judge him or his life.' *Maybe he did something unforgiveable.* She pushed the thought away.

'I don't want him to end up like me.' Marianne frowned, unsure where the sentence had gone wrong on her. 'I don't want to end up like him,' she corrected herself.

'That will never happen,' Shay said. 'You have us and this place and—'

'That's just it,' Marianne said. 'I don't have this place, as it turns out.'

'Yes, you do,' Shay insisted. 'It wouldn't be home without you.'

His gentleness made Liv want to cry. This was what living here had taught him: how to be patient with drunk women. Of course, the bastards had no exam for that.

'Really?'

Marianne's face when she looked at her sister was the same face that used to wake her on Christmas morning, anxious that Santa had forgotten them.

'Really,' Liv promised her.

'I'm not Fred?'

Liv put her arms around her sister and spoke into her hair. 'You're not Fred. You could never be Fred.'

THREE WEEKS LATER
FRIDAY

MARIANNE

The road home was quiet. Rural quiet, not zombie apocalypse quiet. Marianne opened her mouth to tell Ed, but a quick glance showed her he was still scrolling on his phone.

'There are so many summer festivals,' Ed said. 'Not just music, but food, art, literature, the ocean, comedy. A weekend away is not going to be relaxing if we cannot find somewhere without a festival. Look! There is one for scarecrows. And bog snorkelling.'

'Who knew there were so many?' Marianne said, because it seemed an answer was called for. She knew, of course. So did pretty much anyone who listened to the radio from April onwards. Ireland was falling down with festivals.

'Matchmaking, camper vans, red-haired people,' Ed continued.

He had taken a half-day from work so they could beat the traffic out of the city. With the windows down and music playing, she drove through narrowing roads, the sun like a bold child, darting in and out from behind clouds and around corners. Marianne felt a little whoosh of warmth – and something else. Gratitude, maybe.

Ed yawned and stretched. 'Should we stop for something to eat before we get there? What time is the Month's Mind Mass?' He said it as three careful nouns.

'We have time,' she agreed. Would Fred, guest of honour at tonight's little shindig, have said it in a similar way? She didn't think so. Fred would have known that *Mass* was redundant. A month's mind only meant one thing.

They stopped at the next small café they saw. White walls, chairs in muted teals and greiges, extensive tea menu – it was straight out of a Scandinavian style book. It looked a little like Joely's Fish Bar, minus Bert and Ernie, of course. Marianne took a discreet photo to send to Liv. It really was uncannily similar.

'Do you want to go to *Gaofar* before the church?' Ed asked when they had ordered and sat down.

Marianne shook her head. 'I don't think there'll be time. It doesn't matter though, we'll have all weekend there. Liv said they still haven't had many bookings to replace the ones that were cancelled. She's a bit worried about it actually.'

Marianne had been surprised when Liv phoned the day after she left. Surprised and pleased. Since then, they had texted almost every day, Liv careful to update Marianne on the B&B and Ethel. Marianne, for her part, avoided any hint of proprietary interest that might threaten their return to daily closeness. Instead, she kept Liv apprised of anything interesting she came across on the Danish missing persons website. She was in the habit of checking it every morning while she had her coffee. In the evenings, too, sometimes, although she and Ed had agreed to be home for dinner together at least three midweek evenings.

'We drifted away,' he told her. 'A relationship is like a river. Even to stay in one place, you must keep moving.'

It wasn't a perfect analogy, but Marianne knew what he meant. On days when it seemed too organised, too effortful, the Danish website reminded her of how things could be. The rootlessness displayed there frightened her. How easily someone could slip free of everything that tethered them to life.

Marianne plucked a sugar cube from the bowl and let it dissolve on her tongue. Her father would turn in his grave at the idea. Sugar bowls were the next best thing to public toilets, as far as he was concerned. *Sorry, Dad.*

On the website, she was most drawn to the stories of people lost and – more rarely – found. She had posted a plea herself, underneath the photograph the guards had posted of Fred Stille, a still pulled from the CCTV footage in the town. For days afterwards, she would log on, heart hammering, hoping to see a response. So far, there was nothing.

When their toasties came, Ed took a huge bite of the scalding cheese. Marianne handed him her glass of water and watched him gulp it back.

'Will Ethel be at the church?' he asked.

'Yes. Liv said she would be.' Liv had also told her that she wasn't sure if that meant Ethel was finished with Willowbrook. 'Either way,' she had said – and Marianne could hear the effort at cheer in her sister's voice – 'she's almost at the end of the month. She's done far better this time than before. Maybe something you said got through to her.' A kindness, Marianne knew. If Ethel stayed, it was only because she chose to. Her own choice. Her own responsibility. Judith couldn't have been clearer.

'Did you find us a festival-free destination?' she asked Ed before he could say anything more about Ethel. The further from her mother she was, the fonder of her she felt.

Ed shook his head. 'I need to use the laptop to research properly. I will do it on Sunday night when we go home.'

Despite their best efforts, Marianne could still hear the quote marks around the word 'home'.

Time would either solve them or it wouldn't. Kill or cure.

The important thing was that the effort was real.

They got to the village a minute or two later than Marianne had planned. Dempsey Senior was stationed by the traffic lights, waving people into Hanley's field with large slow swings of his arms. No doubt Junior was at the other end of the street, doing the same for the southerly arrivals. This was where Coolaroone shone. In gentle minding. Fred had become something of a mascot, a chance for the village to show its goodness.

'I hope Liv kept us a seat,' Marianne said as they made their way to the church. If not, there was every chance she would get it wrong. She used to sit in the same seat every Sunday when they were growing up, but 'dibs' wouldn't cut it after nearly twenty years away. The day of her father's funeral was different. Her place was assured that day.

She stopped for a moment in the porch, letting her eyes adjust to the gloom. Sure enough, there was Liv, a respectable four seats from the front, waving discreetly. Shay was beside her, with Ethel next to him, on the inside by the wall where she could plausibly get away with nodding politely rather than talking to the neighbours. Marianne took a breath. It might just be all right.

She sat down and Liv gave her hand a brief squeeze. 'You okay?' she mouthed, and Marianne nodded.

The bell rang and Father Mike emerged from the sacristy. Marianne felt herself begin to relax. Much as she hated to admit it, the ritual was a comfort. You knew where you were with a Mass.

At the microphone, Father Mike was waxing lyrical. Not letting his lack of knowledge of Fred slow him down. 'None of us knows what Fred was seeking to move on from,' he said. 'Whether, indeed, he was just anxious to move on to the next adventure. Perhaps he was simply impatient to meet his Lord, or to catch up with a loved one gone before him.'

Dangerous ground, Marianne thought. Although it was a lot of years since she kept pace with the church, so perhaps suicide was no longer a mortal sin but more of a sign of eager devotion. She looked at Liv, but her sister's eyes were closed.

'We would all like to think that Fred, as he chose to be

known, found peace here among us,' Father Mike went on. 'That his last days were pleasant. That – if not enough to change his mind about the course of events he was bent on – it might nonetheless have given him a certain comfort to think that he might have been happy here. While we can wish that he had been more inclined to stay and find out, we have to believe that he was happy for the time he was here anyway. That's all we can hope for.'

To her horror, Marianne felt her eyes filling with tears. She reached discreetly into her pocket for a tissue: nothing. She made furtive pats at her two sleeves, in case she might have stuffed a napkin absent-mindedly up there in the restaurant but again, nothing. How noisy and obvious – how mortifying! – to have to unzip her handbag, remove the little packet, extract a tissue and wipe her eyes. People would think she was doing it for show. Ed's hand was a light pressure on hers as he passed her a tissue without saying anything. Marianne tried to think of other things. A weekend away would be nice. Maybe they should consider going further afield, a city break while they could still enjoy them. If they had a baby, that would take museums off the agenda for a while. She resisted the urge to look at Ed, to see if he had somehow heard her thinking it. It was only an idea, she told herself. One possibility among many. It didn't mean anything was certain.

She tuned back in to Father Mike in time to hear him answering her earlier question.

'I know what the Church teaches about the sanctity of life,' he said. 'But on days like this, I look out among you and see the goodness and kind thoughts that characterise so much of our lives together. I am reminded of the gentle Saint Francis de Sales, who said: "Be who you are and be that well." And if we think about it, isn't there a great self-respect in the idea that we can only be ourselves? If Jesus were to come among us today, then he might say – indeed, he might tweet – that we should be patient with ourselves. We should give ourselves time to be the best we can be. On days like today, we can all hold onto that. In Fred's name, I would like us all to take a moment now to think about ways in which we can be our better selves among those we love.'

Marianne bowed her head obediently, using the moment to withdraw her tissue discreetly from her sleeve and dab her eyes again. No matter how far she moved from the damage and rules of the Church, nothing could get to her like the simplicity and sincerity of individual belief. Father Mike would do well on a TED talk, notwithstanding the collective teenage stiffening up and down the rows at the idea of a tweeting Jesus.

Marianne risked a glance at Ethel, but her head was bowed, giving nothing away. It mightn't be the great sea change the priest had in mind, but with a little effort, she could, she thought, stretch to compassion, if not outright forgiveness.

With no graveside to keep them moving, people milled around the churchyard. This was the part Marianne dreaded. Ed was chatting to Joely's boyfriend – *don't think of him as the drug addict* – by the porch door, with every evidence of enjoyment. So much for not having to stand by herself. If Ed were to end up like Fred Stille, mourned by people who knew him for the shortest possible period, they would still know to put 'affable' on his headstone. But Ed would never end up alone. He liked people too much. And people liked him. Him and Liv, both. That made all the difference. She sighed. Kinder thoughts were hard to come by in a place where you knew you disappointed people. Where they looked at you as if they wanted Poirot but had to settle for Hastings.

'You look like you swallowed a wasp.'

Her mother's voice almost in her ear made Marianne jump. 'Hello, Ethel.' Compassion, she reminded herself. Kind thoughts. She tried again. 'How are you?'

'How are we all?' Ethel said.

What the fuck was she supposed to say to that? Marianne

wondered. What did it even mean? 'Taken up mysticism, have you?' she said lightly.

Ethel laughed and put her hand to one side, like a bird. 'I've missed you,' she said.

Marianne had the horrible thought that her mother was applying Father Mike's words right back at her. Even their two better selves were locked in battle.

'I've thought a lot about what you said that day you came to see me,' Ethel continued. 'I should have handled it better. I meant well, you know. In my head I was doing the right thing but… I don't know that I'm always calibrated the same as everyone else.' She shrugged. 'Especially not with the drink.'

It was as close to an apology as Ethel was ever going to get. 'It hurt,' Marianne said finally. 'It hurt to be told it wasn't really home.'

Ethel made an impatient little movement with her hand. 'You let it have too much power,' she said. 'We can talk about it someday. Nothing is irreversible.'

Marianne looked at her mother. She had put on a little weight and her eyes were very blue against her tanned skin. Maybe Fred was never given a second chance. Maybe he was given plenty only he used them all up. Maybe he didn't know to ask for one, or had nobody to ask. The only certainty was that the living had a whole lot more options than the dead. She nodded. 'Okay. We can talk about it some other day.'

It felt important to be the one to walk away. Three steps in, Marianne realised she had nowhere to walk to. Ed had disappeared and Liv was deep in conversation with Pissabed Hanley. Just as she was wondering if it would look awful if she went to the car, she saw someone waving at her. She made her way over. 'Ellen. Nice to see you again.'

'Despite the circumstances,' Ellen agreed.

She had said the wrong thing, Marianne realised. Made it sound like a social occasion instead of a quasi-funeral Mass for a man who had so little to live for that he spent his last days with strangers before walking into the lake.

'Any progress on finding our mysterious Fred?' Ellen asked. 'I heard yourself and Liv had no luck at the embassy.' Seeing Marianne's face, she shrugged and laughed. 'You know this place. If you sneeze in your own bathroom in the middle of the night, half the town asks about your cold the following morning.'

'I miss that sometimes,' Marianne found herself saying. 'I often think that I could be dead in my bed and none of my neighbours would notice anything amiss.' Shit, she thought, could she sound any more needy and pathetic.

But Ellen was nodding. 'I did a few years above in Dublin,' she said. 'The loneliness of it near about killed me. The day I finally had enough time done that I could put for a transfer was the best feeling in the world.' She gazed off into the distance. 'Better than sex.'

They were still laughing when Ed appeared. 'Even here, it is nice to see you, Ellen,' he said.

Ellen's face lit up and Marianne could see a reflection of the lonesome teenager she used to be. 'I was just telling Ellen we are no closer to finding out who Fred really was.' To Ellen she said, 'Ed here is very rational. He thinks that we need to respect Fred's choice to go the way he did.'

To her surprise, Ellen nodded. 'That's all we can do for him now.'

They chatted for a few minutes about this and that. Ellen told Ed a little about their schooldays, glossing kindly over the part Marianne had played in her misery. 'In a small place,' she said, 'sooner or later everyone has a turn being the laughing stock.'

'What a marvellous expression,' Ed said. 'At home we say "the piss-pole".'

Marianne watched as he chatted to Ellen as if they were old friends. With his arm around her, she was part of it. Folded into that indefinable ease he carried and brought to those around him.

Joely arrived beside them. 'Sorry to interrupt,' she said.

'You lot look like you're having the best time here though, so I'm not that sorry. What did I miss?'

Ed restarted his story of weird and wonderful phrases, leaving Joely and Ellen in stitches.

'Ellen, will I see you at the harvest festival planning meeting?' Joely asked when the hilarity had died down.

'We were just talking about all of Ireland's festivals,' Ed said, looking at Marianne. 'We were trying to choose the one that sounded the most interesting.'

'Look no further,' Ellen said. 'Ours is small and it's twee. The highlight is a procession to the grotto with everyone holding their Virgin Mary statue aloft. You won't know whether to laugh or cry.'

'I can help out, if you like?' Marianne found herself saying. 'If you need it. I mean, it's fine if you don't—'

'Special skills, quick!' Joely ordered. 'Although I warn you, no matter how weird it is, I'll take it. Last year we had a hula-hooping class with Tiny Dillon. It had to be seen to be believed.'

To a hammer, everything is a nail, Liv had said. Well, you know what, Liv, sometimes it is a nail. There are nails, too, in the world. She straightened her shoulders. 'No special skills, as such, but I work in PR, so I could help with branding, promotion, that sort of thing?'

Both women nodded enthusiastically. 'Brilliant. We need to inject a bit of life into it.' Joely lowered her voice. 'Father Mike has great intentions, but he's a bit inside-the-box about everything. Any help you can give us with Noah's Woods would be brilliant.'

'Noah's Woods?' Marianne asked.

'That's this year's theme. You know. Sunken forests? Uncovering hidden treasures right on your doorstep? That kind of thing. It had to be biblical to get Father Mike's approval, but really the metaphor works for everyone. The Catholics were always a dab hand at hijacking the best of pagan festivals. It's high time we returned the favour!' She took out her phone to type in Marianne's number. 'Last chance to bail... Once you're in the festival WhatsApp group, there's no way out, only feet first.' She clapped her hand to her mouth. 'Oh, God. There's me putting my foot in it again. Don't tell anyone I said that.' With that, she hurried away.

'I guess that means we'll be coming here for weekends during the summer,' Ed said as they walked back to the car.

'I'll have to anyway,' Marianne said. She thought about Ed's easy familiarity with Ellen, the way he lit people up by simply remembering them. 'But I would be very happy if you wanted to come too.'

Ed squeezed her hand. 'That's good to know.'

He was right, Marianne thought, as he reached to open the car door for her. It was good to know.

FRIDAY/SATURDAY

ETHEL

Ethel plucked at the nap of her sleeve. She wasn't used to being nervous, not here, in what was supposed to be her own place. The month in Willowbrook had done something strange to time, elongated it so that it felt like a lifetime since she had sat in this church. At least she had the sense to arrive early, knowing that the parish would be out in force. Coolaroone had always loved an underdog.

When Olive and Shay arrived, he hugged her before sitting down. Her beautiful boy. Olive patted her on the arm and told her she was looking well. As if she didn't know that 'looking well' was a synonym for fat. Going home might be looming alarmingly, but her daily walk around the lake would be a welcome return to herself. Parts of herself, at least.

Marianne gave her a nod as she was taking her own seat. That was all she had time for; she was barely in the door before the bell rang. She always liked to make an entrance.

Ethel listened and half-listened by turns, preferring to admire the light falling through the stained glass than focus too much on the rhythm of the Mass. In a certain light, she supposed Father Mike's words could be seen as a general call to goodness. But he missed the crucial point: if everyone was already assumed to be their best selves, what room was there for forgiveness? Judith, with her no-nonsense practicality, would know. She had driven Ethel here herself, dropping her at the church gate and waving away thanks. 'Honour the dead – it's all they have left,' she said, beeping the horn lightly as she drove away. That was the trouble with these kinds of Masses; they had to please everyone and offend no one. Ethel sighed again and Shay turned to look at her, his eyebrow raised. She shook her head slightly and smiled.

When Ethel emerged from the dim of the church, she gave herself a moment to adjust to the late evening sunlight. Around her, people stood in little clusters, chatting about this and that. If she wanted to, she could have joined any one of the groups and been assured a warm response. A discreet *welcome back* even. Marianne stood alone, in the shadows to one side, wearing her usual pained smile. She was a cryptic crossword in herself, Ethel thought. *Impenetrable to light = opaque.* She took a breath and walked towards her daughter.

'You look like you swallowed a wasp,' she said into Marianne's ear, making her jump. She realised the minute she said it that she should have opened with something a bit less likely to draw out her daughter's combative side. Marianne responded with some crack about yoga and Ethel was reminded of Martin telling her, years before, that Marianne had inherited her own sharp tongue.

'I've missed you,' she told her daughter and meant it.

She apologised for her bluntness the day Marianne had come to Willowbrook. It was, she realised only as she said it out loud, what she had come to do. Marianne wasn't ready to hear it and it was hard to blame her. Rejection – even largely imagined – was a hard pill to swallow. 'We can talk about it again,' she said finally and let Marianne be the one to walk away. It wasn't much to give her, but it was all she had.

Shay was easy to spot. All she had to do was scan the walls for a slouching figure. The weeds were gathering force, she thought. When she was back, she would have to come up with her bucket and trowel and sort them out.

She walked over to Shay. 'Will you give me a lift back?' she asked him. 'Spare your old Gran the shame of having to say *Willowbrook* to a taxi driver?' That was a lie. Judith had told her she was happy to come and collect her again. But it was Shay she wanted.

'Let me just get the car keys from Mum,' he said.

That was why the young were restful. They were sufficiently self-absorbed not to bother with anyone else's whys.

Naturally, the car keys came with a side of Olive herself. 'Why don't you come back to the house for a bit?' she asked, as if it were the most natural thing in the world rather than heart-stopping.

Because if I go home, I'll never go back, and it'll be just one more thing I left undone. 'One day to go,' Ethel said instead, as evenly as she could. 'I'd like to see it out.'

When they were safely out past the village bounds, Ethel turned to Shay. 'I am going back, I promise you that. But I need you to take me somewhere else first.'

The two-hour journey passed largely in silence. As they got closer, Ethel watched the landmarks pass by the car window.

'If we took a left at the crossroads, up that narrow road, it leads to the old stone school,' she told him.

Then, 'That small white cross marks where one of the Tom Pips was killed off a tractor.'

And, 'The bridge was where we used to meet the boys on summer evenings.'

When they were through the village itself, she directed Shay left, then right, then right again. 'Pull in here,' she said. She got out of the car, then turned and leaned back in. 'Are you coming?' she said.

'Give me half a minute,' he said.

She moved a few yards away and stood in the falling dusk,

266

pretending not to hear Shay on the phone to his mother. *Yes. Yes. We're at a graveyard, not a pub. Yes. I'll text you when we get there.* What did she expect? she asked herself sternly. Trust had to be earned back.

The graveyard had spread to take over Allen's field and the one beyond. To look at it, a person would be forgiven for assuming the village was doing nothing but dying. She found the headstone with surprising ease, her older legs following the path her younger legs had trodden days without number.

'Iris Ryan. 2 January 1920–14 February 1975. Beloved wife and mother. Whosoever believeth in Him should not perish but have eternal life (John 3:15). *Ar dheis Dé go raibh a anam dílis.*' Was her mother's faithful soul really at the right hand of God? If so, it was hard to picture. She reached out to stroke the stone. 'Hello, Mother. I'm sorry it's been so long since I visited. If St John was right, well, you know everything that's happened since. If you chance across Martin, tell him I hope to be a while yet.' She bowed her head and said a decade of the rosary, touched beyond measure at Shay's voice stumbling the words alongside her.

She took Shay's hand and squeezed it. 'You're a good boy,' she said when they finished the prayers. 'A good man. The best of them. Never let anyone tell you different, you hear me?'

'I won't, Gran,' he promised.

At the graveyard gate, Shay turned towards the car, but Ethel shook her head. 'One more stop.' She followed the graveyard wall, continuing on straight when it began to curl around to the right. A little way ahead, a gate was set into the ditch and she opened it without hesitating. If she stopped to think, she would lose her nerve entirely. Here, time had stood still, the little lost graveyard's failure to thrive evidence that humanity had at last come to the parish.

Her father's stone was small. 'Paud Ryan, 1915–1975' sandwiched between the dates of birth and death of six brothers and a sister, ghosts before she herself was ever made flesh. It was strange to stand there at last after spending years of her life avoiding it. Like a friend she had fallen out with, whose eye she couldn't catch lest the anger might eat her alive.

'They drank two farms between them,' she said, not looking at Shay. 'After my mother died – cirrhosis of the liver, they'd call it now – my father took his own life. He had a fit of depression, I suppose you'd say. He earned that fit, believe you me, my mother had a hard death. The parish priest refused to bury him next to my mother. Not only was it a crime, it was a mortal sin, and so he is out here in the killeen, with the sinners and sailors and suicides, the victims of murder and famine, the unbaptised and the excommunicated and whoever else the Church deemed unworthy of funeral rites. At the time I hadn't enough forgiveness in me to stay in a place that would do this to him. I hadn't enough sense to know it was a curse I should be on the lookout for.' She placed her hand on the rough edge of the stone. 'I'm sorry, Dad.'

This time it was Shay who started the decade of the rosary. Ethel let the tears fall while his voice rose in the gloom.

They were quiet on the road home. Ethel felt wrung out but didn't dare doze off. She wanted to keep Shay company. Or vice versa maybe. It wasn't until he drew up outside the front door of Willowbrook that she spoke.

'The girls don't know how my parents died,' she said. 'I know they should and I'll tell them when I'm able.'

He reached across and bumped his fist gently against hers. 'Okay, Gran.'

Ethel woke with her heart racing in her chest, her body clung to the sheets. She sat up against the headboard and breathed in-one-two-three-four and out-one-two-three-four, the way she had to at the start of the month here. Outside the window, the moon shone on the wet gravel, silver and black as a badger's fur.

There was no point in wondering what thoughts had driven her body to panic. The body – the mind, really – kept its own secrets. Martin used to have nightmares, whimpering and thrashing in the bed. She would lie her head on his chest and tell him it was just adrenalin. That in his dreams he must have been skydiving or bungee-jumping or publicly disagreeing with Mrs Dillon. How good it felt to make him laugh. She missed that trick he had of seeing the best in people. Of knowing that in life you could see something and not see it at the same time.

That Sunday morning was the last group session. Judith had told her that if she wanted to leave that evening, she had to attend even if she sat there like a stooge. Ethel smiled. Sure, what was society without a bit of agreed pretence? She tried to tune out the voices around her, thinking instead of the half-finished crossword in that day's paper. She might have another go at it later on, she decided.

She passed the time by counting the instances of blatant hyperbole from the younger members of the group. It was all 'devastating' this and 'profoundly' that. The closer they were to the end of the month, the more likely they were to be 'in awe of' everything, likely their own strength or humility, depending on how things were going. Sometimes both, in which case, Ethel was sure they would be back again before the year was out. It was hard to tell if they were incurably naive or persistently selling. Her generation didn't have the luxury of either and she was glad of it.

Not that her own cohort were any great shakes. If the youth were overburdened with the sense of their own importance, the old were increasingly desperate to matter in any way at all. Women overshared with the impatience of a child plucking at a parent's sleeve. The session passed with one after the other of them telling the most personal things, as if that would make a mark. See me, they all but shouted. See my pain. *See that my husband slept with our neighbour for a year after I had our third child and I said nothing. See that I kept a tidy house for many years, breaking my heart dusting and sweeping every day, and where is it now, my fine house? While I am in here, who is hoovering the carpet that I saved for two years to buy? See my children – no, you can't see them, because they don't come. I did that to myself.* One after the other, a litany of cries wheeling like seagulls through the air. Whoever it was that said that unhappy families were unhappy in their own way was wrong: other people's unhappiness was every bit as banal as their joy.

When it came to her turn, they were primed to give her the usual thirty seconds of silence before moving on to the next person. This time, however, she cleared her throat. 'Out our way, there's a walk around the lake. Many of you know it. Locals call it "the ring", although I don't care for that name. It sounds too hard for a place that's all softness. Even in the winter, the frost is eased for being near the water.' She looked at her hands in her lap so she didn't have to endure the surprised faces around her. 'There's an air of something about the place. Call it magic or mystery or God. You'd need to be Seamus Heaney himself to capture the essence of it. Anyway. It seemed fitting that the swans, when they came, were black rather than white. At once familiar and unfamiliar. They were a sight to behold. If I was on the way home after a skite, I used to wonder if I dreamt them.' There was a trickle of laughter around her, a flutter of recognition. 'The statue only moved for a few weeks, but the swans moved every day. They were something to hold to. It was a sad day for the parish when one was stolen away. We had TV news cameras down every day for a week and appeals for information, but no one ever found out what happened.'

'I remember that,' someone said and was quickly hushed.

'The one lone black swan swam up and down the same stretch of river every day, tracking to the left bank, the way I stuck to my own side of the bed after Martin was gone.

Everyone felt protective, but there was nothing to be done. Another swan was brought in, a white one, but the widow and widower kept their distance from one another – they weren't to be so easily manipulated just to make us feel better. After a while, the second black swan vanished as well. Some said they saw it heading for the sea.' She sighed. 'Swans can die of heartbreak,' she said. 'They know that some things are not easily fixed.'

They let the silence yawn.

'That's all fine and well,' someone said at last. 'But swans only live for twenty years. If we had that limit on marriage, we'd all be a lot more romantic about it.'

'We mightn't all be in here,' someone else added, to general laughter.

'What does that even mean?' one of the younger residents complained, but Ethel only smiled. She hadn't the time to be explaining the world to people. She had a home to go to.

After, there was a cake with candles. There always was, at someone's last session. 'Make a wish,' someone called.

She was supposed to wish for strength, she knew. Instead, she closed her eyes and wished that time might be kind to them all. That was the only thing worth a damn.

Olive was due to collect her that evening, but Ethel found it unendurable, the idea of an afternoon spent waiting. She had already cleaned her gardening tools and replaced them in the cleaning supplies press.

'The volume of goodwill in here is a threat to my sobriety,' she told Judith, who snorted and offered to drive her home. 'You've outstayed your welcome anyway,' she said, patting Ethel's shoulder.

When they reached the village proper, Ethel turned to Judith. 'Will you let me out here by the water? I'd like to clear my head before facing them.' Her hand, when she pointed, shook embarrassingly, but neither of them mentioned it.

'Tell me again: who are you doing it for? Don't mind rolling your eyes. Humour me, one last time. Who are you doing it for?'

'Myself,' Ethel said. Then, because she didn't want to send Judith away on a lie, she added, 'And Shay. Let him be the teenage stop-out for a while.'

'Go with grace,' Judith said, 'and this time, for the love of God, be a stranger.'

Beside the water, the aspens shivered, the sound a far cry yet from the shimmery chime they would achieve later in the summer. Legend had it that their wood was used to make Christ's crucifix and ever since they shook with shame at the part they played in it all. Martin used to say there was no truth to that story. Hell would have no use for aspen logs, he told her, sure they didn't burn worth a damn in the fire.

Ethel stopped to look over the water. At home, they would be changing sheets and airing rooms. Business was bad, Olive had said the day she visited Ethel, but it was bad before. Olive talked about 'weathering it', but that wouldn't do it. They would have to refuse the slump, do something to get the tourists back. There was no good waiting and hoping. Olive was the same ever, letting life happen to her, as if her future was all determined twenty years earlier. And Marianne, forever the opposite, making one wrong decision after the other. Boyfriends, hair colours, jobs, flats. Her two girls. The earth and the sea.

She sat on her bench and looked out over the water. A sleek head bobbed and she allowed herself to think it wasn't a duck at all but a man clothed in the water itself. She had seen Fred that final day and, in her mind, instead of turning in the gate for home, she accompanied him through his last morning. There were things to live for, she could have told him. Could have told her father. The future was never meant to be imagined.

A sudden breeze lifted the hair off the nape of her neck, bringing her back to herself with a pleasant shiver. Her blood was quiet in her veins. Along the water's edge, the moss was a shy green, bright and surprising.

'Beautiful afternoon,' she called to a woman passing by, but the woman was on her phone and said nothing in response. More fool her, to miss all of this.

'This place will outlive us all,' Ethel said and rose to leave.

SATURDAY

LIV

The Month's Mind left Liv restless. It reminded her of the weeks after Seamus got married, when everything felt like the end of the world. She struggled to get in the shower, even, so sure was she that Armageddon was upon them and she would have to face end times in nothing but a beige towel. Funny how she would rather die than tell him that but could easily picture confiding it to Ruth. Thank goodness for the merciful passage of time.

Rationally, she hadn't expected Fred's Mass to change anything. The chances of his lost family showing up just at the right moment were so slim as to make the cutting room floor of even the hammiest drama. Yet with the Mass over, she felt something unknot and come loose inside her. Maybe it was waiting for Ethel that was unsettling her. Against the odds, she had made it through the month and while no guarantee of any lasting change, that surely meant something in itself. Shay had shared little of their mysterious road trip on the way back to Willowbrook, except to say that Ethel had wanted to visit her parents' graves. She was a bit upset, he said, and seemed to regret not having gone back sooner. Liv wanted to probe, to find out exactly where they had gone, what had been said, but she didn't like to ask him to break Ethel's confidence. Their relationship was theirs to mind. If it had survived the worst of Ethel's excesses, then Liv wouldn't be the one to damage it.

She paused, her index finger poised above the shower door. She wanted, powerfully, for Ethel to be home. For it to be a week from now, a month, a year. To know how it would all work out. The B&B was slowly picking up and she had a family to support. Marianne was upbeat about their chances of attracting new business from artists in the need of inspiration, whether peaceful or macabre, as she put it. They had an engineer coming tomorrow to price the job.

She thought of Fred. Of all the lost souls. The list of unknowns was exhausting. She needed something manageable to balance it out. A good day, she thought. Let today be a good day.

'1 = Future; 2 = Future; 3 = Future', she wrote. Wasn't that all anyone worried about? she thought, then wiped it away.

When the doorbell rang, she opened it to find Paddy Hanley on the other side.

'Morning, Liv,' he said. 'Is Shay ready?

Shay had spent the past few Sundays out working with the animals. Liv was afraid to ask him about it in case he thought she was pushing, but Shay had a bounce in his step on Sundays, that much she knew.

'What are you doing today?' she asked as Shay pounded down the stairs, sitting on the bottom step of the stairs to lace his shoes. If she squinted, he could be eight years old and running out to play with Lucky.

'We're going over to the dogs' home,' Shay said. 'The local vets take a Saturday each, getting the dogs ready for rehoming.'

'Take your coat,' Liv said to Shay, who rolled his eyes and went to the kitchen.

'Thank you for this,' she said. 'It's good for him to not worry about points and exams and all of that.'

'The qualification is only the smallest part of any job,' Paddy said. 'Just so you know, not all the dogs today will make it.'

'That's a bit grim,' she said.

'I'll look after him,' Paddy promised.

She believed him. 'And you? Will you be okay?' She blanched at the idea that he might think she bracketed him with Shay. As one of her son's friends.

'If it bothers you, it only means you're the right man for the job.' He smiled at Liv as they turned away down the path. 'I'll have him back before Ethel gets home.'

Liv closed out the door. This place! You wouldn't know whether to laugh or cry.

She was fairly sure Paddy was waiting for an opportunity to ask her out. The first time round, they hadn't bothered with any of that. It was more that any time they were in the pub at the same time, they would leave and go to his house to have sex. There was never any prearrangement as such.

The first time he came to collect Shay, she had a book in her hand when she answered the door and Shay mentioned later that he had seen Paddy reading it in his office on his lunch break.

'What did he think of it?' Liv asked Shay, but he just shrugged.

'How would I know?'

The image of Paddy – tea at his elbow and feet on his desk, her imagination was quick to furnish the details – occupying the same emotional space made her feel young somehow. Young and fond. Her father's word, as right now as it ever was: it made her feel fond.

If he didn't ask her out soon, maybe she would go ahead and do it herself. What would she suggest though? What did people do any more? A movie? Or was that too teenage entirely? Lunch was a bit casual, dinner a bit stuffy. A gig, maybe? Although anything worth going to would be in the city, which meant a hotel, and she wasn't keen on the idea of reducing them to sex if he had something more in mind.

Marianne was all for the gig-and-overnight idea. 'Once you've mowed the lawn in a pair of shoes, it's impossible to ever again wear them for work.'

'Charming,' Liv laughed. 'Is he mowing my lawn or am I mowing his?'

'If you have to ask, you're not doing it right,' Marianne giggled.

They were reading the papers, with a pot of coffee and comfortable silence between them, when Ed came in to announce he was going for a run.

'Himself and Damien decided to take up running,' Marianne explained as they watched Ed stretch – energetically if nothing else – outside the window.

'Joely's Damien?' Liv couldn't keep the surprise from her voice.

'Apparently he's on a health kick, Joely said.'

'And how…?'

'No idea how it came about. Men and their mysterious friendships. Ed doesn't tell me what they talk about other than to say that *he's lived a life*. Make of that what you will.'

'He might as well have some friends around the place now you're going to be down here a bit more. With the festival and everything.' Liv hated how awkward she sounded. It wasn't as if Marianne had anything to apologise for.

Marianne put down her newspaper. 'About that,' she began.

'There's no need—' Liv said, but Marianne kept talking over her.

'I need you to know that me being here a bit more isn't because I have designs on the place,' she said. 'It's not anything to do with the money or the will or biding my time or anything like that. I've thought a lot about it and it's more about needing to feel welcome. To feel part of the family.'

Her sister's awkwardness was oddly touching, as was the fact that her careful little speech was clearly rehearsed.

'I know what you're thinking,' Marianne continued. 'If I wanted to be part of the family so badly, where was I all along when you were left to run the business and the burden of Ethel. Well, I want you to know that I'm ashamed of how little I knew of what was going on and I'm ready now to be a proper part of things.' She sat back in her chair.

'Now she's fixed, you mean?' They had a little laugh about that. 'Get off the cross, would you? So, you could have been here a bit more and I could have told you a bit more. What's done is done. It'll take us both from here on out. There's enough Ethel to go around.'

'Is it… Do you think it'll be different this time?'

That was always the question: did it work? Liv had visited her in Willowbrook a couple of weeks earlier. Liv assumed they would meet with a therapist together, but when they got there, Judith had waved Liv out to the garden, where she found Ethel on her knees pulling weeds. Liv sat while her mother talked about gardening, all the while wondering if there was some elaborate analogy they had forgotten to explain to her. At the front door, she asked Judith if she thought Ethel would make it this time. 'Sure alcoholics would be the best in the world all the time if they only believed anyone else was real,' was all Judith would say.

'We shouldn't expect miracles,' Liv said. 'Although for the first while it will seem like a miracle, she will be just like she used to be. But it mightn't last. You need to be prepared for that.'

'We can hope,' Marianne said.

Liv remembered hearing about two different readings of the Pandora's box myth. One – the usual one – in which hope was the last thing left in the box, symbol of the eternal well of human optimism. Less well known was the other, darker read. The one that saw hope as the last, final twist of Zeus' knife, the most useless pursuit in which man could engage.

'We can hope,' she said finally.

When the coffee pot was empty, Marianne got up to fill the kettle. 'No Seamus this weekend?' she said, her tone light.

'Not this weekend. Now that Pauline is back in the nursing home, he didn't feel the need to stir himself to come down.'

'Does that bother you?' Marianne asked quietly. 'I mean, jokes aside, are you all right about it all?'

'We were finished years ago only we hadn't the sense to see it,' she said. Repeating the words helped to ground it in her mind, the fact of its being finished.

'Would you hate me if I said I'm glad?' Marianne said.

Liv tried to ignore the familiar twinge of irritation. 'It's not all bad. Myself and Ruth have got really close. We're going to go for coffee during the week.'

Marianne spun around, her mouth open. 'Really?'

'No, you big eejit. Of course not. I slept with the woman's husband and then played nice to her face. The next time we're in a room together, I'll need to have cured cancer if I'm to feel any way human at all.'

There were likely to be many such occasions in the future, she knew. If she was lucky. For now, she was scaling back on the visits to Pauline. Once a fortnight instead of weekly. It was something, she thought defensively.

Time hung heavy, like the air before a storm. Liv shivered and hoped the thought was accidental rather than prophetic. There were still another two hours before she could reasonably leave to collect Ethel. A walk would kill an hour, she decided.

Outside, the day was warm and breezy. The clouds were thin stripes, the sky might have been stitched together with silver thread. She was barely up the main street when she had to stop and tie her jacket around her waist.

'Liv! The very woman.'

Liv turned to see Mrs Dillon, closely followed by Joely.

'Did I hear that you were thinking of expanding *Gaofar*?' Mrs Dillon demanded.

'I don't know. Did you?' Liv said.

Mrs Dillon was too busy talking to hear her. 'Are you sure that's wise? After that terrible review – not that I read it, of course, but I heard all about it – I thought that you were in for a rather quiet season?'

'A good business is always on the lookout for new opportunities,' Liv said.

'That's what I said!' Joely said. 'If your artists' retreat takes off, then I'm sure they will be looking for some artisanal local cuisine! Good business for everyone!'

She couldn't be cross with Joely for blabbing everything to Sheila Dillon. Coolaroone was a small place; word of their new venture would have got out eventually anyway. Liv smiled. 'We're just kicking some ideas around. Nothing is decided yet.'

'Maybe it's time the hotel had a freshen up. A memorial garden,' she heard Mrs Dillon say to Joely as she walked away. 'A beech tree with a bench under it. A nice quiet thinking spot. And Marguerite daisies, they're the Danish national flower, you know. We could serve afternoon tea there. Bring a bit of class to the place.'

Poor Tiny. It would be a *fait accompli* by the time Sheila got back to Dillons.

When she got to the grotto, she slid into one of the seats, genuflecting out of habit.

Overhead, the warblers promised summer. Did birds sing when they were sad? she wondered. Paddy would know. She could ring him and ask him. As simple as that. No mystery, no code.

She closed her eyes to send good thoughts to Fred, as if doing so would hasten them on their way. She couldn't have said where she thought the wishes went. Into the ether for Fred or her father to catch, she supposed. They would have liked each other. It would be easy to picture the pair of them in heaven, sitting either side of a cloud, a quiet game of chess between them. If a person believed in that kind of thing.

Liv opened her eyes and looked at the statue. It looked resolutely back at her. Not a tear in sight.

'You could do the hokey-cokey in front of me, Mary, and I think I'd go on away home and say nothing,' she told the statue. 'We've had enough drama for one year.'

There was enough yet to come. Ethel would be home shortly. Shay had his exams to do and his life to start, whatever that might look like. Marianne and Ed had their own decisions to make. That was the thing with time. So much of it was wasted wishing it to move forwards or backwards, to speed up or slow down. Whether to freeze it or speed ahead and be prepared for what might be coming.

Liv closed her eyes. Behind her, in the distance, the seagulls called to one another. Wasn't it well for them, Liv thought, with no master, only the wind and their own whim? That's what she would come back as, given the choice. Who knew but Fred was one of them, wheeling overhead, throwing his story to the world. 'Now wouldn't that be something.' She said her father's words out loud.

She had a million little things to do. There was a meal to prepare, a load of washing to be hung out, the accounts needed to be finalised, tomorrow's breakfast was still in the freezer. Yet she stayed where she was.

She would listen to the seagulls for one more minute, Liv decided.

One more minute, then home.

THE END

A note on Ireland's moving statues

Grottoes – or roadside religious shrines – are a very common feature of rural Ireland. Many date back to the 1950s, when the Vatican's declaration of a 'Marian Year' saw statues of the Virgin Mary erected in pretty pockets of the countryside so that locals could embrace both the religious and the natural world at the same time.

In the summer of 1985, Ireland was gripped by the phenomenon of moving statues, with several small communities claiming to have seen their statues move. Some saw Our Lady 'floating in mid-air', others claimed to see her 'rocking to and fro', still others saw 'birds fly in and out of her crown'. Those who witnessed such movement insisted there had been no mistake, and similar stories began to emerge at multiple locations. Academics suggested it was an optical illusion, related to eye-brain functioning, while sociologists pointed to the difficult situation in Ireland at the time, with deep recession, high unemployment and emigration, and increasing tension between Church teachings and the changing reality of everyday life.

That summer saw hundreds of thousands of visitors to grottoes the length and breadth of the country, with the devout and the sceptical equally anxious to see for themselves. No definitive answer was found, but the phenomenon seemed to end with the summer. Although thirty-five years have now passed, devotees continue to insist on the truth of their visions and grottoes continue to be an important feature of the Irish rural landscape.

Peter Bergmann

In June 2009, a man checked into a hotel in Sligo town under the name Peter Bergmann. Over the next three days, he left the hotel frequently, carrying a plastic bag but returning empty-handed. CCTV footage shows him never chatting to anyone, using a phone or disposing of anything in the plastic bag. On his final day, he took the bus to the beach at Rosses Point and was seen by several people throughout the day, paddling in the sea and also sitting on a bench overlooking the water. He was last seen just before midnight, walking along the water's edge. His body was found washed up on the beach the following morning. An autopsy revealed that the man had terminal prostate cancer and likely had only weeks to live. The cause of death was found to be a heart attack, rather than drowning. He was buried three months later in an unmarked grave in Sligo cemetery. His funeral was attended by six people, including the gravedigger.

The case remains open until Peter Bergmann is identified.

ACKNOWLEDGEMENTS

Huge and heartfelt thanks to everyone at Legend Press, particularly Lauren Parsons, for being every bit as reassuring the second time round, and Cari Rosen, for handling the novel with such care. Publishing my first novel last year meant a whole lot of extra work for Lucy, Lauren, Tom and the Legend team – to make sure that it came out, that it was read and reviewed and supported, that it found an audience – and they were tireless in their efforts, for which I am endlessly grateful.

Thanks to Kari Brownlie for a striking cover that perfectly captures the tone of this novel and feels so wonderfully quiet after all these noisy months.

Thank you to my agent, Hannah Weatherill, and the team at Northbank Talent Management for their enthusiasm and excitement for this book and for my writing in general.

Thanks to Rachel Nielsen and Sylvia Carr Clebsch, my writing wing mirrors, for gently showing me my blind spots and asking the sensible questions that keep me on track, as well as the wilder questions that get me thinking bigger. Our workshops mean a great deal to me – without them, I suspect my stories would be some nice sentences loosely connected by several plot holes. More string vest than story, if you can picture such a thing.

Thank you to everyone who bought my first novel, who recommended it and gifted it and otherwise helped to send it out into the world. Special thanks to the reviewers and bloggers whose careful reading and considered opinions are invaluable in helping books and writers to find their readers.

Those of us who grew up in 1980s Ireland vividly remember the summer of the moving statues and the wonder it occasioned. A special mention here for my friend Sinéad Hayes, whose fascination at the very idea of it matched my own, and who stood with me in front of the statue in our local grotto every day after school waiting for it to move, until our patience wore out and we went back to reading books.

I grew up in a family of readers and remain surrounded by people who love books. People who happily whip out a book when they're waiting somewhere. People who ask each other, 'Are you reading anything good?' People who believe there's no better gift than a book and no occasion on which it could be anything less than the perfect present. My people. Thank you to my family – Joe, Teresa, Deirdre, Kevin, Eleanor, John, Barry, Mel, Kay, and the littler folk, our next generation of readers, Daniel, Hannah and James. Thanks, too, to my extended family and friends, for support and cheerleading and for not minding when my answers to kind enquiries tend towards the short and grumpy.

Special thanks to my sister Dee, who listened to me outline the story of Ethel, Marianne, Liv and Fred as we walked from Bonchurch to Ventnor on the Isle of Wight during that 2018 summer when, as Irish twins, we were briefly forty at the same time. On that same walk, in St Boniface Church, we came across a plaque that read, 'Within a vault in the yard at the west end of this church are deposited the remains of Thomas Prickett, Surgeon, late of Witham, in the county of Essex, who with piety and resignation closed a life of extensive usefulness on the 6th day of March 1811, aged 30 years.' In *The Ghostlights*, Ethel mentions a burial inscription commending a person's 'life of extensive usefulness', which I include here in recognition of Thomas Prickett and of precious time spent with my sister. Having a sibling who is also a friend means having a touchstone should you ever be in danger of losing yourself: there's no one better at reminding you of who you are and who you're not.

Finally, thanks to Colm, Oisín and Cara, who are endlessly patient in the face of my frequent excuses and absences in body, mind and spirit. And to Ali, who is with me always, and whose bittersweet memory reminds me that time is what we make it.